WENDIGO

THE OTHERWORLD ARCHIVES

DAVID VIERGUTZ

Building a relationship with my readers is the very best thing about writing. I send newsletters with details on new releases, writer-life, deals and other bits of news related to my books. And if you sign up to my mailing list I'll send you something I think you'll like, my terrifying novella, *Peel*.

Details can be found at the back of this book.

BUDDY

FELTON FOREST WAS A PARTICULARLY acrid and uncharted swathe of trees and underbrush that locals from the surrounding town of Barhill refused to call a national park for many years, choosing rather to ignore its existence. Dubbed the Fell or Foul Forest for its stench of rotting meat and sour milk, it was a wonder why anyone had established a township next to such a fetid place. But in 1985, after two hikers went missing, venturing out into what they saw as an undiscovered gem, it gained some attention. Negative attention, to be sure, but it drove enough traffic to the area that the forest grew a cult following, and tourism picked up - at least for a little while.

The story of the missing hikers was buried under the curious rotten smell. After calls for recognition (and funding), the national forestry service finally gave in, designated the area as a preserve, and set up an outpost and trails, adding in an equally rancid gift-shop filled with clip-on-noses and oil-based products (claiming to protect you from gagging while you traipsed through the foliage and imagined you were in a room temperature meat locker.)

No one knows where the smell came from, and scientists

had even tried a small project in 1989 to identify the source, but quickly moved on. It turned out no one cared about why it smelled - they just carried on with their lives, accepted the World's Smelliest Town designator on the city limit signs of Barhill, and promptly went back to ignoring the large stretch of trees. The forestry service fell into the background, the occasional tourist tried to reach the northern ridge where the woods stopped at a small river with a decent current (assuming to go fishing, or drown the smell from their noses), and the world moved on.

Buddy Walsh, or Bud if you knew him well enough, lived in Barhill all his life. As he drove the narrow highway, 55 it was called, for its speed and year built, west from Carlisle to Barhill, he passed a wall of lush trees that blocked out the sun. He held his breath, cursed at the forest, and squinted into the distance. His eyes were slowly failing him, but he didn't care. Nobody wanted to give ol' Bud a ride to the bar. It was Tuesday at noon, and he already stunk of cheap whiskey. His pickup, nearly as old as he was, was clunky and road-walked even at his putzing pace of 30 in a 55. Everyone knew he drank, and everyone knew he took the same abandoned highway from his house to the bar and back. No one traveled on 55, because it was the closest to the forest. No one except Bud.

Some new boy band blared over the radio. Too drunk to care to change it, he instead grumbled as yet another teeny-bopper song came on. They were popular now, and Bud had secretly wished he had died long before bleached hair and earrings made it on full-grown men. By hating the new soft generation and voicing a boisterous opinion about them to all who would listen, he felt he was doing a service to the world. Even the big-wigs at the capitol had predicted the world to end in something called Y2K. For them it hadn't. For Bud, it had. Men were no longer men, cars were built smaller with more plastic than metal, gas went up to $2.00 a gallon, and fruity tourists from the city crossed the state lines to sniff at the Fell Forest.

"Fuck 'em," Bud growled at the radio as he merged back into his lane and rumbled on. He passed a fading green highway sign on the right, shot to shit by a bunch of kids, and smiled. Those were the good days. Now, there were digital music players and video games, and kids spent more time preening than shooting stuff, picking out a movie at Blockbuster, or getting caught making-out on a back road.

"Soft. All soft," Bud barked, spotting his own wrinkly eye in the rear-view mirror. Then, as the corrugated lane marker on the right let him know he was drifting, he looked away, but not before catching a glimpse of a tall shadow, stepping briefly from the wall of trees, then disappearing back inside. Bud didn't slow, and he didn't care. Instead, he reached for the handle of whiskey on his front seat and took a swig. He wasn't nearly drunk enough to deal with that.

Four miles later, Bud inched his truck over a curb on the right and parked in the dirt lot outside a decrepit wood faced building with a sign on it labeled simply "Bar." The sign had long since burnt out, but the people who came to this bar knew it was here before that sign had come about. As Bud shuffled up the ramp (installed specifically for him), a set of teenagers, a man, or a boy rather, in a motorcycle jacket and his trampy girlfriend nearly ran into him. He made note to mention to Doug Prion, the barkeep, to install lane markers on the ramp. He snorted at his own wit and pushed his way inside.

Though the town was rancid and the smell oppressive, the bar itself was at least a partial relief. Filled with smoke, the one-room establishment had grimy floors, worn wooden stools and a natural haze from the cancer swirling the fan. It was perfect for a man, not a girl in a short white skirt and her boyfriend. Doug was at his familiar perch behind the counter. He held a glass in his hand, probably full of whatever cheap swig he had on tap that week, and watched the local news on a crookedly mounted TV. He ignored Bud even after he sat down. Bud didn't need to buy a drink. He just needed to buy people to drink with.

A long-standing joke, Bud dropped a dollar in a tip jar, grabbed a shot glass from the tray on the right and poured himself a drink from his personal stash, a bottle kept near his favorite seat. No one touched Bud's stuff (or handled it for that matter.)

"See that tail?" Doug said without turning away from the TV. He was watching a busty reporter ramble on about the Fell Forest and conservation efforts.

"TV or walking out?" Bud asked.

"Shit. Both." Doug said. "They were visitors, looking for a cool ride to the forest and back to city."

"Did you tell them where to find me?" Bud slammed back his drink and flicked the shot glass.

"Fuck you, Bud."

"Fuck you, Doug."

The two dropped into silence. A few minutes later, the door to Bud's back creeped open and a man much too clean for a drunk pulled up a chair next to him. He still wore his gray and blue work polo and a pair of jeans, pressed, without pre-cut holes the kids were paying extra for.

"Her tits fall out yet?" He asked, his voice hoarse from smoking. Bud rolled the glass on the bar and ignored him. That was his joke, and James Pope fucking knew it.

"No, but your wife's did."

James smoothed back his hair, a habit Bud recognized that came from the 80s and growing up around greasers. He, like Bud, was a relic. Still young, probably in his 40s. Bud had no problem calling him a man none-the-less. He drank real liquor, smoked real cigarettes, and drove a real car made of metal. He also had the hottest wife in town, a transplant from the east coast.

"Probably got a boob job. Would know for certain if I actually saw them once in a while," James mumbled into his cigarette.

"No boob job yet," Doug said to the TV. "I made a down payment though."

"Fuck you, Doug."

"Fuck you, James."

Bud's stool creaked as he shifted his bony ass on it. Despite the jabs, James was a hardworking fellow, caught up in some scheme of his wife's to "invest" in their future by letting *her* work on her career as some sort of high-dollar banking consultant, while he shoved shit at Blockbuster. Everyone knew the story, and everyone knew James. In fact, Tuesdays were reserved for James to gripe about her, with the understanding that Doug and Bud might jab and poke at the situation. They, unlike James, shared the misery of divorce and losing half their shit twice over. James had yet to learn, but if the last few months of Tuesday gripe sessions were any indicator, it was fast approaching.

"It's still a mess," James said lowly.

Oh, here we go already. Normally this starts after a few games of pool.

Bud acted like he was listening by dipping an ear, but his eyes drifted towards the blonde reporting in about the forest service's latest attempts to raise funds for new uniforms, trail vehicles, equipment and other shit that will just end up rotting in a shed somewhere. They never needed anything, but if they were begging for spare change, they weren't working the skunky trails and fighting off mosquitos armed with West Nile.

"She's going there, or at least talked about it a lot," James said, nodding toward the TV that showed the entrance to the park. The camera panned to a large cut stone serving as a sign and a log-built forester station with a round top.

Now Bud was interested. Rebecca Pope was a lot of things. A banker, a workaholic, the nicest set of legs for thirty miles. What she wasn't was a camper, tracker or hiker of any sort.

"She has no idea what she'd be doing, but I promise the words *breath of fresh air* never left her lips." He took a drag from his cigarette, looked it over once to make sure it was down to the nub, and squinted as he blew out the smoke.

"Going to get it going by the moonlight while rolling around in Pepe's sheets?" Bud quipped.

James snorted, lit another cigarette with the butt of the old one. "Shit, Pepe is probably getting some himself. I sure as hell ain't."

"Y'all fighting again? Ain't the Christian thing to do," Doug said, finally peeling away from the television as a commercial about a mail-in video series came on.

James stretched. "I'm not a Christian, and she isn't a practicing one. Holidays, you know? Kind of a guilty thought, it seems. But you won't find a cross in our house, that's for sure. Except maybe an upside down one in my kid's room."

Bud was interested now, fully vested in any conversation dealing with James's kid. He was a Satanist, or so he claimed. Black hair, black eyes, black clothes, fishnets and piercings. He was the type of punk you could hear his music from a mile away while he painted his fingernails on the steps of the school. The kind of kid that always carried a knife and who's bag you wanted to search.

That clammed James up, so Bud poured him a shot from his private reserve. It was worth it. The boy was an oddity in Barhill, and oddities made great bar-talk.

The liquor seemed to lubricate James's tongue, and he continued. "Want to know what's weird? Besides his clothes and the nails and stuff? The kid can read. I mean, really read. He'll put down a book a day, easy, and retain it too. But in school, D+ at best. It's like he doesn't care. Maybe he's sick. Think I should call someone?"

Doug refilled his glass and looked at James and questioned him with his eyes. "Would he even take it if you offered?"

"No. But if I pressed Rebecca, she could mention it. He listens to her. My kid's a Satanist momma's boy. I couldn't get him to pick up a wrench if it meant he could have that tail on the weather channel. All he cares about is his fuckin' CD player."

Bud sacrificed another drink. This was juicy stuff, and the closest he got to entertainment. He lived twenty miles from the town, tucked behind a wall of corn. There were a few things left in this world he still valued; his privacy, booze and drama, especially if he wasn't involved in it. Together, the three gentlemen raised their drinks and continued the small talk until the night caught up to them. By 9:00 PM, it was pitch-black outside. The crickets had come out to annoy them, and James was good and wasted, leaning over his pool stick and squinting.

He shot, swayed, and scratched the carpet on the table. Bud suggested he could do James's wife for him. James slurred something and dumped his drink on his shirt before giving in and shuffling towards the door. He waddled like he had a pool stick hidden up his ass, and Bud snorted, lined up, and sunk a ball into a corner pocket. When James was gone, Bud caught Doug's eye.

"$10 says divorce," Bud grinned mischievously.

"$10 says she's fucking around on him. He works at Blockbuster. Even your wrinkly old ass has a better chance than he does with her, and you don't do anything."

Bud flicked him off, sunk another ball, then drained the last of his handle. He shuffled casually towards the front door. Unlike James, Bud was a professional drinker, and was just drunk enough to think he could manage the drive home.

Before he left, he dropped a ten or a twenty, he couldn't tell, on the counter, and dumped the bottle over into the recycle bin, because he was a conservationist like that, and finally stepped outside. He stood on the ramp and cursed the brightness of the moon, sucked in the warm, foul air, and made for his truck. He removed a moldy blanket from the tool box in the bed and placed it across the seat. The last thing he wanted was to piss himself on the drive home. His jeans were freshly pressed.

2

JAMES

GOD, I've got to piss, James thought, nearly upchucking a belly full of cheap booze after catching a warm mouthful of air from the nearby woods. Whoever the hell thought to put a bar all the way out here ought to be choked. Maybe it was done on purpose. *Whatever, I'm too poor to forfeit free drinks over a little stink.* James clamped his mouth down tight, quelling the stomach heaves. The forest at his back loomed over him, casting a great shadow. Even the moon seemed to be on the opposite side of the sky.

James watched Bud drive off before he contemplated the battle that lay ahead. His car, a bent piece-of-shit, was at the far end of the dirt lot, closest to the road (and furthest from the stink), and he'd have to choose between the stairs, which were spinning in every which direction, or the ramp, which was long and slick from years of wear. He was at a crossroads, risk the ramp and a longer walk, or take the steps. *Steps it is.* It was odd this time of night. Too bright to see, but the bugs were out, and the wind had put up for the day.

One foot over the next, James managed the stairs, slipped on the last step, but used the railing for support. His head felt lopsided and heavy, like a weight was attached to one side, and he drifted to the left. Two blinks later, and he nearly rammed a knee into the front bumper of his old lime green Pinto. It was ancient before it was new. Rebecca, the high-dollar executive, had an image to uphold (so she got the nicer car) and he was just an attendant at a failing movie rental company, so he drove the metal land yacht. He liked to call the car his screaming bitch, because of its insufferable whine when it started up cold and its consistent nagging when its brakes squeaked.

Eventually he'd upgrade when he got a new job, a decision he had come to hate himself for. There were no jobs in Barhill that pay for anything more than the screaming bitch. James fumbled the lock and eventually got it, falling on the cracked leather seat and resting his forehead on the steering wheel. Now, he just needed to get home.

As he turned the beast on, it rumbled, squealed, and squeaked to life, grating on his nerves and threatening to brew a headache.

He had driven Rebecca's car once — around the lot just before they bought it, but after that, she was up in the morning before he was, and the opportunity to take a drive as a family in the new car never came up. When they went somewhere together, it was always in the Pinto. She apparently much preferred to put mileage on the older car (A petty excuse for him to never drive her car again). He worked three miles further from the house than she did, but he had learned not to argue with the woman. She could be a rhinoceros when she needed to be, and evidently that meant at work and at home. But she kept with the excuse, and he resigned to believe she wasn't ashamed to ride in the old green junker. It was just easier that way.

James inched his way out of the parking lot and coasted onto the road, heading east on 55 towards town and his house. It was only a few miles away in a small subdivision of five houses adjacent to the forest. After the houses were built, the people who moved in were mostly high-rollers like Rebecca. *And you too, you're married to her, you idiot.* They collaborated and complained to the township about living so close to the park and the accompanied smell. The township, for whatever reason, gave in and raised a retaining wall. Not to cut off the smell; that, of course, would never work, but to shut up the families in the subdivision. But the subdivision was prime real-estate for what people liked to say the town *could* be.

Most of the folks who lived in Barhill didn't actually *live* in Barhill. Their homes were miles from the forest, but the largest houses were where the land was cheapest, and that was where the smell was greatest. Seeing the house and justifying the stink, Rebecca signed the note on the property without even consulting James, something he tried not to hate her for. After years of waking up in a house he didn't pick out, he hardly got used to it. He lashed out about the smell, and Rebecca filed the complaint. The retaining wall was built, and James was left feeling like the wall was a monument to his wife. Immovable, and not really interested in fixing the problem. Like the wall, she just shuts the people up who have the issue in the first place.

A car was approaching from the opposite lane. Its headlights, the kind no human could ever directly look at, blinded his already sensitive eyes, and James directed his attention towards maintaining his lane. Apparently not well enough, as the other driver leaned on his horn and swerved. James screamed obscenities back and romped on the accelerator. Up ahead were two gas stations on either side of the road. Deciding he needed a break at the halfway point between the bar and his house, he took a wide arc into the brightly lit parking lot. James let his heartbeat relax for a moment before shutting off the car. *I forgot I've got to piss. How could I forget?*

Near the front of the plain, square service station was a man in a green jumpsuit. He sat at the table, reading by flashlight. At his feet was a red box with a flyer stand. He was a representative of the park, collecting donations. *I fucking hate this forest,* James thought, stumbling his way to the front doors. The man, younger than him by at least ten years, barely looked up from his book. James drunkenly forgot his reason for being at the gas station in the first place and couldn't help himself.

"What the fuck is this for?" He asked, nudging the bucket with his toe. It rattled full of loose change.

The forester, obviously annoyed, sighed heavily and judged James with his eyes. "Donations. Completely voluntary. All money goes towards new equipment."

"Y'all don't take enough from hardworking men like me from our taxes? Huh? Or my wife's taxes? Y'all want more?"

The forester sighed again, this time louder, and set his book down. "Completely... voluntary...," he said, a smugness to his voice that James could detect even through his drunken haze. James sized him up. Chunky with black hair, he was a clone of almost every other forester from the area, slightly engorged from a lack of actual work to do. James hated him immediately — as if he represented the forest specifically and had a hand in the stench.

James swayed, his head felt fuzzy. Then his temper flared, and he kicked the bucket again. "Beggars. I hate beggars."

The forester stood up and dumped out his wallet, flashlight, and keys on the table. "Listen man. Go inside, get you a drink, whatever. But don't make me call the cops, alright? I'm having a good night, and I promise I'll tune you up before they even get here."

James snorted. This tree-hugging pansy was trying to shove him off, but he wasn't so easily moved. For a long time, they stared each other down. The forest ranger took two steps forward and stood next to the donation's bin. Inside, the manager watched from behind the counter, but James didn't care. Drunken rage was having a way with his senses, and his judgement. He wanted to hit something. He wasn't particularly strong, but his forester looked soft. Thinking about what could spur a fight was too easy. Instead, he chose to show this beggar what he really thought about him.

Unzipping the front of his pants, James said, "Tune this. You play the skin flute buddy?"

With a forceful grunt he relieved himself in the bucket and looked towards the moon. The bucket chimed and the stink of beer and booze scented urine cut through the smell of gasoline and warm trash. James smiled to himself and looked down in time to catch a fist heading for his mouth. He saw stars as the alcohol briefly dulled the pain. He stumbled back, tripped over his own feet and landed hard on his tail bone.

The forest ranger was on him in an instant. Blow after blow connected with his face. James tried to put up his guard, but the younger, sober man was sitting on his chest and his knees were in his armpits. He was fading, and the blows growing more targeted, harder and faster.

It was turning dark. His arms were trapped, his eyelids felt like they had weights attached to them. Then it was black, and he faded.

⁂

THE FIRST THING James noticed when he came to was the smell of industrial alcohol and the bright LED lights above him. He grumbled and tried to roll to his side, but was stopped by thick straps and a hard metal ring around his wrists. Opening his puffy eyes, he groaned. He was in the back of an ambulance. An EMT was sitting nearby, pressing buttons on a machine with a mess of wires strung from it. He removed a velcro cuff from his arm and said to someone outside the vehicle, "He's fine to go with you."

James looked down at his arm. He was handcuffed to the gurney. *Fuck.* He tried to sit up, and a cop, tall, bald and muscular, was waiting. He helped James to his feet with a firm grip around his bicep and unhooked one end of the handcuff. Everything hurt. His lips were swollen and cracked and there was the lingering taste of blood on his tongue and some grit on the front of his teeth.

James groaned as he stepped down from the ambulance. The cop, a deputy sheriff judging by the tan uniform, swung James's arms around and re-cuffed him. He was drunk and stupid, but not stupid enough to fight a cop. That forester had gotten the drop on him, and he had paid for it. He looked up at the forester, who was rubbing his knuckles, looking entirely satisfied. James bowed his head. The cop escorted him to a patrol car and opened the backdoor, shoved him inside and slammed it home.

James, wanting to apologize for his stupidity, slid the cuffs around his back and pressed the button to roll down the window. The cop and the forester turned and James spat out. "I'm sorry as I was asshole." It sounded good in his head, but the cop wasn't in the mood to translate.

"You're lucky this ranger is in a good mood. He said you tried to steal the change. That's theft from a federal employee, a felony. Instead, you're getting a night in the hole and a public intoxication ticket," the cop said, leaning into the window. He could smell coffee on his breath. Fine. He deserved it, and he opened his mouth to say more, but the cop shook his bald head. James clammed up and looked at his feet. He had brought this on himself.

"Can I call my wife?" He asked hopefully.

"Not tonight," the cop replied. "You can make your call in the morning."

"What about my car?"

"It's blocking the roadway." The cop responded and stepped aside. In his stupor, he had thought he had parked by the gas pumps, but now, his mind clearer with the introduction of pain and adrenaline, he could see he had in fact parked in the middle of the parking lot.

"I'm towing it. Card for the wrecker yard will be in your stuff at the jail. You good, Arnie?" The cop turned to the forester.

The man called Arnie smiled weakly, continuing to massage his bruising knuckles. "I'm good."

The cop left to go talk to the ambulance driver, leaving Arnie to talk to James through the bars. "Not much of a fight in you, but then again, you picked a fight with a guy who's seen some shit. Anytime, anywhere pal, and I'll still fuck you up."

James opened his mouth to say something curse-laden, but the window rolled up as the cop dropped heavily into the front seat. He talked into the radio, muffled by the plastic partition, before sliding the window open and said, "No AC back there, and I hope you like country."

The cop cranked the radio so loud the speakers crackled, and James felt the heater by the floorboards turn on. He stewed. It was the middle of July… in Michigan… and he fucking hated country.

3

ARNIE

SIX YEARS. Six agonizing years Arnie House had suffered working under Edward Gains, the least successful, wannabe business owner west of the city. He was promised a promotion, raises, training and experience, even his own truck. All he had gained from Edward *Gains* was a sore back and a dusty wallet. In 1994, when the towing industry was the worst, and Arnie was nearly *paying* to go to work, he tossed the keys to his ride in the sewer drain and threw his uniform in a burn barrel. But, seeing as the tow truck was his only transportation, he was forced to trek eight miles from the west side of Barhill southeast along the 55.

Four miles in, he was convincing himself not to throw himself into traffic when a green truck from the Federal Forestry Service slowed down next to him. According to the sales pitch the charismatic recruiter gave him, he was just the local they needed to work as a forest ranger in Felton Forest. Without a prospect of a job and an empty wallet whistling with every passing car, he greedily accepted and met the recruiters the following day at the new ranger station. That was six years ago, and he marked the day on his calendar hanging below the viewing window in his office. He valued the six-year mark, because that meant he got a raise. *No promises here, motherfucker. This is on paper.*

He cursed Edward Gains. He was probably dead by now, but this would have been a perfect day to show off. This was his second raise as manager, a position he was still weighing the benefits of. When he took over as supervisor at the park, he was given a truck (the same one he had been recruited in, but a truck none-the-less) to drive the whopping four miles through town back to his house. It seemed the pickup was a perk at first, but after the third or fourth callout about missing hikers, the truck felt like an anchor. He was attached to the forest.

Arnie took a big whiff of a sharpie from his desk, then tucked it into his shirt pocket for later. It stung his nose and made him lightheaded, and he liked the feeling. He removed his feet from the desk, drew the marker again, and took another deep breath. This time, there was a sharp pain behind his eyes and the chemical stench burned. He dug his palms into his eyes and sat back.

"Boss?" Someone called from the other side of the view window. It was perfect to look over the main part of the ranger station. He could keep an eye on his worker bees, buzzing around, helping the occasional customer as they perused the shop and looked over a handful of artifacts in glass cases about the floor. There were only three hikers looking to make quick trips through the park with day passes, and he had enough rangers to tend to them each individually right now. This was supposed to be his alone time.

"What is it?" Arnie grunted, pretending to circle the date on the calendar.

One of the rangers, a spritely young man named Stan or Dan (he couldn't care to remember) with some sort of environmental degree from a snotty school in California, had finished with his customer and was walking towards the window, clutching his stomach. "Sir, I've gotta take the day."

"What the hell's wrong with you?" Arnie asked, looking him over. He checked the time. The clock read 6:15 PM. He looked back at the kid. His face was haggard and sickly.

"Stomach. Restaurant food," he said.

"I told you not to eat there. Even the customers don't eat there," he said. "Fine, but you still have your shift at the service station tonight, 8:00 PM to 10:00 PM. The school basketball team will be arriving and meeting parents there for pickup, it's a great opportunity to fund the cause."

The kid, Stan, or Dan's cheeks bulged, and his eyes grew wide. Arnie knew what was coming next and looked left as the kid upchucked a sloppy mess of yellows, reds and greens on the tile floor. "I suppose I'll work at the service station tonight. It's the last night anyway. Clean this up then go home. I'll see you in a few days."

He didn't wait around to see if Stan or Dan replied and left the office. He held up a cellphone, a generic, well-worn flip phone that only worked in the mornings and dropped calls every thirty seconds. That was his universal supervisor-sign that he was leaving the office. What he didn't tell his lackeys was that he wasn't off on a trail or meeting someone.

He was heading home and would take calls from his house, probably in his underwear, dick in his hand, while he waited for the night to roll on through. If he was going to be out and about in public, he was going to have a clear mind when he did so. Much thought during the day about his promotion and the money that came with it had given him a stiff that made him walk crooked.

Hopping into his work truck, an older model single cab with a camper shell the same pickle green as his uniform, he clicked on the radio and waited for the weather channel. Though the skies were clear, the storms never really drifted this close to the Foul Forest. Something about the elevation broke up the clouds. It was an odd place, and rain meant he could head for the bar on 55 and completely ignore his beggar's duties. The forest service had plenty of equipment. This round of donations would go straight into the general fund, which had already been allocated to his new work truck. *Why spend your money when you can spend someone else's?* Arnie liked the federal government, but only when it benefited Arnie.

The weather channel reported a warm, clear night without any chance of rainfall, and Arnie cursed the radio. He turned the truck over, then romped on the gas, spinning his tires and speeding out of the parking lot. If he blew the engine, maybe they'd just buy him a new one instead of the ass-backward panhandling campaign he was working on now. To his dismay, the pickup had a steady pulse and Arnie sped to his house. After a hard right onto the highway, and a line-drive at 75, he arrived at home and had his member out before 6:28 PM. That gave him about an hour before he had to work the corner with his donations bucket. Not ideal, Arnie would have liked at least an hour and a half. He was a romantic after all.

Ten minutes later and Arnie slammed his laptop shut and cleaned up, wholly dissatisfied. Then, with a thoughtful groan, he started picking up his house. It seemed like the next logical step, as his little retreat was a mess, and he was due for a cleaning. He also knew if there was one thing he needed to turn his computer dreams into a reality, it was at least a semi-acceptable home. Not the musky dumping ground for his used socks and leftover pizza boxes.

His bedroom, an even square off the slightly larger living room, had an abused futon with a mismatch of untucked sheets and an old comforter. His pillow, grimy with drool stains, was the newest addition of only a few weeks. Before that, he had simply stuffed the next-day's clothes under his head for a few hours of tossing and turning. It made for a quick dress in the morning before work.

Arnie left the room with the bed still a mess, but most of the floor was clear. Upon closer inspection, he remembered *why* he was leaving things on the floor in the first place. It covered the various stains, some from him, others from whatever animals the previous renters of the house had (it was a rental, and therefore not his problem), and others of unknown origin. About the cleanest thing in the place was a console plugged into a precious flat-screen TV in the far corner. It didn't have a speck of dust on it; that he made sure he wiped down every day.

Arnie thought about the game system and blamed it for the way he looked. The hours he spent in front of it wreaked havoc on his appetite to the point he'd have to purchase bigger pants this week — the second time this year, and his acne was out of control on his face. His thinning brown hair and pudgy cheeks did him no favors, either. It had gotten so bad he had removed all the mirrors from the house except one behind the door in the laundry room.

He picked up a stained ball-cap and considered wearing it, but ended up throwing it in with the rest of soiled clothes in his room. A few minutes later after his back ached from stooping and delivering dirty clothes to the hamper in the bedroom, Arnie gave up, snagged his latest read from the bedside table, and a backup from the shelf in the living room and checked the clock on his way out the door.

He could get thirty minutes of reading in before he was supposed to be at his post, pail in hand, new truck on the mind. He didn't dare share the fact that he loved to read. Only shut-ins and losers read beyond what they were required to. But Arnie could read anything. It was an addiction. From stories about zombies to haunted houses, he loved them all, and his current book, a tale about western Indian migrations and bloody territory battles, was book two of a series he had started earlier that week.

His job as supervisor was perfect for reading copious amounts of books and reaping all the benefits of higher pay by delegating every responsibility he had. Early on, after accepting the position as park manager, he routed all complaints through an email address he controlled so he could filter them before they even hit the Major's desk in the city. So far, he hadn't had a single reprimand and things hummed nicely. Now most of his time was spent hiring people.

A short drive later, Arnie pulled into the parking lot of the local stop-and-rob outside of Barhill on 55. It was one of two service stations and the only one open late, having been privately owned by a hot-shot in the city. He controlled several gas stations in little towns, and would appear from time to time. You could tell he was around by his smell. His cologne probably cost more than Arnie made in a month. He would appear, check on a few stations in the area, grab a piece of tail from which ever town, and return them sometime in the morning, the top down on his convertible. He'd slap their ass as they got out, wink at them, then speed off, ready to do it again the next week. Arnie wanted to be like him, whoever he was.

Parking behind the station, he used the back door to get inside, waved to the cashier manning the counter, and dragged the change bucket with its red flyer pole along the sidewalk and out front. Then he settled on a bench with his book in his hand. Close to the end, about two or three chapters, as the blood and gore were getting good, a lime green Pinto inched into the parking lot and stopped in the middle between the pumps and the store. Then, a worn drunkard in a Blockbuster uniform came stumbling out and approached him, a scowl written across his face.

Fucking great. Here we go. Arnie thought to himself and pretended to read the page. Something told him he wouldn't be finishing the book tonight.

4

REBECCA

REBECCA POPE DIDN'T KNOW a damn thing about camping, but she could learn, and she could read, a trait her son Jr. had luckily inherited. What he didn't get from her was his lack of care towards anything that wasn't music or meant to draw shock and awe from those around him. Right now, he was slinging both. Rebecca carried a handful of printouts on camping and set them on the counter in the kitchen. Some of it was just-in-case type stuff, others were instructions on how to put out a fire or deter bears from entering the camp site. She had the instruction manual for the new framed tent she bought earlier that day, and for an emergency radio. She had also added a recipe for *Pudgy Pies,* a campfire sandwich baked in a wrought iron skillet with any kind of filling she could imagine. She hoped Jr. would make them with her.

You just have to get him out there, then he'll talk. He won't have a choice.

Jr. was sitting across from her, his dark eyes glazed over. He had a book propped up on his uneaten toast and his head leveled on the counter. She had started a conversation with him about his father, James, but he refused to acknowledge he heard a damn thing.

Rebecca resorted to talking to herself, pretending Jr. was listening. That way, she could say she tried. "He got out the next day. That was probably his rock bottom, but it also told me that I was tired of waiting around. Tired of wondering what dumb thing he was going to do next."

She glanced over at Jr., whose eyes had left the page. They met in the middle, and he promptly returned to his reading. "I know you won't understand it now, but this could be good for us. A chance to try something new. Start over. It also gives your father some time to work on his own demons."

"Don't say that," Jr. grumbled. She hadn't even noticed he had turned his CD player off and tilted his headphones onto his neck.

"Don't say what?" She asked.

"Don't say demons. He doesn't have demons. He's a drunkard. A has-been. A wash-out. I'm surprised he got this far."

Though Jr. was right, Rebecca wouldn't tell him that. Instead, she looked him over and frowned. Despite his outward appearance, he had grown to look like James. So much so that he no longer asked to be called Jr. and preferred to go by just James. She wouldn't let that happen so easily and kept with his nickname. Once she heard James was arrested, she broke the news to Jr. that she had gotten an apartment and was filing for divorce. Jr., being as astute as he was, quickly put together the timeline. "I'm guessing it's a coincidence then that he got arrested. Therefore, you've been planning this. You already got this apartment, and the divorce filed. You were just holding off on telling me."

She nodded. "That's right, Jr."

"James," he said, his eyes drooping, if only for just a moment.

Jr. insisted his name was James, after his father. But over the past few days he was more apt to snap at the mention of him.

He was finally showing some emotion, and while it was nice to break through his shell, it all came at a cost. Jr. was behaving like an asshole.

"Fine. He had an addiction. But he wasn't a bad father, really. He just wasn't ever there. I suppose this is my fault in a way for taking on this new job. Whoever thought putting a banking headquarters in the middle of the countryside was a good idea is an—"

"Mom," Jr. interrupted. "You wanted to be on the road by 11:00 AM. It's 11:30, and I'm getting a headache from listening to your justifications on why you left him. I get it, and I don't care. Let's get this shit-show underway."

Before Rebecca could retort about Jr's language, he had flipped up his headphones and was back to reading. She couldn't be mad, not when he was so right. She could try to be distraught about his language, but even that could be dismissed. He was sixteen, and about to be on his own in a few short years. Besides his recluse behavior, she didn't have many gripes. He was smart. Brilliant, actually, and went through a book a day. He had a proclivity to emerge from his dungeon for food during the summer-time, or for a few hours at a time when he wanted to go get a new CD from the store. Besides that, he had a cellphone that he never used and a TV with a heavy layer of dust on it. He was an oddity, the opposite of her husband, but his eyes, face and name were the same.

James was a wrench turner, a do-er. Jr. was a reader and an intellectual (but lazy as all hell). James had a fully stocked toolbox. Jr. had the most well-organized and immaculate book collection that could put the local library to shame. Two chances, and she had ruined her relationship with them both.

"Good point. Well, the car is packed, we're leaving my cellphone behind, right? And taking yours? Good. I don't want to risk getting a work call, because you know me, I'd probably answer it. Let me just check that I have the ingredients for the pies one last time. Excellent. Off we go!"

Rebecca took Jr.'s phone from his outstretched hand and dropped it in the box on the counter, then the instructions for the food and the tents, and followed him out the garage door. He held it for her, his headphones making her wince as they blared death-metal, and he locked the apartment behind her.

The trunk to her souped-up black sedan was already packed and waiting to receive the last box as Jr. plopped into the front seat. The garage smelled strongly of rubber and paint. Rebecca lived in the feeling of a new place, with new opportunities for change, for just a second longer before closing the hatch and sliding into the driver's seat. She started the car and they left the garage into the mid-morning blaze. A few turns later they were cruising down the 55 heading towards Felton Forest. Rebecca rolled the window down and let the wind scoop up her hair. *I can fix this. I can repair this.* She thought to herself, her true feelings breaking through her bustling outer shell. *I have to fix this before Jr. ends up like James.*

The ride to the State Park was uneventful and predictable. As Jr. spent most of the time with his eyes glazed over while less-than-jolly tunes ruined his eardrums, the short car-ride only facilitated more of the same. Luckily Rebecca's stores of patience for the music, the hermit attitude and the apparent lack of care towards anything were about to be renewed. She was hopeful about this trip. Time away. Time alone. No electronics. No books (which she guessed was what Jr. realized was an acceptable reason not to say a damn thing or engage in any kind of interaction), and no James. Not that James wasn't the problem, he was, but not in the sense that what he did impacted her directly. Not anymore.

He took care of the house, went to work, and drank. Occasionally, he'd ask for a date to the movies, or lay on the couch under a weighted blanket with her, but it was superficial. By being out here, without James waiting in the wings, she could have a break from him.

He was going to need the time to think too. The divorce papers she had sent shouldn't be a surprise, but he will be shocked none-the-less.

Rebecca slapped the blinker and turned left off the highway on to a drive marked by a decorative wooden fence on both sides and a sign with the name of the park: *Felton State Park.* While anyone other than the residents of Barhill would have stayed as far away from the stench emitting forest as possible, she had grown used to it, and was happy to have it nearby. She found nature comforting.

She located a parking space where there was a gap in the fence and a trail ran north, directly into the thicket. Jr. pressed a button on his CD player and the rancid howling stopped, and Rebecca had to stop herself from smiling. It was finally quiet. Nothing but the bugs now. Instead, she directed her elation of the moment towards Jr. and said, "This will be good. I'm excited." The words came out hollow and Jr. forced a smile back, a small but purposeful one, where only the corners of his lips curled upward.

He got out of the car last, and Rebecca began removing things from the back seat. Moving on to the trunk, she could have sworn she saw Jr. slip the CD player and headphones into his pocket. No matter, maybe she could push him into the river and ruin the fucking thing. Once she had triple checked the contents of the bags to her neatly typed packing list, they finally hefted them up onto their shoulders. Rebecca's was heavier, having chosen to carry most of the water while Jr. carried clothes and other camping essentials. Her bag was also sturdier and came with a support strap for around her waist. He didn't complain.

She felt a budge in her pocket. Apparently, when they stepped off to check in with the ranger station, she had ritualistically grabbed her cellphone. Keeping with the plan, she unlocked the car and shoved it under the seat.

She looked at Jr. once she locked the car again. "Yes. I've got mine," he said, patting his breast pocket and heading towards the large circled-top building with mirrored windows and a wood-cabin exterior. *Snarky little shit,* she thought.

5

J R

Jr. HELD the door for his mother, resulting in a blast of frigid air. Their footsteps fell heavy on the hardwood floors and echoed as they walked towards the check-in counter. Hidden behind the tall counter was a young girl who he'd consider in his range. She wore a green jumpsuit like the other rangers, but hers said *cadet* on her collar. She was rotating between flipping through her magazine and pecking away at an expensive-looking cellphone. She looked up as Rebecca stood patiently waiting.

"We need to check in, please," she said.

The young woman briefly glanced at James and he felt himself blush, then pretended to be interested in a display case showing a detailed map of the forest, taking note of a particular area shaded and marked, "Untrailed. Dangerous".

"How many nights?" The girl asked. Her voice was sweet and soft. Jr. felt his arms begin to sweat and became acutely aware of the odor coming off his body, the sourness of a day in long pants and sleeves in the middle of the summer. Even the forest's natural malodor couldn't compare. Outside his own lack of confidence, his thoughts drifted to what the girl would be like, her lips parting, her blonde hair draping over his face...

"Two nights. Checking out mid-morning on the third," his mother's hard, prominent shrill cut into his imagination.

It wasn't a very strong thought. He didn't have much to work with, experience-wise. Sure, he had kissed a girl on a dare once, but it was awkward and resulted in the clanging of teeth. Beyond that, he had what the internet could provide when his parents were at work and a wrinkled magazine tucked under his bed from which he had swapped the centerfold for a busty WWF star wearing black pasties. Jr. shook his head. He was about to be knee deep in the shit-forest with his mom. That thought ruined the moment, and he pulled away from the display.

"Which campsite do you want? We have most of them available. The park is pretty much empty," the girl said again. "You'll be quite a ways away at either of them." *I'd like to be alone with you at one of those sites.* Pressure grew behind his zipper and he swept across the room to where he couldn't hear her. His eyes caught a glass-top coffee table centered between three wicker chairs. On the table was a book. It looked out of place. Jr. went to it and picked it up.

It was black and titled Caprock Haunts in gold foil on the spine. The front had an ornate cross embossed into the cardboard. He flipped it open, and it split at the natural fold. Examining it closer, he saw it was half-book, half-cutout. On the left were pages talking about the exploits of a paranormal research firm (he had never heard of them, and he knew quite a few) in Texas, followed by prayers, a glossary, and hand-drawn photos of a wide range of supernatural creatures. There were geists, named haunts like Belford Manor (which he also hadn't heard of) and the Wendigo. Then there was a host of other short stories and personal letters from a few of the people who had written the book. There was one consistent name through it all.

The main curator of the publication was a man named Dwain Cooper.

Wanting to find out more about Mr. Cooper, Jr. passed the cutout (empty, of course) but took notice of what it might have contained. It looked like it had slots for a vial of some sort, a square hole for a small item, maybe a necklace, and a larger center-piece for a cross. Then there were a few more pages, each one with striking, almost horrifying images of demonic creatures of mixed parts both animal and human, words in what he recognized as Latin (though he couldn't read the language... yet), and finally, he flipped to the back page.

"Ready to go?" Rebecca asked.

Jr. grumbled and slid the book into his back pocket as he turned around. It was a smooth move, and his mom didn't notice. She stood hopefully by the door, a pass with their site number on it in her hand. Jr. walked out first, his mother on his heels, but she quickly bustled in front of him. She put the ticket in the windshield of the vehicle.

Jr. lagged behind. He wanted to think about the book (which he found intriguing) and got his mind off this bullshit attempt to play house. His mom had been an okay parent, but a horrible mother in every sense of the word. Most of the time, she could be located under a mound of paperwork, working well into the night (when she was home), or sometimes sleeping at the office. When she was home, she was distant, probably thinking about work, while his dad drowned himself to sleep overnight in cheap booze and misery. Why did it take a divorce for them to realize he existed and suddenly want to play house? He had two years left of school. After that, he could finally get a few moments away from them. This trip was the opposite of what he needed.

His mom started on the trail, well-worn with compressed dirt, but not paved. To all sides was grass, which would normally be somewhat welcoming, but the forest had other plans. Jr. had to breathe loudly through his mouth to prevent the smell from seeping into his nose. The two trudged on in silence but stopped at a sign just before the tree line which loomed ahead as if it was waiting for them. It was a faded version of the map.

Jr. looked it over. "Which site did you choose?" He asked.

Rebecca smiled as if she had won a prize. "Twenty-five. Right here." She pointed towards the number on the map, but Jr. recalled which one it was. It was furthest in, the longest hike, and closest to the river to the north, and wedged on the edge of the restricted zone to the right.

He looked it over and she apparently read his mind. "The off-limits area just isn't trailed. It has a fence around it."

"I don't care, mom," Jr. said in a low voice, and turned back to the path. It was a straight shot through the woods. At their backs, the sun was still high and provided ample light for the journey up the draw. The markers on the outdoor map said the furthest peak was over two miles in. Two long, sweaty, grueling miles. If it was possible to hate his mother any more at this moment, he would. If they knew him at all, this was the least likely place they'd find him.

His boots crunched lightly on the path as he fought to control the whirlwind of thoughts running through his head, from how his dad was doing to the book in his pocket. Rebecca sighed forcefully when they passed under the canopy and were covered in shade. As many had stated, and would forever say, Felton Forest could have been a wonderful place if not for the unexplained rot that constantly assaulted their noses. Jr.'s eyes watered and he felt for the book. Maybe he could read it by flashlight when his mom went to sleep.

Up ahead, the path wound to the right behind an over-zealous grouping of old trees that were fighting to reclaim territory. It was a blind curve, odd for the forest, as most of the shrubbery was evenly spaced enough to see between them. But as Jr. began to notice, the further they moved inward, the closer the trees huddled together. Unexplainably, his heart raced as they came upon a curve and the trees had once again thickened. All around them, the ground was obscured by a mess of green vined plants with triangular leaves. Once he rounded the corner, his heart relaxed, and he glanced at his mother, who had been unexpectedly quiet.

She was marching on, her face dripping, the heavier pack with the food doing a number on her energy and causing her to sweat profusely through her track jacket. Her hair was matted and Jr. felt a pang of guilt. Just as he opened his mouth to offer to take the bag, as a way to wave a white flag, there was a rustling sound from off to their right. His mom must have heard it too and stopped. Then Jr. felt his lungs seize in his chest. There was something deeper in the brush. It was white, with horns, and had deep cavernous eye sockets. Despite the high-placed sun, the thing was wrapped in shadow, and appeared to be looking at them.

His mind sped back to the book, to the creatures he saw. Goat headed monsters with claws and scales and fur. Rebecca clicked on a flashlight and sighed. She had apparently been holding her breath, too. He inched closer and saw it was, in fact, a goat head, but not like his imagination had created for him. It was hung by the horns on a heavy chain draped across a horizontal branch. On the ground was a white bucket with streaks of blood on it. Rebecca shined the light away from the beast to the left, a little further up the path but still within a stone's throw. The body of the animal was laid in the brush, its fur matching that on the head. Then Jr. understood (as his mother apparently did not).

"I thought you can't hunt in the State Park? It looks like someone gut that goat."

Jr. shook his head. "When an animal dies, it's gutted and

tossed aside so other animals can eat it, that way the innards don't ruin the meat."

"Yeah…" she said. "But why take off the head?"

He shrugged. "When male deer are killed by a car, the Game Wardens will cut the head off so it can't be mounted. Maybe this goat-ram-thing is the same way."

It sounded good enough in his head, and his mom appeared to agree with him by holding out a folded copy of the park map. Taking it, he felt a moment of regret for letting her take the larger pack. She was clearly struggling, not just with the hike, but with everything, and he could see it in her eyes. With her forehead caked with grime, and her chest heaving from their bout of excitement, she looked tired and regretful. *She wanted this* was the only thought it took for him to change his mind about humping the bigger bag.

He walked on, his heart calming about ten minutes later. He consulted the map but couldn't get his bearings. Everything appeared the same, and the canopy blotted out the sun. He guessed it was only about a mile to the campsite, and it was growing darker by the minute.

6

JAMES

EVERYTHING HURT. His head from a hangover, or withdrawal. His back, from laying on the concrete plate mounted to the wall that the Wayne County Sheriff's Department dare call a bed. And his face from getting pummeled by one pissed-off forest ranger. James hurt, and he had an odd feeling it wasn't over. He had been there two days, having since earned himself another night after spitting on the magistrate. A kinder punishment than he deserved, the frequent-flyer in the cell with him explained (as he scratched at invisible spiders on his arms). "Normally, spitting on the judge or a cop is an easy felony, and Alcona County doesn't play," the tweaker said.

Thanks, local meth-head. James scooted closer to the cold gray wall and shut his eyes as time ticked on slower. It knew he was waiting and was doing it on purpose.

Hours later, the cell rattled open and a burly-looking woman with a butch cut and dark hairs on her arms yanked him up by his bicep and nearly tossed him out the front door with nothing but a ticket for public intoxication. Maybe someone was taking pity on him. Using the paper to shield his eyes from the sun, he looked down and realized his hope had been misplaced. They still had his shoes inside.

Motherfucker. Well, I am not pushing my luck. I need a new pair anyway. Tail tucked between his legs, James contemplated calling Rebecca, but she was at work, and would never drive the miles from her job just to take him home, and he didn't have the guts to call Jr. either. Then, he realized he couldn't. They were already in the woods by now.

Face swollen, head pounding, feet aching, he turned towards the west to start his walk of shame back to his empty house when the sound of a car rolling up behind him made him stop and turn. It was a Wayne County Sheriff. James sighed and hung his head. He hadn't done anything wrong, and he was sure getting let go from the jail was a good sign. Maybe this was the deputy that arrested him and was back to gloat.

When he got out of the car, he immediately knew it wasn't the same cop. He was older and moved like he had sand in his joints. His uniform was pressed, and he had just a patch of silver hair.

"Mr. Pope?" The cop asked, holding out a packet of papers, already sure that he had the right man. How many James Popes were there getting let out of jail? James took the papers, assuming it was related to the charges.

"Yeah, that's me," he mumbled. There was a cover letter, which he hadn't gotten a chance to flip over before the deputy said, "You've been served, sir," and turned back to his car. James watched him drive off. Maybe he owed money, and it was finally catching up to him. He lifted the sheet. There, clearly across the top, was the headliner he was not expecting. *Petition for Divorce.*

"Divorce?" James said aloud and glanced over the form. It looked real enough, and that cop was real enough, too. The fact that he thought it was a fake just solidified that he was wholly not expecting divorce paperwork. They had never really fought, but then again, he hadn't tried very hard in the relationship either. She'd rather work, and he'd rather drink. He thought there was an understanding. *I guess not.*

He went through the entire packet, letting the sun back on his exposed neck and the hot asphalt nearly melt his socks to his feet. It was all real, and Jr. was mentioned too, as well as child support. He couldn't believe it. Well, he could, but it didn't mean he wanted to. Suddenly he felt like all eyes were on him, though he stood alone, shoeless, in the dust-bowl outside the plain chain-link fence topped with concertina wire that marked the jail-house yard. There wasn't even a car in the parking lot, but he couldn't help but feel like he was being watched.

His anger boiled over, no longer suppressed by unexplained paranoia. But he wasn't just angry. He was livid. After everything he did for Rebecca... move out here, take this shit job in this shit town, give up his career and his sanity. Just for her to leave him and take Jr. away from him, and then take even more money for child support? She made more than he did. She owed him child support. There was no way this was happening. He didn't have a dime to spare. They had always kept separate accounts. Every month, they paid their share of the bills and transferred money to a joint account for groceries and half of all other expenses. His account was empty, if not negative, at the end of every month. They always paid the bills, but there was never any extra. Now Rebecca? James guessed she had seven figures squirreled away.

His thoughts flashed between Jr. and the money, just like his eyes darted left to right across the page. It was all standard stuff, but he was hoping he'd find something in there where she had at least given him a bit of leniency.

Then near the back, he read something. She had left him the house. Well, not really left it to him. She was dumping the mortgage on him. *What the fuck? I can't even afford an apartment. She's not just leaving you; she's burying you.* James felt ready to explode.

If he could, he would have smashed something, anything, he could get his hands on. She was bleeding him dry and taking primary custody of Jr. too.

His rage pumped newfound energy into his body. James rolled up the packet, tucked it under his arm, and started running. Though sharp rocks cut his feet, his lungs burned, and his bladder threatened to burst from the need to pee, he still ran. He ran westward into the sun, letting the light blind him. He didn't care. He might have been running into traffic along the 55 but he still wouldn't care. All he cared about was what he had left. The few dollars in his pocket, and the bank account they shared for the compiled bills. She would get her damn money, but it would be hers. Luckily, the closest ATM was at his favorite bar and that was worth running towards.

Of the eight-mile distance between the Sheriff's Office and the bar, James ran four of it before mis-stepping and scraping his big toe so his sock ripped and the tip bled. Then he walked the remainder at a snail's pace, every mile further driving his irrational plan forward. *Want your money? Fine. You'll get it. Whatever's left, that is.*

Finally, by mid-afternoon, the bar came into view and the rest of the trip felt so much better. Along the way, he pulled his cellphone from his pocket, turned it on and dialed Buddy. He was already there. He said he'd have a drink ready for him. James replied he'd need the top shelf stuff and when he asked why, James only responded, because it's all gone to shit. He closed the phone and hung up. Fifteen minutes later, he was nursing his blistered feet on an old high-backed chair. Doug was there too, playing pool by himself while Buddy read the divorce paper, a $20 bill randomly laid in his lap.

James helped himself to the expensive stuff, having since set his card on the bar with instructions to Doug to not only keep it open, but don't call the ambulance until he knew he was dead. Doug smiled, though James didn't ever mention that he wasn't joking. He fully intended to go comatose with all the swill he could get down, and the most expensive stuff too. Doug looked like he appreciated the business.

He took another shot of a clear tequila with a name he couldn't pronounce. There was a layer of dust on the label and Doug had tried to explain where it came from. James didn't care, he just needed it to do the job. It was smooth as water going down, then rested warm and heavy in his belly. He leaned back and closed his eyes. Even if he drifted off into a dream, he'd still wake up in a nightmare. Nothing he could imagine could be as bad as this. Taking money was one thing. Being in debt over child support with a mortgage over your head was a death sentence. Not to mention the damage it would do to whatever frail relationship he had with Jr. Surely by now, since Rebecca was throwing the book at him, she would take the next two days to reinforce to Jr. why his daddy was such a dirt-bag.

This was all too well thought out. All too well planned. And he hated Rebecca for it.

"It says here you get to keep your house," Buddy said, twisting around in his stool from the other room.

James didn't open his eyes to reply. "We owe on it. Market went to shit. If the bank called our note right now, we'd be out a house and $40,000."

"Ah. Well, no wonder she wanted you to have it. Any idea where she moved to?"

"No, Doug, but I suppose you can shoot your shot since she's on the market. Probably looking for another sucker she can bleed dry."

Doug cleared his throat. "A bit harsh, man. Aren't you going to try to fix things? People bounce back from divorce all the time. Maybe it's an ultimatum."

James sat up and massaged his feet, eyeing the exotic bottle on the end table next to him. He knew what this really was. The divorce paperwork didn't outline the specifics, but he knew what it was. He got arrested. He was a liability. He could tarnish her image with the bank or whatever. Maybe he was a bad influence for Jr., who was already on the brink of a mid-life crisis at sixteen.

He poured himself another drink. "When you start giving away houses, moving out, dividing the children and filing for child support, that to me is a sign of done-done. If there was reconciliation, we are long past that."

He shot the drink skyward and slammed the empty glass on the table, knocking over an ashtray on his foot. "Great," he mumbled to the floor as his cellphone started buzzing. He didn't recognize the number right away, but eventually put it together. The family's numbers were all the same, except for the last four. Rebecca's was saved. This one was not. He assumed it was Jr.'s. The rest of the number was the same and the kid never used it. Feeling woozy, he flipped the phone open and saw the whole text message was a jumble of numbers.

"What the fuck?" He asked, squinting at the bright, artificial light.

"What's that?" Buddy asked. He had been peering over his shoulder, probably inching towards the good booze.

"I have no idea," James said.

"I think I do," Buddy replied. "I think those are coordinates."

7

JAMES

JAMES DIDN'T THINK MUCH of the message and snapped the phone shut. He assumed Jr. had finally gotten around to playing with his complicated phone functions (a purchase from his mother) and had pressed a key somewhere. He didn't agree with spending that much on a phone that he'd never use, but it came out of Rebecca's account, so he moved on. Come to find out, it was more like a computer and had an entire keyboard and a screen that spun open. Still, the kid wasn't interested in it. James kindly suggested she return it because he had the same phone for many years and hadn't felt much need to upgrade. No-one ever called, and he called no-one.

He slid the phone across the top of the bar so it tilted over the edge and fell out of sight. He then dumped his head in his hands and let the gravity of the revelation that he would be alone for the first time in sixteen years rest squarely on his shoulders. It was heavy, depressing, and crushed what little plans he had for the future. Everything revolved around maintaining the status quo at the house, and that was now turned on its side.

Doug inched closer, having since abandoned the ritualistic

cleaning-of-the-glass and Buddy had even poured him a drink from his coveted private reserve. It was going to be a long night for all of them.

Four hours and half-a-handle later, the three men were sitting together behind the pool table, passing the bottle. Doug had locked the front door to the bar and turned off the exterior lights, and resigned himself to helping his friend drown away the memories of his marriage. Buddy had mostly remained silent, taking deep gulps of the swill whilst the others sipped and sighed at the powerful concoction. Before long, their eyes were drooping, their tongues slurred and stumbled, and their faces went numb.

"That dumb bitch didn't even ask me if I wanted to move out here — she expected me to be okay with it," James preached to the leg of a pool table while he sat with his back against the wall. "Then, next thing you know it, she's already put money on a house I hadn't even seen." He finished with a huff of air, then laid his forehead on his knees. The world was starting to spin. He was drunk, hammered actually, and getting home would soon be a struggle. Especially if the numbers on his phone blurred so much he couldn't dial for a cab. He didn't dare ask Buddy for a ride. Everyone in the whole damn town knew not to ride with or near Buddy.

"What're you going to do?" Doug asked. It was a superficial question. One which James knew the answer to immediately. *Absolutely fucking nothing.*

"I'm guessing it's about time I ask for that raise. Our manager just moved off to work at the new Circuit City in Watershed Valley, but I'm still too new at Blockbuster to put in for his job. Looks like a raise it will have to be if I'm to afford all this bullshit." James kicked at the pile of papers with his fate written all over them, and a fresh footprint.

"To you, and may that broad get lost in the woods for good." Doug raised the bottle by the handle, its amber liquid sloshing gently about the bottom of the container. He drank from it, nearly hurled, stuffed it down, and leaned back accomplished. James didn't toast back. Instead, he took a shallow sip, his final for the night, as he too felt queasy, and hefted himself up. The room swam in a flurry of artificial light and plain brown walls broken up by old band posters from the 80s — now a whirlpool of sickening color.

He held still long enough to regain his upward balance and stumbled towards the bar. He made it in three steps. Thankfully, someone had retrieved his phone and had left it out for him to find. He flipped it open and hissed at the overly bright screen, then squinted until his eyes adjusted. He found the number he was looking for in his contacts and dialed. A second later, James slurred the address into the phone, then puked a combination of bar-nuts and whiskey all over the floor. Embarrassed, he looked up to see both Doug and Buddy had passed out in the other room.

"Pussies," he said to himself, wiping his mouth with his sleeve, then stalked to the front door, and out into the rancid evening air. Outside, it was the same stillness that always loomed over the bar. The forest up and behind him towered over the small building, the moon just high enough to bathe the dirt lot in shadows.

"Maybe you'll get lost in there," James said, staring up at it. He imagined Rebecca wandering through the dark, clueless to the ways of the outdoors. *She'd probably wipe her ass with poison ivy.* He imagined Jr., having gotten sick of her, walking off on his own, remembering to follow the stream that ran north-south along the central path that all the local hikers took. He'd emerge a few hours later. But Rebecca... they wouldn't find her for a few days. Maybe weeks, if she had gone too far in the wrong direction — after the coyotes and bears had gotten to her corpse. The bugs would crawl about her pale skin while she laid in the dirt, maggots falling from every orifice… rats scampering out of her rotting mouth…

The blaring of a car-horn broke James from his trance. It was the booze making him dream such terrible things. He loved his wife. Even with the divorce, he still loved her. He had spent the last few hours in a drink-fueled rage, spouting angry words with angrier men who hated their ex-wives. But not him. He wasn't them. He wouldn't be a Doug or, God-forbid, a Buddy. He could be reasonable — sane. The horn honked again, and James winced. "Fuck, alright man," he growled, then traced the railing with his fingertips as he followed the ramp around until he met a yellow city-cab with black lettering. The driver, a young man with lightly tanned skin and bushy eyebrows, leaned over to look at him and held the door shut but spoke through the window.

"Cash. You got cash? You're drunk. Gotta know you have cash," he said.

"What? Sure. Whatever dude." James dug his wallet out from his back pocket and fanned it open to show the fresh set of bills. Apparently satisfied, the driver pushed the front door open, and he slid inside.

He gave out the address for his house. "618 Windamere."

The driver nodded, put the car in gear, and left the bar behind. Meanwhile, James let the mild summer night blow against his face. For whatever reason, it helped calm his already sensitive stomach from another upheaval. A few minutes later, the car came to a squeaky halt in front of a plain black mailbox with the numbers 618 displayed in gold on the side. He didn't move, instead looking up at the house that was both so familiar and so strange to him at the same time.

It was a two-story home, with light yellow siding, red faux shutters and a maroon front door. It sat on a cul-de-sac with four identically laid out homes, but his had the biggest yard and the longest driveway. It had a wrap-around porch and a screened-in back patio that had never been used. James knew what awaited him when he went inside. It would probably be empty, or close to it. Rebecca would have moved her shit out during the day while he was working. *Sly bitch.*

"Mister. The total is $47.50," The young man broke his concentration before the anger compiled into shaking hands and gritted teeth. James fumbled with his wallet, grabbed what looked like two twenties and a ten and handed them to the man. Then he let himself out of the car without another word and began the long, treacherous walk up the house. It stood over him, like a dull referee, judging by his drunken waltz. Somehow, by the grace of God probably, James made it to the garage and had to punch in the code three times before his fat, blurry fingers found the right combination.

A short walk and a light-switch later, he was inside, having come through the mud-room into the kitchen. He scanned the island, hoping for a note, a letter, something from Rebecca maybe explaining things. But it was empty, cleared from the night before. He walked along the wall, passing quickly over the glass doors to the unused patio, to the metal sink, over the coffee maker, then on to the refrigerator where there was an empty to-do list attached by a magnet. James picked up a marker and wrote in wobbly letters *survive,* snorted, then grabbed a beer from inside.

He closed the refrigerator, cool drink in hand, and turned the corner into the hallway, then froze. There was something in the dining room. It was still and tall, with a long, pointed snout and antlers that spread across the back wall. James's heart leapt into his throat, all drunken thoughts having been replaced with sheer panic. His feet refused to budge. Each breath was laborious and came with a stabbing pain in his lungs. Finally mustering the courage with a plan to run, James reared back and threw the beer at the thing and waited.

It didn't move when the can smashed against the window

and busted open on the floor. Then James stepped off to the side so more light poured in from the hall. Relief washed over him.

He was staring at the curtains. White window treatments ruffled across the top. They were back-lit with the moon outside and gave off an eerie glow that looked like there was an animal, like a large elk or a buck in the room with him.

James forced each breath to come out deep chested and full. Then he scolded himself for being so stupid and jumpy. It was the booze doing this. He dreaded what dreams would show up in his sleep, but decided he would solve the issue with the curtains on the spot. He crossed the room through the dark, grabbed hold of the curtain and pulled it so the rack bent out-of-shape and the nails plucked from the sheet rock. Fresh moonlight swathed the room and his back as he turned. Retrieving a replacement beer from the refrigerator, James dumped the curtain in the corner and headed upstairs.

Once in his room, he dropped his pants and his phone glowed in his pocket. He pulled it out and saw that the same text message from earlier that day had come through again with the same cryptic set of numbers. It had been sent hours after they were supposed to have been back. *Coordinates,* Doug had said. With a clever thought, James dug through a dump-box set on the vanity until he found what he was looking for. It was a faded green and white business card for the forester station set near the base of the woods. Dialing the after-hours number, he said, "Those goofy tree fucks know this stuff."

A few rings later and the line picked up. A man on the other end of the line replied in a groggy voice, "Yeah?"

"Uh. Hi, yes. My name is James Pope. I was wondering if you or anyone you work with can tell me if what I've got here is coordinates."

There was a pause while James waited. "Mr. Pope, this is Arnie House."

"Hello Mr. House. Anyway, the numbers are…"

"I figured you'd be in jail longer."

"450 north — what did you say?"

"I said, this is Arnie House. You pissed in my bucket before getting your ass kicked the other night, and I thought they'd hold you in jail longer."

"Oh shit." James said. He had probably meant to say it to himself, but alcohol loosened his tongue. "Listen man, I'm having a rough time… I'm getting worried about my wife and kid. They were supposed to be back from…"

"Yeah yeah, I get it man. It happens."

James sighed into the phone, "Thank you for understanding…"

The man on the other line, Arnie, chuckled in a squeaky voice. "I said it happens, not that I'd help you."

"—wait. You said you get it though? Listen, I think something happened to them…" James didn't understand. *Wasn't Arnie going to help? Wasn't that his job?* Sure, he was a drunken asshole the other night, but he did go to jail for it.

"I do get it. I get that you're a piece-of-shit. I get that you're a jerk. And I get that you need my help. Which, I will be happy to report I am refusing to give you. Have a nice fucking night. Don't worry about your wife and kid. They sound better off without you."

Before James could tell Arnie what he thought of him, the line went dead and he was left with his mouth agape and his hand shaking. It took him several more beers and trips to the refrigerator (and bathroom) to calm down enough to get to sleep after that.

And luckily, while his subconscious vowed for revenge against the pudgy weasel, Arnie, it also begged his body for sleep, which he reluctantly agreed to give it. As James plopped back on the cool king-size bed with down pillows and weighted blanket, he stared blankly at the off-white ceiling, watching the fan spin. He laid that way until pure exhaustion overtook him, straining his eyelids, and threw him into a dream world impossible to forget. A dream world filled with the forest that surrounded their little town, only there was no end to the trees, and the thing in the dining room waited around every bend.

8

EDGAR

A NEW DAY, but with the same struggles.

Edgar Wiles's bones creaked, his back ached, and his skin hung uncomfortably loose about his neck. His hand rattled the keys to the front doors of the service station unintentionally. He cursed his age, his hands, and buying this damn store.

He had retired many years ago when Barhill was just a nickname, and farms still dominated the un-forested land surrounding the settlement. Without much else to do he took to reading and ran out of books in a month, having outdone their collection. He also grew weary with the constant click of his wife's knitting needles as they huddled together in a single-story farmhouse (not including the flooded basement). Coupled with her judgmental eyes creeping over her glasses and occasional jab about his choice in books, Edgar desperately sought a hobby. Luckily, he came from a time when more work could be considered a pastime and left retirement to work the register at Barhill Oil, which he later purchased (from a likewise dying old man) and renamed to Edgar's Bait and Beer.

Now, the building was the perfect excuse to get away from his wife.

It had a bright red glowing sign that stayed lit 24/7 and contrasted the off-white cinderblock walls. It was so bright, Edgar couldn't look directly at it, but he left it, because it was an unintentional beacon of his current health status. *If the sign is lit, Bonny hasn't killed me yet,* he'd joke to anyone who'd listen. But no-one came into Edgar's Bait and Beer. Not because of his prices or his personality per se, but probably because of its location, having been set back closer to the tree line off the main highway. The property butted against a privacy fence to a fancy neighborhood — the fanciest in town, actually.

Edgar finally managed to get the key in the door, unlocked it, and went inside. It was still early. The moon and sun were competing for space in the sky, and the horizon was blocked by an oppressive wall of trees. Reaching blindly in the dark, Edgar flipped the heavy-duty switch between the shelves on his right and braced himself for the harsh overhead lights to come on. After a few seconds, there was a hum, a click, and the LED's lit the small shop. He let out the breath he wasn't even aware he was holding.

He meandered to the coolers near the back, flipped on their lights and walked to his favorite spot near the register (where he'd perch for the next eight hours) He didn't do a lot these days, and he liked it that way. Once he had moved in and established a rhythm in the shop, he dragged the TV from the house and set it up. He eyed it like it was a long-lost friend. Ancient with only three channels, the TV was stationed in front of a lawn chair and an old modified wash basin that smelled like fish.

This was the closest he'd gotten to the woods. His old chair, the gurgle of running water with the hint of a fishy river. He'd already promised himself he'd never go into the park again. Not with what happened the last time. He had set up this command post where he could waste away and reminisce. The memories were enough.

Before he sank into the chair, Edgar turned the TV on, tapped it twice to get the channel to adjust, and sat back. It was in black and white, but as the temperature increased outside, the program, some paid advertisement about knives, would turn to color. Until then, he draped his fingers over the edge of the wash basin, letting the cool water creep over his fingertips while little minnows nipped at his nails. He dosed off thinking about leaving the town for good and dying on a beach somewhere. When he finally did doze off, his mind was void of dreams — that pleasure had been taken from him a very long time ago.

SOMETIME LATER, the shop door opened and a little bell jingled. Edgar startled himself awake, having been snoring, and wiped the sleep from his eyes. The clock on the wall read 9:45 AM, which meant he'd been out for three hours. It was odd to get any customers, let alone someone this early. Grumbling, he got out of his lawn chair. It creaked just like his bones and he made for the far wall where he could see the head of whoever had so rudely disturbed his sleep. If he was going to disrupt him, by golly he was going to be helped, whether he wanted it or not.

"Looking for something particular?" Edgar inquired. The man in the corner, bent over and peering into a refrigerator, turned his head. He was haggard, with stern overgrown eyebrows and long in need of a haircut. His face was shadowed by a beard that contoured his sharp jawline.

"Just Shiner Dark. Ran out down the street," he said. His voice was rough, deep, and menacing.

"We don't sell beer until ten on weekdays. But if there ain't any right there, I can grab some from the back for you while you wait."

"Sure," the man said, standing up. He wore blue jeans and

light gray and blue top that bore the logo of the video shop in town.

"You're Edgar Wiles, right? I've heard of your shop, just never stopped in. I live behind you."

Edgar paused and turned on his heels. "Yes sir, but don't listen to what they say about me, especially if *they* is my wife. And who might you be?"

"James. Pope. I appreciate it, Edgar. I'll mind the shop for you."

"Thank you," Edgar said, walking around the bend, past the bathroom, then entered the overflow cold storage. He came out a moment later carrying the beer and set it on the counter.

"I'm going to make a phone call while I wait, if that's okay?" James nodded at the landline.

"Go right ahead. Dial nine first for local. But no long distance or I'll have to charge you."

"No problem," he said, lifting up a card to read the number and starting the dial-tone on the receiver.

Edgar noticed the card was one off his board mounted by the ice cream freezer. He had a lot of cards up there, most of which he had memorized, as they hadn't changed from when he first received them at his grand opening years ago. Some were carried over from the previous owner.

The particular card James was holding made his heart sink. He hadn't forgotten it. In fact, he had left it up as a reminder. That card, with its subdued gold-lettering, light touch of green near the top and a picture of a baby deer, belonged to Joe's Tracking.

James must have caught him eyeing the card because he said, "Know anything about this guy?"

Of course he did. He knew everything about Joe Corrinth of Joe's Tracking. In fact, he was a part owner in the business many years ago, handling most of the actual services while Joe managed the backend, equipment and booking. He was a skilled tracker, just like Edgar, but he wasn't as seasoned. That business had long since shut down and their relationship, both personal and professional, dissolved in silence.

"Nope. Not even sure he'll answer," Edgar lied, hoping it was convincing enough, and wishing even more that the lie was true. He didn't need Joe calling him. Then again, if he did, it was his own damn fault for leaving the card up.

"Oh well, I'll give it a try."

Edgar couldn't do anything but nod along as James dialed. He waited in earnest, holding his breath, staring at the phone while James eyed the cigarette rack behind him. Then, on what should have been the last ring, the line picked up, and Edgar choked on his own spit.

"Hi, yes. This is James Pope. I'm looking for Joe's Tracking."

He was sure he looked insane for staring, so Edgar forced himself to turn away and fiddled with the register, all the while his ears tuned to pick up the conversation. He was feeling stupid now for keeping the card up. He did what he could to decipher what was being said based on James's side of the chat.

"I understand, sir. But this is important. I got this cryptic message. I think they're coordinates. I can't find anyone to help me... yes sir... I can send them over."

James read off the numbers from his own phone. Edgar went over them in his head. After a few moments, he narrowed the location down and gasped, unable to hold it in.

"Yes, sir. Okay, sir. Thank you. I guess I'll go on my own. Thank you. Bye now." James hung up and replaced the receiver, then dug around for his wallet. Edgar was frozen, his fingers hovering above the register, tapping the keys lightly as he shivered.

"Apparently I've forgotten my wallet."

Edgar snapped out of it, "What did Joe say about your mystery location?" He blurted out. He already knew where they went, or at least the general area, but it was like an achy cut on the bottom of your foot that could be real but only if you actually looked at it.

"Something about the restricted zone of the park. Near the northwest."

Edgar forced himself to remain stone faced. "Didn't know there was such a thing," he lied.

"Me neither. Apparently it's up off the beaten path, to the north-west, around the backside of a big hill. Hey listen, I don't have my wallet. I think I left it in the cab last night. Can I just give you this and pay for the beer later?" He was holding out a handsome watch with a black leather strap. "It's worth a few hundred at least. A gift from my ex-wife. I'll come back for it with cash."

"Yeah. Sure. Whatever," Edgar said, taking the watch and dropping it into a change slot on the register. He was on autopilot, the gravity of the call overtaking most of his normal functions.

"Thank you," James replied, scooping the case of beer off the counter and heading for the door.

"Wait," Edgar said just before James was gone. "Why do you need to go to the restricted zone?" He asked, then followed up with, "If you don't mind."

"My ex-wife, or soon to be ex-wife, is there with my son. I need to know where to find her body" He smiled mischievously as he headed out the door. Edgar couldn't help but feel like there was more truth to that joke than James realized.

9

JOE

JOE CORRINTH STARED into the microwave, the only piece of technology in the break room. There wasn't even a damn TV. He had taken his break two hours earlier, having been rattled by a phone call. It was both unexpected and concerning, as it came from someone he hadn't heard from in over a decade.

He had kept his number, just like all the others he had gotten over the years, and programmed it into his phone, regardless of his intent to never call him again. Least of all, he hadn't expected a call *from* the person. A vow of silence was an implied vow of no-fucking-contact of any kind. Thoughts swimming, he settled on making his lunch early in the roach-infested break room with the half-functioning microwave provided by the glorious Outdoor Pro Shop rather than get caught daydreaming on the storeroom floor.

The ripe chopped chicken and stale rice spun about, popping, taunting him. It knew he would hate it. Hot or cold, it didn't matter. The dish was six days old and though it hadn't grown fuzzy with mold, the bacteria inside surely had time to consummate. It was either the chicken or go hungry, and he had learned long ago what hunger could do to a man. His choice seemed obvious.

Packing the Tupperware that morning, he quickly threw it in a plastic bag before scuttling out the door. Years ago, nearly twenty, he would never have been late to anything. The military had taught him that. In fact, he would have been thirty minutes early if the order was to arrive fifteen minutes early. Most of his habits instilled in him as a soldier had faded with age, as his body refused to keep up. But there was one thing that never went away; his iron stomach and his powerful will to drive through the pain. His leg twitched in response, reminding him of what true pain was. True pain wasn't stepping on an IED and losing a limb. Pain was working at an outdoor shop for twenty years in constant discomfort, too fucked up on painkillers to do any other job. Then being reminded of the bomb every day as the cheaply made prosthetic dug into his skin. He winced and bent over, twisting the shaft a bit until the ache went away. He was no stranger to pain, but that didn't mean he wouldn't try to avoid it.

One second before the microwave was supposed to beep, Joe yanked it open and pulled out the unsavory meal — a slight sourness to the steam. Meal in hand, he limped over to a stiff plastic chair and matching table (which were chained together to prevent theft) hugging the wall where he could see the only exit, leaving no-one at his back.

His fork hovered by his mouth and he was about to take his first bite when his boss, a piss-ant of a man with a comb-over and stringy neck beard poked his fat face into the room.

"Got a customer up front. Looks like a city guy. Could use your expertise." Joe hated his boss. A raw, visceral hate that was reserved for the dumbest of people. The greasy manager took advantage of his position by barking orders and purposefully interrupted what little time Joe had cordoned off for himself.

Almost like he was retaliating against a man he knew was better than Outdoor Pro Shop.

He pushed the dish aside, somewhat thankful to have a reason to put it off, but no less aware of the hunger jabbing him in the stomach. He ignored the feeling to indulge his joke of a boss.

"Yeah. But I'm starting my break over," he snarled. It was a command, not a request. He glared at his manager, who held his gaze for a half-second longer than he liked, but eventually, the weaker man backed down and disappeared back around the corner. Joe smiled a bit. *I've still got it.* He walked onto the main floor and instantly found the customer his manager was referring to.

He was bent over a set of turkey-calls, his eyes glazed over with confusion. But his head darted side to side. Tall and trim, he looked out of place in the outdoor shop.

As Joe walked over, the hint of stale booze hit him. Only for a second, then it disappeared under a mask of laundry detergent and cheap cologne. Then, with his best facade of giving-a-shit, Joe put on a weak smile and cleared his throat so the man looked up. "Is there something I can help you with?"

The man shook his head quickly then went back to eying the turkey-calls.

"They aren't in season, if you had planned on doing any hunting," Joe followed up, not appreciating being ignored for just trying to help. *You interrupted my lunch to look at turkey-calls. I AM going to help you. Whether you want it or not.*

"I need a whistle, a mirror, some all-weather matches and rope," the man said into the rack. He rattled off what any internet search would say you needed for an emergency pack. What this guy needed was an intervention.

"Well, you won't find any of that over here. Come on over to the next aisle. Most of the camping gear is over here."

Joe walked off with the man finally pulling away and

catching up. He turned around the next isle where there was an entire section of similarly branded orange tools.

"What's your name?" Joe asked.

The man reached over and grabbed an overpriced compass with a viewfinder. "James Pope. Call me James."

Joe stopped. *This was the man that called him about the coordinates earlier. This was the man who called from Edgar's place.* He decided to gather more information before revealing he was on the other end of that particular phone call. The restricted zone was named that for a reason, and it took a serious cause for anyone to want to go there.

He knew all about the restricted zone, and had helped cultivate the rumors about it over the years. Steep cliffs, mountain lions, bears, poison ivy, venomous snakes... rumors of which all did well to keep people from going there. The truth, however, was so much worse.

"What are you needing this stuff for? Maybe I can help you narrow things down."

James picked up a fixed-blade knife and compared it to a machete wrapped in cardboard, as if they were comparable. Joe rolled his eyes.

"I'm heading into the park. I haven't heard back from my family. I got a cryptic message with coordinates and a forest ranger told me they pointed at the restricted zone."

I ain't no fuckin' forest ranger.

"Do you think they're lost?"

"No, but they outstayed their listing. They were supposed to be back today. I called my wife's cellphone, and it went to voicemail. The same with my son."

"What about the park cops? Or the rangers? Did they say they'd go up?" Joe asked. He knew the answer, but he was trying to spur more information out of him. It was pretty uncommon for anyone to *want* to go into the restricted zone. There were a lot of signs. Fences. Even fines for wandering off the beaten paths. If someone had gone there and had gotten lost, there would be hell-to-pay if they got out. In fact, the rangers were so good at keeping people out of that area that Joe was almost excited. They might call on him again for help, just like the old days, and his manager could promptly suck on his expertise. If the rangers called him, it meant a payday. That was the protocol, or at least had been for many years. If someone gets lost in the restricted zone (rare, but it happened), call Joe's Tracking to get them out. He hoped the policy hadn't changed...

James dropped the machete into his hand-basket while Joe dreamt about the money, only to have the dreams chased away by the memories of why he retired from the tracking business in the first place. The visions of what waited for him in the Fell Forest. The thing that left a scar across his back. A warning.

"I'm going to have to go in alone. The rangers are pretty sure they're just running late or decided to stay an extra day. They have warning signs and stuff. Plus random patrols up there. I tried to call to get a handle on the location, but I pissed off the boss over there and he wouldn't tell me anything. But I know they were only supposed to be gone two nights."

"Do you have any experience in this sort of stuff?" Joe asked, already knowing the answer.

James paused and considered the question. Joe could tell the answer by the look on his face. "No. But it doesn't matter. We aren't doing so great. I could use this, you know. To show I care... I don't know why I'm involving you in my marital problems. Anyway. I didn't get your name."

"People call me Mr. Corrinth. Are you ready to ring up?"

"Nice to meet you. Yeah. I think this is as good as it gets."

Joe led the way to the counter on autopilot, his brain running a mile a minute. He knew he'd be making a phone call after James left. Too much of what he said was coincidence, it wasn't just a set of missing hikers. It was all adding up, and though Joe wasn't a total believer of superstition, there was one thing he knew about the forest. The fence, the signs, the rumors, the random patrols and the fines, were all built with a purpose. To keep people out of the restricted zone and let still waters lie. But Joe had unfinished business there. Not including a hefty payday. He just needed to lay the seed and watch the panic-tree grow. And when the panic-tree grew, money fell from it.

He finished ringing James up and when he left the store, Joe rushed back to the break room, his fingers barely able to click the buttons fast enough. The phone rang once and then someone picked up. He could hear the person on the other line breathing.

"Edgar, I know you're there. And I know this guy James called from your place. Folks have gone missing, and the rangers will be calling me soon. We need to talk."

"Joe. We can't. We swore."

"I know what we swore, Edgar. But we can finish this. It takes three of us, and I think we found the third. It can work this time. We tie up loose ends, get paid, and get gone. It'll be worth it."

There was a long pause, but Joe held steadfast. This was a negotiation. Edgar had sworn off the forest. Joe had laid out the bargain. Whoever spoke first, lost.

"I take it he just left your store," Edgar asked

"Yes. With camping gear. He's going up soon."

"Let's be ready when he gets there," Edgar said.

"Do you want me to tell him?"

"Of course not. Tell him when he won't have a choice."

Joe sighed. "Done."

Edgar sucked in air. "One more thing."

"What's that?" Joe said.

"I don't care what training you have. Try to leave me on the mountain, and I'll fucking kill you."

"Same," Joe said dryly.

"I'll see you shortly," Edgar said. Then the line disconnected.

10

JAMES

JAMES LEFT the outdoor store feeling more ill prepared than when he had gone in, but he was short on time, and the cab waiting for him was cinching down on his already suffocating wallet. He crawled into the back seat. This driver, an older, but more courteous man, was kind enough to deliver his wallet from the previous night — intact — with what little money he had still inside. As James sat on the hot leather seat, he reminded himself to tip the driver whatever he could. This drive was going to empty his credit card completely. He'd have to rely on the cash, and hoped he'd be left with enough after the ride that it wasn't insulting.

"Felton State Park," he told the driver, who only nodded and cranked the air conditioner. It whined, but soon filled the cabin with frigid air. While they drove, James began emptying his purchases into a simple backpack he had found in a closet at home. He didn't have much beyond what he got from the store. A flashlight and crank-radio, an extra set of batteries, some granola bars and two bottles of water. He also had a long fixed-blade knife, a spool of rope, a bundle of tinder and a whistle. All of which he had no idea how to use to his benefit, but figured he'd rather have them than not.

Ten minutes later, the cabby entered the highway and then took the first exit. James stared out the window and watched the sign move by in slow motion. *Felton State Forest, Visitor's Center, next exit.* James's heart beat faster in his chest, a lump forming in his throat and an uncomfortable sweat brewing on his lower back. He shifted in the seat and went through the items in his bag once more. Then, his cellphone buzzed in his pocket, causing him to jump. He let out a growl at himself for letting it happen; he was not so easily rattled, but his nerves were acting up.

Thinking about it, he hadn't been this nervous when he sky-dived for the first time, got married, or had Jr., but something in his subconscious was telling his body to be prepared, and James was ignoring it. He wiped his sweaty palms on his jeans and opened the phone. On it was another message from his son. It said one word, a word so powerful he nearly hurled.

Help.

James had to force himself to remain calm. He could tell the cabby to speed up, but it wouldn't change anything. The entrance to the park was coming into view on the left. He perked up, head on a swivel, checking for Rebecca and Jr, perhaps walking towards their car, or hiking out on one of the trails. Like he'd be so lucky. Instead, he was heartbroken to see that the parking lot was empty except for a fleet of forest ranger trucks parked behind the circular visitor's center. The cabby came up alongside the brown building with long, thin windows and a large wood carving of a tree mounted on its face. There was a wrap-around awning across the backside that overlooked a scenic valley used for events and could even be rented (why anyone would want to rent out space in the world's smelliest forest, he didn't know).

There were a series of smaller buildings in a line matching

the brown-wood exterior. Also carved into a large plaque on the side were labels identifying their usage as storage, a spare office, and equipment. James pulled the three largest bills from his wallet and handed them through the window.

"Keep the change." He wasn't sure how much the tab was. Truthfully, he didn't care. He needed to go. There were more pressing things at hand.

He swept the bag over his shoulder and left the cab behind, then followed the sidewalk inside. Dimly lit with a vast ceiling, the large theatre like room gave his footsteps an echo. At the far end of the building, he found a young girl sitting behind a desk with a digital music player in her hands and large headphones covering her ears. She didn't look up. James quickly grabbed a day-pass from the rack on the counter, scribbled his name on it and slid it over so it fell into her lap. She glanced up, annoyed, and intentionally took her time looking over his information before dropping her headphones around her neck.

"Day passes are good until five. It's five fifteen."

"That's fine. How much for an overnight?"

"We don't sell overnights after five. You'll have to come back tomorrow."

James's face grew hot, and he leaned over the counter a bit.

"I need to get into the park. My wife and kid are up there, and your useless people said they can't find them. Check the log. They were supposed to be back by noon today."

The young woman, unimpressed, repeated the same statement in an even more monotone voice, her eyes dull. "It's five fifteen."

James couldn't help but raise his voice. "I don't care what fucking time it is. Screw the pass. I'll be heading towards these coordinates." He scribbled them down from his phone onto his pass. "Looking for my wife. I'll deal with the fine later."

"You can't do that, sir."

"Argh! Listen..." He glared at her badge. "Elli, tell your

useless manager where I'm at. Maybe he'll send someone who actually knows what they're doing…"

"Is there a problem?" A familiar voice called from behind him. James turned to see none-other than Arnie. If he didn't have to find Rebecca and Jr, and had more bail money, he would have clocked him on the spot. He waddled up, arms crossed on his fat belly, looking amused at the spectacle. He smiled, stretching his pockmarked skin, temporarily hiding the blemishes from years of picking at acne.

"I don't have time for you," James said, turning on his heels and prepared to brush by him.

"Now then. Elli said you can't come into the park. If that means I have to kick your ass again and send you packing, this time for trespassing, I will."

James could tell he was relishing in the temporary bout of power. He contemplated knocking him out and heading into the forest anyway. That would surely draw the cops and help him find his family sooner, he hoped. He was sober now, making the fight more likely to spin in his favor if he struck first. Arnie was heavy and clumsy, but James could take a hit, despite not actually knowing how to fight.

"How about we not go for round two?" Arnie asked slyly, then took a step forward, his gut nearly touching him. "Unless you want to go back to jail. Probably enjoyed being someone's bitch." There was a chemical smell on his breath.

James inched forward. He could feel the heat of Arnie's skin through his shirt. Any brush of their clothes and James would hit him. The two men squared off. Elli was silent behind the counter. Then, the door to the station opened with a creek and slammed shut. Two people walked in their direction. James balled his fists.

"Arnie! Enough of that," the voice called. James's eyes darted to the side and he couldn't believe who it was. It was Edgar. He was walking slowly, but stood tall. He wore a tan ball-cap, a light-blue fishing shirt, unbuttoned near the top with a bandana protecting his neck. He also wore a pair of cargo-pants and green hiking boots. To further add to James's confusion, the clerk from the outdoor store was next to him in a similar outfit. Both men unslung two identical packs and set them on the floor.

"Leave him be. He can pay your fees later. Same thing with us," Edgar said.

Whatever was going on, it was enough for Arnie to back down and eye up the newcomers. He seemed to recognize them both, and his face shifted into a loathing scowl reserved for someone who you truly hated.

"What're you doing here?" He hissed, eyes darting from Edgar to the clerk.

"Joe and I will be escorting Mr. Pope into the forest to retrieve his wife and son. We are his guides into the restricted zone."

James was confused, then he put the puzzle together. Joe… from Joe's Tracking. But how did he and Edgar know each other? Joe had also said he wouldn't take the job. None of this was making sense.

"Our people have her logged out as of noon today. Her car's gone too. An expensive black SUV. Checked the logs myself," Arnie said.

"What? That's bullshit." James said. "I got a text from Jr. asking for help…"

Edgar held up a hand. "We believe you. This wouldn't be the first time Arnie has lied about these kinds of things. Come with us, James. Let's go find them," he said, turning off, leaving Arnie standing bewildered.

Edgar not only run him over, but he also ended the conversation with a statement of fact. James couldn't help but smile slightly as he left the station behind. But as soon as he got outside, he was filled with more questions than he had breath to ask.

Once the three of them were alone, it became a race to speak first, with James being the loudest and most emotionally charged.

"What was that about? Do you two know each other? Someone tell me what's going on."

Edgar waited for him to finish, fiddling with a strap from his pack that went around his waist.

"This is Joe. From Joe's Tracking. We have... a history. Look, we're running out of daylight, so we have to know. Do you have money?"

James was taken aback and stumbled his words out, "Yeah. I mean, my house is worth a penny. My wife and I have some in savings but we're divorcing..."

"Okay, so at least one of you has money? Great. Then understand this. If Joe and I are going to help you, you have to help us, got it? Arnie is lying. He probably towed your wife's car when she didn't show just to be an ass. Joe and I have a history... with Arnie. Call it bad blood, but know he isn't going to help you. And without him, the foresters do nothing. He's a piece-of-shit, but unfortunately, he runs this show."

James's jaw dropped. He knew what this was. This was a shakedown. They knew no-one would come. Maybe even conspired with Arnie. But why were they gearing up and putting on such a show? Maybe they really did want to help.

"How much?"

"One hundred thousand." Joe jumped in. "That's fifty for each of us. Not that how we split it matters, but we're being honest. Just like we're being honest when we say this park is the most treacherous place we've ever been. And your wife and son — if they are at all like you —have wandered into the restricted zone. Without us, they're fucked. The longer it takes us to get up there, the harder it will be to track them."

James didn't know what to do. He could figure out the money later. Rebecca's car was still worth at least forty. Maybe she had some in savings or a retirement account somewhere. Whatever the case, he needed their help, so he was forced to do the only thing he could do in the moment. He lied.

"We've got plenty. Fifty each."

Joe looked him over, then glanced at Edgar, and they both nodded to each other. "Follow our commands," Joe started. "Every single one if we're getting out of there alive. The first of which, is not to ask us about Arnie. Because we haven't and won't talk about that man ever again. Follow me. Stay close — Edgar will always be at your back. And no matter what happens, keep moving."

11

REBECCA

INITIALLY, Rebecca felt good—no, rejuvenated, as she and Jr. began their march into Felton Forest. She had a map, plenty of supplies, and an idea for a dessert she thought he would absolutely love. Then, while gathered over the peace meal, she could finally talk to him and maybe explain her side of the divorce. If she was lucky, she could get him talking while they hiked. But to her dismay, not fifty yards up the beaten path, she looked back at Jr. to see he once again had his headphones on and was staring blankly ahead. Even as they crossed into the wall of trees and the smell became so strong she had to breathe through her mouth. His mouth opened a hair too, but no words came out.

Overhead, the thick canopy nearly blocked out all the sun, and the trees huddled neatly together. There was a steady chorus of bugs and mammals, humming their call to arms, and a gentle crunch of fallen leaves on the path at their feet. It was marked by thick branches, sliced smoothly across the top and standing three inches tall. It was cute, cool, and at a grade just steep enough to break a sweat, but not so busy it barred them from making small talk. Rebecca felt it was not only a need, but a requirement that she and Jr. talk this trip. She stopped in the middle of the path and he lowered his headphones looking confused.

"I said we weren't going to be messing with electronics. Put it away."

There was no retaliatory comment, eye roll or sarcastic winding of the cord, only a gentle hair flip from his overgrown mop about his head and the same emotionless stare as he pushed forward, this time leaving Rebecca in his wake. She was now following him, their conversation non-existent. He had changed everything, but they had accomplished nothing. Along the way, she tried multiple times to engage him with questions about anything, from what the names were of the musicians from his favorite band, to if he had given any more thoughts about what he was going to do after high school. That latter seemed like an ongoing battle to not only make a decision but make one that would lead to any kind of future. Currently, his plan consisted of starting a band and getting a degree in music theory.

Rebecca could only explain why it was a poor decision in so many ways before she finally gave up. He'd have to figure it out the hard way. Her next topic of choice would have been his dad, but that was best left for over the campfire.

Nearly half a day later, both of them were covered in bug bites, their boots were soaked through with sweat, and their lower backs ached from unbalanced packs. Rebecca signaled for them to stop, having taken the lead sometime mid-afternoon, and removed her map and compass from the pack. She wasn't lost, but she found that using the compass, understanding their heading, and where they were in relation to the visitor's center helped alleviate the host of what-ifs swarming in her ever plan-ning mind.

Jr. seemed to take an interest in what she was doing and joined her, even offering a water bottle to drink from. Rebecca shook her head gently and pored over the map. But after a few seconds, something happened that made them both ignore the map completely. She could tell Jr. was looking at the same thing she was. The compass was spinning freely. Jr. took it up himself, now interested, and spun around slowly, the dial still moved irregularly, never stopping in one direction.

"Maybe it's busted," he said, handing it back. "We don't need it anyway. We can stay on this path and get there. We can't be far off."

"Maybe," Rebecca replied, then had a brilliant idea. She shoved the broken compass away and sorted through her pack until she felt the hard corner of a new book. Removing it, she set it on her lap and retrieved a headlamp from the front pocket of the bag. It was growing darker by the second, and her digital watch told her it was nearly 7:00 PM. Clicking the light on, she held it out for Jr. to hold while she looked through the book.

It was about survival techniques. A lot of it was basic but useful as it explained the most likely scenarios to have to use the skills listed, and it had plenty of pictures. Jr. seemed even more interested and hovered overhead. Rebecca flipped through the pages and found the section she was looking for.

"There. Directions on how to make a compass with a needle, a leaf and some water. Think you can handle it?"

Jr. didn't answer and took the book. A few minutes later, he had a hole in the ground, a needle from the sewing kit, and a leaf. He poured the water from a bottle into the hole until it no longer soaked in, floated the leaf on the water, then placed the needle in the middle of the leaf. It gently rotated, and Rebecca held her breath. A few seconds later and the leaf pointed up the path, the same direction they had been going before they stopped.

Rebecca smiled, looked up, and saw that Jr. looked pleased with himself. He closed the book and tucked it under his arm. She didn't mind. It was for him anyway, and a trick to get him to talk when nothing else worked. Only she had hoped to use it as a last resort.

After the leaf compass, Jr. lead the way, finding purpose to the stay in the woods in the form of knowledge gained. Rebecca was also able to clear her mind about the compass, though the forest had gone completely dark. She and Jr. walked side by side using both expensive LED flashlights and headlamps to light their path. She had bought the best equipment for the trip and that gave her the confidence to travel into the hours after dusk.

Just when she was about to consult the map once more, there was a break in the path and it veered right, whilst the rest of it continued north. On the left-hand side of the trail was a wooden marker with the campsite number carved into the side. They trudged along into a small circular clearing with a well-worn fire-ring made of stones and a little grill that had rusted through. If not for the marker, she'd have had no idea the camp-site existed.

Twenty grueling minutes later and their tents were set up and the fire started to take. Jr. had found a stump large enough to sit on and had dragged it closer to the fire and was now reading the survival book by flashlight. She gave him the time and focused on making the campfire pies. Using the wrought iron bread-shaped device, she loaded two pieces of bread, some butter, cherry pie filling and sugar into one side and closed it. Hanging it over the fire, she roasted the contents and flipped it at regular intervals. After the first one was made, she dumped it onto a steel plate. The scent of warm baked goods mixed with cedar wood from the fire. Jr. looked up as Rebecca started the second one.

"Want to try it first?" She asked. Jr.'s face was shadowed by the flashlight. He clicked off the light and Rebecca noticed how he resembled James so much. It was almost painful.

"Why are you doing this?" He replied, cold and dry. Rebecca wasn't prepared.

"Doing what? This trip? I told you already. We need this. To regroup, reset, synergize as a family."

Jr. snapped the book shut. "Oh, don't act like I'm some fuckin' employee. Families don't *synergize,* and it takes more than two people to make a family."

Rebecca wasn't ready for the outburst, knowing neither what to say nor how to process it. Her frustration boiled inside. With James, with Jr., with work, with all of it. It compiled together and was shoved deep down, masked by her drive for success. But now, it seemed like it was all about to come out. The flood gates were open.

"What the hell do you know about family? You spend every day sulking and listening to trash music. You wouldn't know what to do if it didn't include dreaming about how terrible your life is. Your father and I love you Jr., but we can't keep going on like this. We're like two people living in the same house, completely unrelated."

"My name is James, and just because you're divorcing dad doesn't mean you get to dump all the memories we have. You don't get to erase our family!" He was standing, bellowing, his voice echoing. The bugs had all grown silent and were listening in. "You know what your sin is, mom? Pride. Pride and ambition. Both of which became a perfect substitute for a family. You're just as much to blame as dad is. You worked so hard, you forgot to work on us. Well, good job. Now you get to work all you want, and you burnt the fuckin' pie. Goodnight. I'm counting down the hours."

Rebecca blinked twice before the smell of burnt bread hit her and she saw that the iron she was holding was smoking. She dropped it in the dirt and popped it open to find blackened crust on both sides. By the time she looked up, Jr. had already gone inside his tent and zipped up the door. His flashlight clicked on and his shadow showed he was reading again.

Then, without warning, she broke down. Head in her hands,

her tears dripped shamelessly into the dirt. Not for the food, but because the same thing that had happened to the pies had happened to her family. She held them over the fire, hoping they could take the heat, but ended up burning the crust beyond recognition so everything stunk and no-one wanted anything to do with it. Now, there was only a single pie remaining, off to the side, cool to the touch, and covered with ants.

Rebecca cried until the coals died down and the fronts of her legs grew chilly. Then, alone and with a painful bruise from where she had sat back on her tailbone in the dirt, she crawled into her tent and laid on her side on her bedroll. Arms tucked under her pillow, she watched Jr.'s shadow sweep the pages in the book until exhaustion took her, and the night-bugs resumed their song.

12

JR

Jʀ. ᴡᴏᴋᴇ up the next day in a pool of sweat. The tent had turned into a sauna before the sun was even up. Birds sang, little animals dove through the underbrush, and the forest itself seemed to shake itself awake. He rolled over, his back sticking to the mat. He hunted for a fresh shirt and shorts. He'd sleep with the door open and let the mosquitos have at him if it meant he wouldn't be this hot ever again. As he turned, something dug into his side. Reaching blindly, he discovered the little black book, Caprock Haunts. He had finished it that night in the privacy of his tent using a flashlight. It wasn't particularly long, nor detailed. It was more of a novelty, really.

Turning it over in his hands, he appreciated the amount of effort put into the design. The book was, in fact, well done in its construction. From the clever cutout with the supernatural warding items like the holy water and the cross, to the text itself, which was as entertaining as it was informative. Caprock Haunts is, or was, a paranormal research firm based in Texas, and what appeared to be a flimsy operation on the surface (based on the low-rent shopping-center photo), turned out to be a well-run business highly regarded and respected in their community. According to the book, Caprock Haunts started in 1967 and was originally named Roswell Hunters, and took up a renaming as well as a new location when they received a hefty donation. From what the book also said about their timeline, Caprock Haunts moves to wherever the action was and had taken cases all over the country

Overall, it was almost comical and made for a quick read as the spells, wards and incantations placed at the end of the text grew more absurd the more he read. Jr. decided the little book was cool enough to make his bookshelf and maybe one day he'd look them up.

"Jr.?" His mother called from the other side of the tent. "Are you up?" What a stupid question. Of course, he was up. How could anyone sleep in this humidity?

"Yeah," he said, not wanting to show his frustration.

"I'm making pies. Going to try powdered eggs in them," she replied, sounding like a whipped dog. This was how she made you feel dumb. Even though he was the one who blew up the night before, she was extending the olive branch and waving the white flag. She would use that fact to force an uncomfortable conversation later. Wicked but effective. It was a business strategy, Jr. knew. He had read the book she had learned it from.

He answered by unzipping his tent and coming out into the morning air. It was just as he had expected, another level of humid, and his hair stuck to his head. With a quick swipe, he brushed it back and sat on the stump by the fire. His mother had already mixed up a batch of instant eggs and was heating up the dumb square shaped pans by leaving them in the embers. He eyed the burnt and abandoned pie one from the night before, covered with sand and ants.

"Good morning," she said. "We should talk. There's something you said I don't agree with." *Jesus, she couldn't even wait until after he'd eaten.*

Jr. pushed himself up from the stump and walked towards

the edge of the camp, then circled back, looking for any reason to not have to be stuck here and take part in the conversation. Diving into his tent, he found his green plastic military canteen with a cloth strap. He stood off to the side of their camping area and upended the bottle over his head. The water was lukewarm, but soothing from the prickly heat growing on the back of his neck. He ran his hand through his hair, letting the water soak it until the bottle was empty. *Just one more day,* he told himself, returning to his tent. Meanwhile, his mother waited patiently for him to be done. He went for his pack instead.

It was well organized, but he needed to refill his canteen, or so he told himself to avoid the conversation. He could also refill the jug from the bottles. He had taken six total, plus his canteen, which held two quarts. His mother carried another twelve, along with all the food. It was enough for one day, with the assumption they'd have to shower by gathering stream-water from a hanging plastic bag. As Jr. dug for the bottles, he heard the empty crinkle of plastic as his fingers brushed up against them. A moment later, he emerged, confused. All the bottles in his bag were empty. Outside the tent, he showed his mom what he found. She raised an eyebrow but eventually pressed him to speak his mind.

"What's the deal? Do you want one of my bottles?" She asked.

Jr. shook his head, "They're all empty."

"What? What do you mean? Like you drank six bottles?"

He shook his head again more furiously "No. I drank from my canteen yesterday and finished the rest of it today. All my bottles are empty. Look," he said, turning the bottle cap, so it clicked as he broke the seal. He tilted it to the side to show there weren't any holes in the side and even slid aside the flap to his tent to show that none had leaked out. Rebecca bustled over to her tent and a few moments later, there was a soul-crushing crinkling sound as she emerged with a handful of bottles as well, all empty.

"I don't understand. The heat couldn't do this. And there aren't any holes either. The tops are all sealed."

Jr. could see a break in his mother's hard exterior. She was out of her element. As much as she planned and plotted, prepared and researched, she was anything but a survivalist or a camper. She relied on equipment and articles before basic skills such as how to get clean water.

She perked up, a little smile on her face. "The stream. We can boil water from the stream and refill the bottles. It'll be fine!"

For a moment, Jr. hoped she would give up so they could march down from the mountain early, but before he could come up with a rational rejection, she was already gathering up bottles from his tent and packing them in a lightweight neon green dump-pouch.

"I'll be right back," she said, smile still on her face. "Mind the fire." And she was off, heading along the beaten path, then turning left onto the main route that smacked directly into the stream. Jr. watched her leave, then picked up a stick and played around in the hot coals.

He examined the tip glow red, and fall off, and did this several times, along with snuffing the end out in the sand. Chin in hand, he was getting near dozing off when he heard something that made his stomach flip over.

A scream, long and crackled with pain, coming from outside the camp.

Jr. leapt up, flailing about madly for the first aid kit in his mother's pack, and snatched up his cellphone while he was at it, then sprinted out of the camp and down the trail to the left. It dropped into a gulley, and he broke into a down-hill controlled run-fall. A short distance later, the path ended at a wall of overgrown brush, but he could see where people had cut through it, and he smelled moisture in the air. Then, as if to signal him,

Rebecca screamed again. This time, she sounded close, her voice cracking in pain.

In a mad scramble, Jr. dove through the thicket, ignoring painful vines and over-zealous branches that scratched at his bare legs, face and arms. Up ahead, he saw a burst of color, the neon-green bag, and he sped up, too panicked to cry or call out. He spotted his mother, laid on her back, clutching her leg, and as he got close, he understood why.

Her ankle was twisted at an odd angle and was already swollen. He didn't have to be a doctor to tell it was broken. There was even a spot, just above the joint, where a bone pressed up from behind the skin. Rebecca's face was a combination of tears, dirt, and fear, all wrapped up in a healthy dose of pain. Jr. dropped down next to her. He reached out and grabbed her arm. Her skin was clammy.

Without a second thought, he retrieved his phone from his pocket and dialed 911, but it wouldn't ring. He checked it again and saw that he had no signal, and even worse than that, his battery was somehow down to a single bar. He had less than a half an hour before it'd be dead, and no-one would know they needed help.

"It won't go through and the battery is almost dead. I need to get to higher ground," Jr. said, looking around. Then he spotted something on the other side of the river. Something clearly out of place. A chain-link fence had been erected beyond the river bank, and beyond it in the trees was what looked like a deer-blind.

Spurred on with a purpose, he filled his mother in on his plan. "There's a deer-blind just across the river. I can get there, scale the fence and grab a signal. I can see you from there. I'll be right back."

Rebecca only managed to nod and wince, then rolled so she could take her pack off and reach for the first aid kit. She found the medium sized pouch, black with a bright red cross on the front and heavy-duty zippers and dumped out its contents, wincing. A pill bottle fell out, and she snatched it up and swallowed two pills from the container without water.

"Oxycodone. Expired but effective. From when I got those teeth pulled," she struggled to say. "I'll be fine. Go."

Jr. ran for the bank and found a gently gurgling stream that passed over his knees. He dismissed removing his shoes for the sake of time and waded across, thankful actually, as the rocks along the bottom were smooth. A few yards from the riverbank was the fence. It was old. The aluminum was faded and warped in some areas. There were a few spots where branches had fallen and damaged the rungs holding it up, but it was still sturdy and ran east and west through the forest. Jr. placed his fingers through the holes and climbed to the top before dropping hard to the other side. He looked back and saw the neon green bag and his mother's rough shape laying amongst the leaves.

Turning around, he sprinted the remaining distance to the deer-blind and exclaimed out loud when he saw it had a solid ladder still attached to the side. "Yes."

He climbed it a rung at a time and did a quick peak inside checking for snakes or other critters. He only saw a handful of sticks and some leaves. He pulled himself the rest of the way inside and tried the phone again, which showed a single bar of service. He dialed 911 and waited with it against his ear. A screeching sound assaulted his ear a moment later, and he tried again, only to have the line go dead, and on the third try, it was left on *dialing...*

"Fuck!" He screamed, shaking it. Then tried one last option.

On the next screen he found a program for a map, and pressed a button *send his location*, but realized he didn't know how to send it to the police. Without much of a choice, he selected the only number in his contacts, the contact labeled

Dad. He pressed send. Then, just in case, he opened a text message, typed *Dad* again for the contact, and wrote one word.

Help.

Mashing the keys with shaky fingers, the phone died before he could tell if the message got out.

"No! Damn!" He screamed at it, holding the power button, but it was no use. The phone was dead. Years of frustration, the divorce, pent up rage, all culminating in this. He dropped his head as his vision went blurry, and he sniffled once then lashed out, punching the side of the deer-blind, a hollow thunk following each blow. He managed to remove the top layer of skin from his knuckles, and a single teardrop cascaded towards the ground from his eye. Through his quivering, rage-filled eyes something odd caught his attention. He flexed his stinging hand and leaned off the ladder. There was something odd about the trees. Climbing down, he got a better look at what he had seen from above and gasped.

On the rear side of the tree nearest him, a thick oak, were three massive gouges, each about six inches long, like a bear or mountain lion took a chunk out of the bark with a swipe. He put his fingers in them and could feel that they were deep. Looking around, he saw that this wasn't the only tree with deep cuts on it. There were more. They stretched all along the riverbank.

13

JAMES

THE CANOPY SEEMED to loom over the trio as they walked along the narrow, beaten path between the legs of the forest. James had kept his head down for the most part, refraining from speaking with Joe or Edgar, though his mind was ablaze with questions. Most of which had come about in their last conversation, and had almost nothing to do with what was clearly a shakedown. He needed something, something bad, and they had raised the price as far as they believed his wallet would open, because he had no choice but to work with them. That made sense, in a perverse way, and based on Joe's and Edgar's preparations, equipment and demeanor, he trusted they knew what they were doing, despite the extortion scheme. *Was no-one really coming to help his wife and son?*

A few yards ahead, Joe stopped in the shadow of an enormous tree, whipped out a knife from a sheath attached to his belt, and carved the letter 'A' into the bark. Edgar paused as well and drank a few sips from a water bladder hanging off his hiking pack and peered off into the deeper parts of the woods. More questions came to James's mind as he looked on, and Joe must have sensed it.

"The forest, this forest in particular, plays tricks on the mind and the lighting. We carve letters along the way to get a sense of time in the dark. Each letter represents an hour." Joe finished reseating the blade and pulled out a map from his back pocket.

James wandered over to him and couldn't help himself, curiosity working his mouth for him.

"I don't understand. Why the fees and the mystery? Why all this pomp and circumstance? What's this crap about the foresters? Since when won't they find a missing hiker?"

"Look. You want something from us. You need to trust that we know what we're talking about," Joe said.

James shook his head. "No. You need to trust me too. If this place is really as bad as you say it is, then I deserve to know what's going on. I've lived here for years and have never heard of hikers going missing with no-one going to get them. That just doesn't happen."

"It happens here," Edgar said from behind. He sounded morose.

"Edgar, stop." Joe said.

"No," Edgar replied. "He's right. He deserves to know. He's not going to blindly follow commands. We aren't soldiers, Joe."

Joe pulled his hat off and smeared back his hair, then wiped the sweat on his pants. He smacked at a bug near his neck and dropped his pack before squatting back and plopping down. He looked like he was working up what to say as he massaged his leg, then James noticed one was quite a bit thinner than the other. Joe caught him looking and lifted his pants, revealing a prosthesis in various blacks and grays speckled with carbon fiber. It was a high-performance prosthesis. James couldn't even tell he was an amputee, he moved so well.

"No. But I was. And I've been deployed twice, blown up once, and can promise you this. I'd rather get blown up again than get lost in these woods."

James averted his eyes. "Listen, I appreciate your service and all, but please explain..."

Joe held up a hand, cutting him off, and looked to the right, like there was something there looking back from the crowded line of brush and tree trunks. James waited, wondering what was in this park that could spook a combat veteran this badly. Joe looked off, back the way they came, and spoke like he was recalling a story he had written out in his head many times before.

"Years ago, this forest was just that, a forest. There weren't any paths or campgrounds or even the foresters. But one day, a group of hikers took interest in the place, the smell actually. They had some sort of online blog, and word spread like crazy. People came from all over to explore and hunt down the source of the smell."

He sipped on a hose from the water bladder. Edgar leaned up against the tree, looking up. It was near three in the afternoon, but the trees were so lush and dense, it felt like it was nearly dusk.

"Naturally, a few people got hurt. Falls, broken bones, dehydration. Stupid shit. Still, experienced hikers and trackers came. Even hunters. Like the place had never been available until then," Joe scoffed. "What happened was hunters stopped being afraid. There were always whispers about these woods — the tourism just made it even less scary."

It was starting to get interesting. He didn't know the forest had a history. He thought it had always just sort of been there.

"I'm almost done," Joe continued. "All was well until some hikers went missing, and it was just when I was getting out of rehab for my leg. I've got a skill set, and I'm not afraid of much, so I saw a business opportunity, and started my tracking and guide services with them. I couldn't find them, so I notified the forest service, and they came in for a survey. Within three weeks, they had engineers cutting a path, erecting a fence and establishing the forester headquarters. From then on out the restricted zone was established too."

"So why was it restricted?" James asked.

Joe paused for such a long time that James was about to repeat the question. "I don't know. All I know is the foresters claim anyone who goes over the fence is on their own. I've asked a few of them about it, and even explored the perimeter myself, and the only thing I can guess is the terrain becomes impassable. I was even able to pull some satellite imagery of the restricted zone and it looked like nothing but steep cliffs with rock bottoms where you could fall to your death."

"Jesus. I guess they assume if you went over the fence, you're dead? My family is too smart for that. They'd see the drop off."

Joe worked on getting on his feet and once he was up, he stretched his back. "You'd think so. But as you can tell, it's a different kind of dark out here."

He began to walk off, but James felt like the conversation was cut short. "What about Arnie? Why won't the foresters help?"

Joe glared at him. It hadn't gotten any darker, but there were shadows guarding his eyes. "Fifteen years ago, a couple with a lot of money, older folks, came looking for their kid who had gotten lost up there. They swore he was still alive, despite it being a week since he went missing. The foresters found a red hat near the fence and that was it. The family contacted us and paid a lot of money to search the restricted zone. So we took two people on and counter offered with double the cost. The parents agreed, and we went up."

"Did you find the kid?"

Edgar led out a huge sigh and Joe groaned painfully. "Can you just listen?"

James bowed and looked away. He felt like a little kid, but he was a mix between interested and worried.

"We crossed into the zone and continued the search, camped the night, and searched as far south as we could before having to turn around. Turns out, the restricted zone is just more forest. There are no cliffs at all. No steep drops. Nothing... but on our way out... one of our guys got hurt. So bad, we had to leave him and come back with a litter."

Edgar shuffled behind James. Overhead, the trees seemed to lean in to listen to Joe's story.

"Edgar and I left and got back within a day and a half, grabbed the litter and returned to find that the two new people were gone."

He trailed off and fiddled with the strap along his waist. "We searched for four more days before coming out, starving and exhausted. We didn't have a choice. They were just gone."

"Who were they?"

"Arnie's older brother... and Tim Breaker, my best friend. All we found was a bracelet, one I had made from his dog-tags."

Joe sighed, his eyes wide, looking at James's feet, but not really looking. The memory was obviously painful, and now he understood why Arnie had so much contempt for Joe and Edgar. Not just because he was an asshole. He blamed them for leaving his older brother behind, though it seemed they didn't have a choice and nearly died themselves trying to make it right.

"We haven't been up since, but Edgar is getting older, and I have a bad leg. We were going to search the zone while we looked for your family. For closure, you know? We just needed a reason to come up here. If we can't find the remains this time, we're taking the money and moving as far away from Felton Forest as we can. I can't deal with the memories anymore."

Now, James could tell Joe was done with the story. Though it was an exorbitant amount of money, he didn't feel so bad now about the cost. Joe wanted to move on. Same with Edgar. But they had to relive a terrible memory to do so. In all, they were killing two birds with one stone.

"I get it. Let's find my family. I'll keep my eyes open," James said, hoping there was solace and gratitude in his voice. One way or another, he'd get them their money.

14

JOE

JOE'S LEG ached more as the terrain shifted, and his leisurely stroll quickly became an uphill climb. His prosthetic wasn't designed for the kind of pressure he was putting on it, as it was designed for a younger, lighter man. Luckily, he only mis-stepped twice before he got the hang of the grade on the hill. So far, the leg had held up.

It was near dusk, and the campsite where they'd be staying — the same one James's wife and son were supposed to be at — should be coming up on their left. Joe was pretty in-tune with the layout of the park on this side of the fence. Everything beyond that might as well have been the moon in terms of his familiarity.

Finally, when the forest went to sleep, and the birds stopped chirping, he paused for a moment to get out his headlamp. He didn't have to say anything. James was watching his every move, and Edgar, though decrepit, was sharp and wasn't falling behind.

Joe found his lamp in the side pocket of his bag and clicked it on. James and Edgar mounted similar lights to their hats as well. Two bright lights looked his way as he crossed over to the nearest tree and carved a 'D' into its base. Then they were off again, huffing along in silence as none of them could bother with conversation when the bugs nipped at their exposed skin, the inside of their legs were raw and chaffed, and their nerves worked to sever what feelings of confidence they might have had.

Joe was okay. Edgar seemed better. James was frantically swiping his head from tree line to tree line, making the shadows bob and weave, like they were dancing.

"Cut it out," Joe grumbled. From behind there came the sound of a misstep, but it seemed James had taken the hint as his headlamp settled ahead.

Somewhere in the ominous dark, a branch snapped, and the three paused in unison. Joe slid his shirt aside, unveiling the holster to a .45 semi-automatic pistol, a replica of the model he carried in the service. He unclasped it, gripped it tight and felt relief from the pistol's weight. He listened intently, unblinking, though sweat ran alongside his nose and stung the corner of his eyes. Little bugs bounced off his forehead.

He was still for a few moments longer, but nothing came. He signed, holstered the weapon, and clicked the retention strap back into place. He'd have to answer for the gun as soon as they stopped, that he knew, but there were always things in the woods that warranted a firearm. This forest was no exception and should, in fact, be the prime example of *why* you should bring the biggest damn gun you could carry.

There were no more disturbances all the way to the camp site marked number twenty-five, but they did stop to peer into what looked like a black hole in the middle of the path. While the campsite was directly to their left, there was a deep pit up ahead.

"The river is down there. Then on the other side is the fence. Even the moon doesn't shine down there. We will continue at sunrise," Joe told James, who stared longingly into the dark, as if his wife and kid were about to stumble their way out of it at any minute. Edgar eventually had to steer James away by the shoulders.

"C'mon. Let's get a fire going and eat."

The scene unfolding in front of Joe was not only expected of James, but annoyingly stereotypical. As Joe worked to set up his tent, James was dashing around the outer rim of the camp site, having since abandoned his equipment upon recognizing his family's tents and bags. Joe did a peripheral search for obvious clues, but felt like he knew what to expect. Their gear was here, and they weren't. Combined with a lack of obvious distress, it wasn't a good sign. You never leave your gear.

Edgar must have assumed the same thing, as he didn't concern himself with the camp site and instead used nearby brush and sticks to build up a decent fire. He stayed well within the ring that marked spot number twenty-five.

"Rebecca! Jr.!" James ran about, calling into the dark, circling the site like a dog at the end of its leash. After a few annoying minutes, Joe had to intervene.

"James. Shut up and sit down. You'll need your energy."

He stopped and stared. Joe squinted as his lamp shined directly in his eyes. "They could be close. Why aren't we looking?"

Joe stoked the fire with a stick, then slid a saucepan over the coals. Inside was a salty soup with chicken and rice.

"They would have found the camp in the daylight. All they had to do was find the river and follow it back until the bank broke at the path. The coordinates you gave me were nowhere near here anyway. Now sit down and eat."

James choked up, the muscles in his neck stiffened. He looked defeated. But eventually, he dropped his gear and sat down. Joe saw there were sweat stains in the shape of the straps on his shoulders. He retrieved a pouch of peanut butter and a bottle of water from his bag and Edgar helped himself to some soup. Then, the three huddled around the fire, staring into the coals until they died down to warm orange embers.

Joe decided it was time he and Edgar were alone to discuss what was going to happen next, and casually invited James to head off to sleep, offering to take first watch. He didn't seem to have a problem with that and chose to sleep in his wife's tent.

He crawled inside and went to close the door. "What time are we getting up?"

"Dawn." Joe said. "We'll wake you."

James nodded, pulled himself in, and zipped the door shut. Joe thought he could hear him sniffling. Then, after a few minutes, it was quiet, and he and Edgar moved in close.

"What are we doing, Joe? What are you hoping to accomplish?"

Joe rubbed his palms into his eyes. He was tired. Not just from the hike. This was a different kind of tired. His very *soul* felt tired.

"I'm just trying to make it right. We find his family, do what we need to do, and we can both be out of here for good. You can sell the shop, and I can quit the store. It's a win for us all."

Edgar wheezed, then dug in his pack. He found a silver flask and spun the top, offering it to Joe first. He accepted it and sucked down a mouthful of the booze. He wasn't surprised to taste a pungent brandy made from blackberries. He smacked his lips and handed it back.

After Edgar took a drink, he said, "Yeah, but why now? Why, after all these years?"

Joe didn't have an answer for that. When he first got the call from Edgar's place, his initial reaction was going to be hell-no and please forget my number. But after advising James over the phone to contact the foresters, he knew that was the wrong decision. If someone had gone to the restricted zone, it was the foresters who used to call him (probably because no-one was stupid enough to go there but him).

"Fine, don't answer that, but what happens next?" Edgar asked, clicking off his headlamp, his face half-illuminated by the orange coals of the fire.

"We do what we did the last time, only we don't mess it up. We have a third. We always knew it'd take three." There was a finality to his voice. He believed everything he was saying, even with the odds stacked against him. Edgar left the conversation alone. Spinning the top on the canteen, Edgar sat up from the log, walked around the fire, then knelt painfully to open the door to his tent.

Before he got in, he paused on his knees to look at Joe, though it obviously pained him to do so. "Hey, Joe."

"Yeah. Edgar?"

"I doubt we'll make it off this mountain alive. We barely did the last time, and we were younger men back then."

"We'll make it," Joe said firmly. He could tell Edgar was serious, but they were both tough, and knew what to expect in some regard.

A few minutes later, just before the fire had died down completely, Joe removed a map, separate from the one showing the main grounds and hiking trails. A map only he and Edgar knew about. A map that was incomplete.

He unfolded the worn piece of paper and examined it by firelight.

Similar to the park map, the trails were drawn in, as well as the borders for the restricted zone, the fence, a deer-blind and a few other landmarks. He referenced the coordinates James gave him and added a large X where they landed, deep in the heart of the unexplored area. *Well, not exactly unexplored.* He sighed and glazed over another X, marking where he and Edgar had last seen Arnie's brother, and their friend, Tim. Near that location were a few words he had etched a long time ago. Together, they created a triangle in a gulley. A chokepoint in the forest where the trees grew so tight they were nearly impassable. It was down there that Joe and Edgar had carved out a narrow path.

Along the windy route were the words *feather spear, spiked log, deadfall*. Joe folded the map up and tucked it away before the memories caught up to him.

"I'm coming for you," he whispered.

15

JR

Jr. MADE it back to his mother in what should be considered a record time for any human. Though the message on his phone said it had gotten through, it immediately died afterward, taking his hope with it, leaving him to return to his mother, praying she had a backup plan.

Then, his uncertainty and worry were replaced with terror upon finding the scratches on the trees. They were massive, and indicative that whatever had done it was tall, powerful, and angry enough to mark dozens of them. He settled on the likelihood it was a large bear. Nothing he could think of had claws that big.

He chose not to worry his mom about it when he got back to her. Instead, he started working through what he remembered from a basic first aid class he took in high school and the book he had taken from his mother.

He found her quickly, leaning against a sapling, breaking out in cold sweats despite the warm, pungent air, shimmering with heat waves off of rocks near the riverbank. She was whimpering and gripping her legs just above her injured ankle. It was swollen, angry red, and hot to the touch. Her skin turned white when he pressed it, and she screamed in pain.

"Sorry. I'm so sorry, mom," he said, sliding over two straight sticks he had found on his sprint back, and removed his belt. He placed them alongside her ankle, then used his belt to cinch it down around her calf. She screamed again.

"I'm sorry. I had to splint it. I think its broken, and it looks like you're bleeding under the skin."

He peered down at his mother, the once proud, confident woman now appeared frail, sickly white, and broken. Her eyes drooped. Rather than doing nothing, he recalled what he could from the book. Splint, ice, painkillers, get help. He had done everything, and felt like he had done nothing.

Between the time he had run for the deer-blind and now, the pills she had taken appeared to have started to kick in. She just sat still, head on the sapling, staring off even as ants marched down her shirt.

Jr. stooped and brushed them away. "How're you feeling?" He flipped through the first aid kit on the ground near her side. It was built for basic cuts and scrapes, not broken bones.

"High. But I know I'm hurt," she mumbled. "If you're looking for the icepack, it's gone."

"Well shit," he said, not caring if she'd get angry at him for swearing.

"Did you get a message out?" She asked, her eyes opening just a little more. Overhead, a bird called loudly.

"I think so. There's an odd fence and a deer-blind on the other side of it. I got one bar before my phone died."

She snorted. "Perfect."

"Have you tried moving yet?"

She shook her head. "As long as I don't move, the painkillers do their job. When I stand up, blood rushes into my ankle and it gets ten times worse. You should go back to the campsite. Leave me here. Come back with food and those iodine tablets so we can at least have clean water."

Jr. remembered she had originally come to the river to get water, anyway. Peculiar, as they had packed enough clear water for the entire trip. It's what weighed her entire pack down in the first place. He brushed it off and his mind went over sanitizing drinking water. Then it moved on to the facts about surviving. The human body could go only a few days without water, and a few weeks without food. *Weeks. Why was he thinking about weeks?*

It should only be hours now. His message had gone out. His dad would put it together. He'd do anything for the family if it were dire straits. Of that, he was sure. But should he tell his mom that he had only reached his dad instead of the police? What about the foresters? Either way, there were plenty of chances of being rescued, and even if they had to stay an extra night, soon, people would come looking for them.

"Mom. Someone will show up. We need to get back to the camp. It's going to hurt, but we can take it slow. I can carry you a bit too." He tried to coax her into moving, but her eyes drifted closed, and she dribbled a bit of spit onto her shirt. He felt a pang in his heart as he wondered if she was dead or dying. Her eyes flicked open for a second, just long enough for her to say, "Tired. Need to rest."

Jr. sat back and looked at the bottle of pills, which clearly had a warning on the front advising of potential drowsiness. He wondered how many she took. He dumped them out in his hand and saw there were nearly twenty remaining. Plenty for the trip back.

He also wanted to think what his dad would do at a time like this, but realized it was wholly farfetched. He'd never go camping, therefore there was no way to know what he'd do.

Truthfully, he didn't know much about his dad. But if they were as similar as his mom claimed (as she so often did when she was angry at one or both of them), he supposed all he'd have to do was look inside himself to see what his dad would do. He tried, and when he did, he came back to the same answer. He wouldn't know what to do, because he'd never do *this* and therefore, his dad would never do *this*.

Jr. settled on letting his mom rest until the pain subsided enough for her to move at least a little. Then they'd head to the camp where they had the most chance of being found, for it was an impossible thought to consider her hiking her way out.

After some time, he must have dozed off laying in her lap and only awoke to the sound of a large branch snapping in the distance. It was behind him, over the road, or where the road should be, and deep within the brush. Jr. sat up quickly, wiping sweat from his face and rubbing the blurry vision from his eyes. He gently shook his mom awake, and she stirred.

He heard it again, this time closer. Then, there were heavy footfalls and the nearby trees swayed violently. Jr. could only stare.

Then he saw what was coming from the brush, and it made him whimper.

A great black bear, with small beady eyes, a tan nose and shiny black fur, meandered through the thicket. It had claws two inches long and teeth nearly the same.

It was the biggest damn bear he had ever seen. Scars ran along its face and back. Bright red blood and sinew dripped off its mouth from its latest kill. And it was heading right for them.

JAMES

JAMES AWOKE NOT from the frightful calls of some animal in the dark, nor from creatures whisking through the air or scuttling on their bellies through the dirt.

He awoke to a deep, lonely silence.

At first, sitting up in his tent, he had imagined a moment when the forest went deathly quiet, and all sounds stopped at once. He had been sleeping, or as close to sleeping as possible, having nearly screamed into the pillow beneath his head the night before. It smelled like Rebecca. Clean, barely scented from the wash, it smelled like her perfume had rubbed off from when she was carrying it. Instead of yelling, he slammed his fists against the ground and rolled over so his nose was directly on the spot. He fell asleep almost instantly, then jerked awake sometime later... because it was quiet.

After strapping on his boots, James unzipped his tent and crawled out. A light-red glow from a handful of coals marked the hotspot between the tents. Pressure built under his belt.

Slipping back into the tent, he grabbed his headlamp, stretched, attached it, and clicked it on. Both Edgar's and Joe's tents were dormant, and their doors closed. (As if he had expected them to join him in the silence). They didn't appear to have the same concerns about the quiet. Overhead, no birds called, no bugs chittered, and even the things that crawled on their bellies lay still. It was so odd to be in a place teeming with life but so silent; it was maddening.

What was more troublesome was the stink of the forest that never went away, but instead came about in waves for them to walk through, versus outside the trees, where the stench laid like a haze over the town.

A stinky cloud must have been floating nearby, because as he relieved himself near the back of the campsite, the smell hit him, and his stomach turned over. For a second, he had forgotten to breathe through his mouth at all times, and the stink made its way deep enough into his nose to have its full effect.

"Fuck this place," he murmured to himself after recovering, finding a decent tree to lean on and relieving himself. He yawned and clicked off the light for a moment. When he was done, he zipped up his pants and turned the light on again and yelped, backpedaling and tripping over his own feet. He fell back hard against the tree and whacked his head so he saw stars.

Firm hands gripped his arms and James saw it was Edgar. His face was stark white as the powerful headlamp flooded his skin. His eyes were wide and his pupils were large dark disks.

"Get up. Quickly," he said in a gravely voice. "Get that fucking light out of my face."

"Edgar?" He asked as he was yanked to his feet. Edgar was old, but he was strong and his hands were as strong as vice grips.

"None other." He sounded tired. Like he had just woken up, too. "Now shut up and come with me." He walked off back towards camp. The little red light on his shoulder blinked at regular intervals, and his headlamp clicked on. James could merely see his feet as he walked through the camp toward the main road.

"What? Where are we going?"

"I said shut it. Joe found something."

James's first reaction was to ask for clarity, but he clammed up quickly and explored what exactly Joe could have found, and why he had found it in the middle of the night. He could have been out for a piss, just like him. Nothing else made sense. Nobody wandered the forest at night. Nobody wandered the forest alone. Nobody but Joe…

James caught up with Edgar and matched his step. He was suppressing his footfalls by walking heel-toe, his head-lamp sweeping left to right across the light-red clay, river rock and leaves. He thought he was looking for tracks.

A few paces later, the trees broke to both sides, and they arrived on the main path that ran north-south. James remembered that heading south would bring them back towards the entrance to the park, and north would drop them into the river if they weren't careful. Edgar cut left.

The road ahead was so dark, the forest looked like it just ended in a deep well of nothing. No stars shone through the trees, no light from the moon lit their way. Without their head-lamps, they'd be lost with only their thoughts. Edgar pushed onward, as he didn't seem to share James's apprehension. The old man hunched over and continued on, his footfalls rhythmic and purposeful as to avoid tripping. Even on the well-worn path, the occasional rock jutted out from the earth and threatened to take him down. James thought one fall, and Edgar would probably be down for good.

Regardless of the direction the path took them, he felt like they were heading down. Down into the mouth of some yawning beast. Soon, they were nearly leaning back and letting their footsteps catch them on the way down. Whatever drove Edgar into these woods left James feeling like the old man had a secret. He risked everything, a fall, broken bones, dehydration, and fatigue, by being out here. He was well past the age where hiking was a possibility in the best of circumstances. Whatever brought him out here... was more than money.

A few moments later, the theories about what he'd do if Edgar actually fell drifted away. Up ahead, the gurgle of the stream began to grow out of the silence. For a while there, James wondered whether they were even going in the right direction. He didn't think the river was that far away.

Then there were stupid thoughts about the forest changing, moving on its own. Like it wanted to keep them there.

The riverbank came into view, as well as Joe's backside. He was holding something, looking over it with his headlamp, while standing with his toes just inches from the bank.

The waterway was nearly thirty feet wide, but it was shallow, and the rocks slippery, making travailing it at night a death wish. This he had been told more than once.

James knew it grew deeper the further downstream you went. It grew deeper, then it broke over a waterfall. All of that had been depicted on the basic maps provided to hikers in the park and advertising around town.

James recalled the large red X marking the waterfall, and the yellow and black caution ribbon along the water that marked the post-of-no-return. The point where the water took you... no matter what you did.

Joe turned as Edgar and James arrived behind him. He was holding a florescent green bag. The waterproof kind with hard plastic supports at the top that were meant to roll over. He flipped it over to show the initials on the side — R. P.

Rebecca Pope. His wife's bag.

James opened his mouth to share his elation at finding some evidence of his wife's location. The bag meant they were on the right path. But a burning question came to mind when he flipped it over again. A question he wasn't sure if he wanted the answer to. There was a streak of red on the back. Joe smeared it with his finger to show him. It ran when he touched it.

"Where'd you find that? Is that blood?"

He looked somber, James's headlamp giving his face an unnatural, ghastly white glow.

"Over there." He pointed towards a set of trees. There was a sapling laid over on its side. "Got up to pee. Noticed a path through the forest where something big walked through. I followed it down here and found this bag laid up next to a tree."

"But the blood? Was there anything else? Did you see anything else?" James was near mania waiting for news.

"There were tufts of hair. Some claw marks. I don't think this blood is human, too thick. Maybe a bear, or some kind of big cat. There's a streak of dried blood on top of a pile of leaves too, and someone had leaned up against a tree for some time. I think they fought an animal off."

James about jumped. They had fought something. That meant a lot of things. It meant they weren't losing hope, and were trying to stay alive. There also wasn't a body, and only a streak of blood that wasn't human. Hearing these things from Joe made him want to hug him.

"There's more," Joe said. "I also found a pack." James's excitement boiled inside. They were so close.

"Where?"

"In the water, just off the edge, caught on a log. I tried to get it with a branch but the water took it. It's only a few feet deep here, but it will pull you down in an instant. Whoever came through here fought the animal defensively, then chose to risk the river, and lost their pack along the way."

James could only stare.

"This isn't a good sign, James. There's a channel in the river, straight down the middle. If someone stepped out of that channel, they'd be on slick rocks and under the current in an instant."

"What're you saying?"

Joe handed him the bag. "I'm saying your family risked the river to run from whatever's out here and we're either going to find them over the falls… or on the other side of the fence."

"Over there?"

"Yeah. In the restricted zone."

17

EDGAR

JAMES WAS in over his head, but did his best to mask it. Edgar admired that about him. Whilst someone like him voiced his concerns, or wined or was pessimistic, Edgar came from a different time. During his prime, the slightest showing of weakness was quickly weeded out and squashed. No-one believed a weak man. Weak men turn tail and run. Edgar wasn't a weak man.

It was this conviction that drove him to return to the woods, that silenced his lips as his every step sent shooting pains up his leg and into his back. It was this conviction that quelled his mounting fears as the group headed deeper into the forest. His body was old, but his memory was fresh. He remembered what was waiting for them.

Seeing the bag in Joe's hand brought these memories about, regardless of whether he wanted to relive them or not. But even as images of what happened before ran through his head like a movie on three-times-speed, he showed no weakness, and forced his face to be still. Choosing instead to act like he was examining the water, Edgar brushed past Joe and James, and stood at the riverbank, jamming his fists into his pockets.

It was so dark over the river, and only grew darker the further they went.

He remembered that above all else. It could drive you mad—make you see and hear things that weren't there. That wasn't the case all those years ago. The dark wasn't driving them mad. They knew there was something waiting, hiding, watching.

Edgar kicked at the riverbank, the sand softly dribbling into the still water at the river's edge. A fishy scent brought a reprieve from the oppressive stink of the forest, then was quickly swiped away. He looked out over the water and could clearly see what was on the other side in his mind's eye. A fence, then more trees, a path, and a cave. The crunch of leaves from lightning-fast footfalls in the dark. Then a flash of white. Teeth, claw and the screams of his friend as his flesh was rent from his bones...

"Edgar?" Joe called from behind. "Are you alright?"

Edgar sighed and turned. Of course, he wasn't alright. This place, this forest, had a *pulse*. It was alive, and it was too much of a coincidence that what they were experiencing was so very similar to his haunted memories that were as old as the ache in his bones. "Yeah, I'm fine. There's nothing for us here. Let's head back to camp until morning."

Joe clapped James on the shoulder and steered him up the berm. James looked back to make sure Edgar was on the same page.

"What do you know?"

Edgar was taken aback. Perhaps James wasn't as dumb and oblivious as he thought.

"Nothing."

"What do you mean, nothing?" James said over his shoulder as they arrived in the camp. Joe checked his watch and must have decided going back to sleep was useless. It was almost 5:00 AM. Sunrise was soon, and that meant they'd need to be up.

Edgar walked to their meager wood pile and began sizing up kindling and brush to burn, all the while ignoring James's question.

"You told me you two were the best. I'm paying you for what you know."

Edgar groaned as he crouched by the skeleton of the previous fire and set up the new kindling, stuffing leaves and small sticks under the larger logs.

"All I know is what we've told you. We've been here before. We've lost people before... and we've found people before. That's all you need to know."

James must have mustered courage from somewhere deep down, as he didn't seem like the guy to welcome confrontation, but he stepped next to Edgar so their feet were almost touching, towering over the frail man. Edgar sighed, determined not to let this develop any further. *This is how it starts. The arguments. The yelling. The fighting. It will sense your rage. It will feed on your anger and fear... and when you are hurt, it will come for you.*

The words rang true in his head as they were his own words. His subconscious was predicting what would happen — just as it had happened before. He knew it all would come to be if they were here long enough.

Pushing himself up by his knee, he turned his headlamp, lighting a bush behind a tent.

"I'm not going to argue with you. We can't afford to argue out here," Edgar said, choosing his words carefully. He caught Joe resting his hand on his gun, then glanced down at James's balled fists. His lips were pressed into a thin line, and his eyes locked forward.

"I don't want to fight. I just want to find my family, and the best way to do that is for us to work together," James replied, appearing to relax slightly, his bony shoulders slumping.

"I've told you everything I know," Edgar lied. He gave

ground and turned away, then froze. Over Joe's head, beyond their circle of cut brush and into the maw of darkness, a branch swayed. James kept talking, but Edgar didn't hear him.

Joe caught his eye and quickly followed his gaze.

"You told me you lost Tim and Arnie's brother and…"

"Shut up, James," Joe snapped.

"But I'm confused because both you and Joe left, you know, the experienced guys… and left them alone," James continued, his tone growing more heated.

"Shut the fuck up!" Joe screamed, drawing his weapon.

James stopped his tirade as Joe's voice, rattled with fear, echoed off the trees. Edgar hadn't said a word. He couldn't. His voice was lost in his throat.

Something was coming through the brush.

"Or what? You going to shoot me?" James said, mocking Joe, turning and placing his hands on his hips. He glanced in the direction the others were looking and froze, letting out a cross between a whimper and a gasp.

Then, there was a loud snort, and a shadow parted the thicket.

A great black bear, walking on all fours, approached them, sniffing at the air. Its face was covered in scratches from years of hunting through the undergrowth. Its powerful muscles rippled beneath a black shiny coat. All Edgar could focus on was its claws and equally large teeth.

It had dried blood caked around its nose and mouth, and its beady eyes sized up each of them individually. Nobody moved. At least James was sensible enough not to run. Joe's hand quivered. Edgar knew why he didn't shoot. Even the .45 would have to hit the bear square in the head to drop it, otherwise, it'd just piss it off. It was too big of an animal, covered in too much fur and fat.

The bear plowed through the clearing, running between

James and Edgar, who each fell back as the beast thundered by. There was a loud snap and a flash as Joe fired, then rolled out of the way. As Edgar tripped over his own feet, he landed on his rear and smacking his arm against a large flat rock. It shot into his elbow and shoulder. His eyes swam, and he fought the urge to scream as white-hot pain radiated upward with every heartbeat.

The bear passed him by and ignored him completely.

He caught the glimpse of white and pink tissue, the whiff of iron and sweat, and the stink of decay. As it ran huffing through the clearing and into the thick brambles on the other side, its footfalls shook the dirt. And then it was gone.

Edgar replayed the scene in his head like it was a bad movie, forced to relive what he thought would be the last moments of his life. The shadow moving through the dark. The parting of the branches and the stink of blood. But it was James who pulled him out of his nightmare.

"What the hell, Edgar? Are you alright? Why didn't you tell me you saw a fucking bear?" James pulled him up by his arm and looked him over. "Jesus, man, you look pretty banged up."

"Yeah. I'm good," Edgar croaked. He wasn't good. He was far from good. Black bears were not uncommon in this area, but they rarely came through the grounds, and especially not when people were around. If you left a bag of food out, they might stroll by. But they mostly left well enough alone.

"You don't look good. So what do you think happened? Think it was just passing through?"

"No. Didn't you see the gash on its side?" Joe answered, holstering his gun and beginning to pack up the tents. Daylight was breaking, and the treetops were gaining a bit of a glow.

"So what? Bears can get a scratch from time to time. Maybe a big cat or a mountain lion like you said. I heard even boar can maul you…"

"No." Edgar said lowly, hissing at his now-swelling elbow. "It was running. It was scared."

"Scared by who?" James asked.

"Not by who," Edgar replied, getting up. "By what."

18

REBECCA

REBECCA LEANED UP AGAINST JR.'S back. He had to be getting tired. He'd been propping her up for hours. But her head was swimming. A feverish haze sat over her and left her in a constant delirium. She no longer felt pain, her body having gone numb from their romp through the forest. That much she could remember.

First, she broke her ankle. Then Jr. found her when she screamed... and then the bear. The five-hundred-pound beast that sent her and Jr. into a mad scramble, broken ankle aside, back down the hill, over the river and to the other side. Then, without checking to see if it was following them, they ducked through a hole in the chain-link fence and ran until she collapsed.

Jr. had supported her weight with her arm over his shoulder and dragged her until he was out of breath too, and they were thoroughly lost. That was hours ago. And now, they were paying for their misguided, panicked run into the dark forest; their packs were gone, and their pockets were as empty as their stomachs. The type of lost that was *forever*. The type of lost that made you feel like God himself couldn't hear your cries.

Rebecca desperately tried to maintain her composure, opting instead to help Jr. help her. Currently, he was moving around, fidgeting with something. He hadn't lost his nerve, or if he had, she couldn't see it.

"What are you doing?" She asked softly, then looked around, as if the bear would hone in on their position. In their flight, they had inadvertently stumbled upon a shallow cave and chose to huddle near the front, waiting for daylight. The back was dark and grew narrow, reminding them of a tomb. At first they didn't want to stay there, but thought it was better than sitting out in the open.

"Digging a hole," he said from just outside. "If I can find some water, a leaf and a piece of metal of some sort, I can make a compass like before. Then maybe we can head south until we reach the river."

He sounded optimistic, and Rebecca appreciated it at that moment, for she couldn't do that. She had the opposite. All she could think about was her stupid plan that led her and her son into the situation to begin with. And with her doubt of that decision, came her doubt about James. Was she making the right choice? Was it what she needed? What about James? Was she abandoning him? Was she being too harsh? All these unimportant questions filtered through her mind, but she was thankful for the reprieve and focused on what Jr. had said, "Where can we get a needle and water?"

He stopped moving. "I haven't gotten that far yet. I need the river to find water, but I need water to find the river. I can't tell what time it is, and I can't tell if it's going to rain. All I know Is that I don't want to just sit here," he responded over his shoulder.

She continued to stare at the smooth gray wall of the back of the cave. Jr. looked outward. Neither of them would sleep that night.

Jr. fidgeted and Rebecca shifted on her numbing rear, then

winced painfully as even the slightest jarring of her leg caused intense bursts of pain.

Her stomach turned over once, reminding her that they hadn't eaten since the day before. Jr. was right, however—water was more important. She couldn't remember the last time she'd relieved herself. Call it nerves or emotions, but something as mundane as peeing felt undeserved. Secretly, she was ready to punish herself. She wasn't prepared for this romp through the woods, and Jr. was going to pay for it.

"Have you tried the cellphone?" She asked, though she already knew the answer. The phone was dead, the last of the battery had been spent calling the police. A worthy cause.

Jr. paused a moment longer than she had anticipated and said, "It's completely dead." His words were stretched out, and there was a hint of an inflection on *dead.* She was corporate, and that meant a constant game of chess was played around a polished wooden table by men in stiff suits, haggling over budgets and investments while the pool-boy plowed their wives at home. She had to be ruthless, and she had learned to read people. Because if she could read them, it gave her a distinct advantage when someone knew something she didn't. Jr. had made the call—but there was deception in his words. She decided to level the playing field.

"There's something else," she replied. She knew better than to point out that she thought he was lying. That would only lead to confrontation. Instead she chose to go with an open-ended question.

"What something?" He answered without looking at her. It was a non-answer. She pressed further.

"Did you get a hold of someone?"

More direct, but the details were nevertheless open-ended.

"Yes," Jr. replied, perfectly still.

"The police?" She inquired. This was the moment where he'd lie or cave.

"I tried to call them."

She pounced. "Tried means you didn't. So who did you call?" Now she'd get the answer out of him.

He breathed deep. "It was all too fast. Your leg was broken, the battery was dying, and I couldn't get a damn signal. I called once, and then fearing I wouldn't get anything out, I sent a text message too."

"Who'd you send a text message to?" More direct. She stared intently at the wall of the cave. It stared back.

"The only person in my phone. You know I don't use my phone."

"Who, Jr.?"

He paused. "I got a message to dad, I think. I think I got him our coordinates."

Rebecca wanted to scream. To lose all control and wail like a child. She wanted to beat her fists into the dirt and cry into a pillow until her lungs hurt. It was falling apart, piece by piece. The camping trip, her leg, the divorce. Now, he'd have a reason to come running up the mountain and try to save them. That wasn't what she wanted. She wanted to be away from him.

"That's fine," she said dryly. She'd have to wait to handle this. Jr. didn't need to see a breakdown. He needed to see her as the strong mother he'd always known. That way, it'd contrast to his father's callous, lazy self. The same man that would be bringing the cavalry up the mountain. She knew he'd bring an army. Because it would mean he wouldn't have to do it himself.

"It'll all be fine," she told herself, but her heart raced. Down by her side, she scraped at the dirt and rocky floor, her finger-nails catching the tiny grains which embedded themselves in the soft tissue underneath. It made a drawn-out scratching sound.

Her cool, collected nature was bubbling over. Beyond the nurturing mom she wanted to be, her true character was rearing its ugly head. The natural self she used on James and in the board room. It made her want to slam the back of her head into Jr.'s for not listening to simple instructions.

Instead, she started to say, *it'll all be fine* again, but there was a snap and a pop in the distance. She couldn't help but turn around. Ignoring the strain on her eyes, Rebecca peered into the forest, but nothing more was heard, and thankfully, nothing was seen.

"It sounded like a tree falling," she whispered.

Jr. did his restless shift again and said, "It sounded like a gunshot, mom." He paused. "I'm sorry about all this — what I said earlier back at the camp. I'm sorry about your leg and I'm sorry about you and dad."

Rebecca frowned, "Why are you sorry about your father and I?"

"Well, one of us has to be sorry, and since neither you nor dad ever apologize for anything, I figured I would."

Rebecca's heart hurt. It pained her to hear such a mature explanation out of a young man who had acted like a normal teenager should up until now. He was growing more like James, even when he wasn't around. James was the forgiving one. The one who was judged as meek and pale. Not a coward, James would never run, but he was never aggressive either. Jr. was taking the passive approach, acting as the voice of reason. He was acting like her husband, when all she needed sometimes was just a good fight.

Rebecca stopped grating her nails and said, "You don't need to apologize. I'm the one who got us into this mess." That was true, and drew attention away from the fact that the sound was surely a gunshot, and that they were most likely fucked if James wasn't bringing a mountain of help with him.

JOE

THIS ALL HAS TO END. *I have to end it.* Joe looked his prosthetic over while he was already on the ground. The joints rotated and bent properly, but his boot had slipped off the foot and the laces were untied. It was all for show. Joe knew the leg was fine, but his heart was threatening to burst from his chest — sitting down covered up his quivering knees. He hadn't been this scared in a long time, and the feeling was all too familiar. What scared him then was what scared him now.

James started walking over. Joe glanced up. The pistol was just out of arm's reach and both he and James shared a look at it, then at each other. Before Joe could stretch over and grab it, James had bent at the waist and gingerly picked it up between two fingers, like it was a fetid rat a cat had dragged inside. Joe stared at him. *Give it back. You're in over your head,* he said with his eyes. It was a standoff broken by Edgar clearing his throat loudly, looking outward towards where the bear had come from. James blinked twice, then hesitantly held the gun out. Joe snatched it, jammed it into the holster, then struggled to his feet. *He knows. He knows something's up. You should just tell him.*

"Where to?" James asked innocently.

Maybe not.

After dusting himself off, Joe withdrew a map from his pocket — a bare map, lacking his personal notes. He held it out, dodging a look from Edgar, who also knew about the other map, and pointed to a spot beyond the river, deep into the woods northwest of the tree stand.

"There? The map isn't complete. It's shaded out. Are you sure that's where we need to go?" James raised an eyebrow.

Joe nodded. "Edgar and I have been that way. It was a long time ago, but there are a few landmarks that will give us bearing, plus the trees aren't nearly as thick, so we'll be able to see the stars."

James put his hands on his hips, appearing to mull it over. *It's not like you have a choice.* "Alright. Let's go then."

Joe, who forced back a sigh of relief, watched James pack up their tents, and even collected some of what Rebecca had left behind. There wasn't much that they could take, as most of it was redundant, but he found a black book with gold lettering inside Jr.'s tent. While digging through Rebecca's bag, he crunched something underneath him and held it up. Joe and Edgar turned to see James holding up an empty water bottle, looking confused.

"I don't understand."

Joe rolled his eyes. "They were drinking water, that's a good sign."

James picked the bag up and turned it over. A dozen empty bottles fell out and onto the ground. He picked them each up individually and peered through them.

"What're you looking for?" Joe asked.

"There isn't a drop of water in any of them. It's as if the water just evaporated."

So it knows we're here already.

"It's hot out here, man. Don't worry about it. The river is nearby. They probably refilled what they had from there. If they were smart, they would boil it. I don't see a pot anywhere around here, so maybe they took it with them," Joe reassured him.

Again, another lie. He had to force his head not to turn and look at Edgar. James seemed to take his answer as reasonable, collected a few more supplies than began marching down the path and towards the main road.

"Are you alright?" Edgar asked James.

He stopped and turned. "I guess so. I don't really know what to make of all this. But I'd rather not sit and talk about it here. You said the bear was running from something. I can't think of what that might be. I just know we have to get to my family before the bear or whatever else does. You can explain what you meant along the way."

Edgar nodded and looked at Joe. Joe's lips curled downward and his eyebrows came together. *Hiding your fear behind confidence. Impressive.*

"Fair enough. Let's get going. We'll be fine without the lights. The sun is coming up, and it's easier to see on the other side of the river."

James twirled on his heels and strode off and out of view. Edgar lagged behind, clicking on the waist band of his pack and sipping from his bladder.

He spoke in a whisper. "Their water is gone. It's already started."

"Of course it has. The crazed bear wasn't a good enough clue for you?"

"Whatever, Joe. Let's get this over with. James is catching on, you know. He knows why we need him, he just hasn't said it yet." Edgar tried to turn, but Joe's hand shot out and grabbed him by the shoulder.

"Fuck that. He doesn't know. And he won't. The plan hasn't changed in ten fuckin' years and it's not about to. We set the traps. He's the live bait. If the creature has marked the wife or the kid, we need to find them, too. But it will come for the weakest first, and that's him."

Edgar sighed. "We know it marked the family. Their water is gone. They are gone. It's going to drive them mad before it eats them. The same thing happened before, remember? Arnie's brother, then Tim…"

"Shut it. Just stick to the plan."

Edgar snorted, then rubbed the sweat off his neck. "Plan? We don't even know if those traps are still in place. There is no plan."

Joe went around him and stood in his way before he could walk off. "They are. I know they are. Because they're made of steel and wire, not sticks and twine. This was a solid plan before. It's a solid plan now, as long as you keep your shit together."

There were footsteps on the path, then James reemerged around the bend. "Are you guys coming?"

"Yeah," Joe said. "I was just helping Edgar with his pack. Old man can barely move first thing in the morning."

James gave a weak smile. "Cut the guy some slack. He made it this far."

Without another word, James took off again, followed by Joe and finally Edgar.

Joe caught him out of the corner of his eye, pulling a plastic bag with an envelope inside from his pocket and setting it under a rock near the fire. Joe said nothing. He had done the same, but he left his letter on the front seat of his car, along with his wallet and ID, carefully laid out next to it. He could guess what Edgar's letter said, but if it was anything like the one he wrote, it was an explanation, covering up a warning.

He had written a suicide letter, lying about a deep-set depression he had hidden, and had chosen the forest as a place where he'd like to die. That way, no-one would come looking for his body if he didn't make it out alive. Hell, after it was all over with, he might just act on that letter anyway. *Because you deserve it. You deserve to be forgotten.*

Arriving on the main path, Joe turned left and caught up to James, leaving Edgar walking behind the others, slowly, but steadily. He took his place up front and braced his leg as he descended the steep dirt ramp leading down to the river. There was a click in his step as he walked. The prosthetic might have been damaged after all.

A short while later, the bubble of the stream filled their ears, along with a dampness that made the forest stink stick in their clothes. There was a hint of fish and damp mud as well. Joe stood at the bank, then eyed the wall of trees to his left and right. He found two sturdy oaks, a few years old, and removed a ball of string from his pocket. He started tying one end off to a tree on his right, then the other on the opposite side, while James looked on curiously. When he was done, he tied off to the center of the line, now strung across the path, making a T-shape.

"I'll go first," he said, walking down to the bank. "I'm using the string to mark my path. I have to feel where the current isn't as strong. Once I've made it across, follow my line. I'll tie it off at the end, and whatever you do, don't slip, otherwise the river will take you."

Joe waded straight into the water, stepping lightly at first, then gaining confidence. It was like memory was coming back just before each step. He could feel the smooth rocks under his feet, and the powerful current pushing on his legs. The water was chilly, but refreshing. About fifteen steps later and he climbed the embankment. "Okay!" Joe called from the other side. "You're next, James."

20

JAMES

REGARDLESS OF ITS CALM, gently waving surface, the river was exactly as Joe described, a hidden danger with a powerful current. Each step he took was meticulous, but eventually, using the string dangling over his shoulder, he gained enough confidence to step quicker. Edgar didn't wait for him to cross and entered the stream just a few paces behind. The frigid water came up to his knees and the uneven riverbed made each step difficult. By the halfway point, he was more afraid of slipping than of the current. But every few steps, there'd be a moment when the water rushed quickly by his foot just before he stepped down, as if it was waiting for an opportunity.

"Keep moving. Don't let it distract you. Use the string and Joe to line yourself up. I'm relying on you. I can't see like I used to," Edgar said. His gruff voice was calming in the quiet. For most of the trip across the river, he had been subject only to the noise of his own heartbeat and that was giving him a headache.

"Sounds good," he replied, thankful to hear anything beyond the river's gentle bubble. He glanced up from his feet and down river, where a great shadow blocked their vision.

The sun had yet to light everything, giving the river a

tunnel-like appearance, and the tree lines to either side were endless walls, and there were no doors except for the one they came through. Despite the wide-open space, James felt trapped.

Then there was movement. A blur of gray, quick and low, skirted the top of the water, causing a brief splash. Then a second and a third, crossing the river into the restricted zone on the other side. James froze and Edgar did, too. He could hear him breathing and wheezing uneasily behind him.

Apparently, they had both seen the same thing, but it was James that reassured Edgar despite his unfamiliarity with his own words, "It's not doing us any good to sit here," he said, and pushed onward, each step feeling heavier than the last.

Water sloshed on either side of his legs. His footfalls were not coming nearly as far out, and they weren't as purposeful. Driven forward by angst, James quickly waded the rest of the way and emerged on the bank. Joe seized both James and Edgar by the arm.

"What the hell was that?" Joe asked.

Edgar put his hands over his head and focused on taking deep breaths. James keeled over. "Something ran through the water... further down river."

"I'm sure it was nothing. A bird maybe. Sometimes the bats will pick bugs off the surface," Joe said. James shook his head but thought it best to leave it alone. He knew what he saw, and Joe was too calm. It was tall, fast, and covered in fur. In truth, he was starting to suspect that Joe and Edgar were hiding something.

From their story about Tim and Arnie's brother, to the way they looked at each other, to Joe's badass front and Edgar's coddled nature. James wasn't stupid, and he couldn't read people like Joe could (Or his wife, for that matter), but he could tell when someone was afraid.

If there was one thing Joe and Edgar shared, it was mutual feelings of utter terror, as neither of them wanted to be in the forest, but they were forcing themselves to. Money could only go so far. There was another reason for them being here, and finding their friend's remains after a decade wasn't it. They would have searched for them a long time ago. Their story was falling apart, and James was determined to get to the bottom of it. He needed to know if these men really intended to help him find his family — because he couldn't do it without them.

Soaked pants and squishy boots aside, James waited for Joe to check the map again, but he didn't seem to need it. There wasn't a path to be seen, but he appeared to know where he was going, and ducked between two branches. The next few minutes were spent dodging trees and twigs that threatened to take out their eyes until they arrived at a chain-link fence, ten feet high. Expecting to climb, James grew confused as Joe cut left. He followed, and further along the fence was a section that looked like it had been ripped apart.

There was a gaping hole in it and more of the same dimly lit forest on the other side. Joe passed through, then James and then Edgar. Joe pushed on and the further he went, the more spread out the forest became. He stopped next to a large tree, wide enough for them to all sit next to, and sipped on his water bladder.

Finally, James couldn't wait to ask, "Do you know where you're going?"

Joe sipped again, closed his eyes and bounced his head softly against the tree behind him, then removed the map. He pointed at a spot inward from the fence and showed that the large tree was marked with a circle.

"This is us. In a few hours, we'll go to this rock formation. From there we'll cut west until we run into this." He dropped a finger next to a square that looked like it was in the middle of nowhere in a field of gray and green.

"What's that?" James asked. He wanted to know the plan, not just be along for the ride.

"Old ranger station. We'll rest for an hour there and eat. After that, there is no more shelter, so we'll need to keep moving."

"Shelter? Shelter from what? The bears?" he asked dryly.

"Yeah, the bears. Like the fuckin' bear that we saw a few hours ago? If that's all, it's time to go." Joe sipped from his bladder and hummed to himself, his eyes closed. James's blood pressure skyrocketed. He wasn't one to be dismissed, especially not by people he was supposed to be paying (regardless of the truth of it), for their expertise. He had questions, and he needed answers.

"Explain the fence."

Joe rolled his head back and forth with the melody. Edgar inched a little closer, watching.

"Explain the fence. Because it doesn't make sense to me," James pried. "So the foresters put this fence out to deter everyone from coming in here? That's it?" James's voice was raising beyond a harsh whisper and building into a yell. He continued without waiting for an answer. "Things are starting to look fishy on my end. Why the gun, Joe? Why a handgun and not a rifle if it was to protect you? Why the dismissal of everything going on, like the water bottles and the thing in the river? And what the hell could cause a bear to run scared like that? I think you're full of shit…"

Joe was up in a flash and had his hand around James's neck. Edgar stepped forward to intervene, but Joe glared at him. James fought against the death-grip. His fingers inched up his face on towards his eyes, creeping forth to gouge them out. He was quickly fading, staring into Joe's crazed snarl, his upturned lip quivering, showing teeth.

"I owe you nothing, you piece-of-shit. I'm doing you a favor by finding your family. You're paying me to get you in and out of here alive, not to explain every little bump in the night."

"Joe," Edgar said. "Give it a rest, man."

"No!" Joe screamed. Spit flying from his mouth. James felt lightheaded. He clawed at Joe's arm, but he didn't budge. He even tried to reach towards the holster in a puny attempt to go for the gun.

"We had a deal. We stick to the deal and the plan. There is nothing out here other than your wild imagination and your pathetic family. I am so tired of yellow weaklings with money and a complex calling the shots. You follow me, my every word and order. Do you remember that part of the deal? I owe you nothing. Now shut the fuck up and get in line. We're moving."

Joe relaxed his arm and James managed to pull away, gasping and clutching at his neck. He nearly passed out, but it confirmed what James was thinking. He didn't see anger in Joe's eyes. He saw fear.

21

REBECCA

"WHAT'RE YOU DOING?" Rebecca asked. She could feel Jr. moving around, more than he usually did to get comfortable. They'd been sitting in the cave for a half a day at least, most of it in silence, and most of it still, except for the occasional break so they could relieve themselves. Though time seemed to pass normally, nothing about their situation appeared to get better. She tried to look on the bright side.

The cave was warm, having been heated year-round as the forest never dipped below seventy. What worried her was there was no shift in the lighting, no raising of the ambient temperature or slow, drifting sunbeams angled over the forest floor. Overcast was the norm, and everything was still.

Even when the sun should have come into its full glory and broken through the canopy, the area was dull and lifeless. As peculiar as it was concerning.

Jr. got up and stretched. Rebecca crawled to the edge of the cave and leaned back against the wall. She saw Jr. had his CD player in his hands, turning it over. He also pulled out his headphones, but before she could tell him it was okay to listen to his music, he snapped them in half. Rebecca was taken aback. He didn't look angry or upset, his eyes darted left to right, thinking, as he removed the remaining cable from its plastic housing. He then popped the player open and pulled the CD out, ran the rope through it and hung it outside the cave on a nearby branch. He had created what amounted to be a highly reflective marker. *Smart kid.*

She hadn't thought to mark the cave, but if she had, she wouldn't have used his headphones, instead sacrificing the laces from her own shoes.

"Now they'll be able to see us," Jr. declared, crouching down next to her. He looked tired, his face streaked with dirt and hair greasy and disheveled. She couldn't imagine she looked any better.

"Good idea. I would have used my laces."

"I know, but how would you hike out of here, then? Besides, now you owe me a new pair," he added slyly. "Let me look at your ankle."

Rebecca nodded, shutting her eyes. It hadn't hurt for about the last hour, even when she moved. It just felt numb and swollen. She let Jr. take care of the business of pulling up her pant leg. He had thin, careful fingers and was gentle when lifting her leg to rest it in his lap.

She heard him gasp. But with the way he was sitting, she couldn't see what he was looking at. He hissed, as if feeling her pain.

"What is it?" She asked, twisting to see.

He paused longer than she liked before setting her leg down softly and saying, "It'll be okay."

Her heart racing, Jr. slid aside, and she nearly fainted. Her ankle was a discolored, swollen stump. Black and angry red, like a turkey leg from the fair. Blood had pooled around the broken bone and when she touched it, the skin was hot and stiff like it was under pressure.

"Jesus! What happened? It's just a broken ankle," she cried, turning off to the side to look at her heel. Then, she saw something that really worried her.

Just above the lip of her shoe was a small indentation with a blackened scab recessed in the skin. It had become necrotic and was starting to die. She wasn't a doctor, but she had enough sense to know that when skin died, it first turned shades of green, then black.

"Oh my God, mom," Jr. said. "What do we do? What's happening?"

Rebecca started to cry, looking up at the roof of the cave, tears streaming down her face. She was going to lose her ankle if she was lucky, her life if she wasn't. If someone didn't hurry and get her to a hospital, the dead flesh would poison her blood if it hadn't started already. She stiffed Jr. of the details.

"I'll be okay. I don't have a fever yet, which means it hasn't infected me yet. We still have time."

"How do you know? It's fucking black, mom. How did it just die?"

"I don't know, Jr., but I need you to stay strong for the both of us. Don't you lose your cool. I haven't lost it yet, so neither can you." She grew stern, masking her growing dread. What she had said about her ankle was a guess, but it sounded right, and her tone sounded hopeful which she, of course, didn't really believe. But with James as their rescuer, she was feigning hope for Jr's sake.

Her mind went to a technique what was known as *fake it until you make it.* She'd fake the hope and the planning and the dismissive nature in lieu of a complete breakdown. She owed that to Jr. for putting him through this.

He nodded, wiping away tears that were beginning to form and lowering her pant leg. Then he crawled next to her and laid his head in her lap. She brushed at his hair softly, her memories taking her to better places.

"Do you remember that time we thought it was a good idea to road trip to Galveston a few months ago?" She asked him.

He snorted, then forced a laugh. "The trip where we drove through the heart of the country and into Texas during the middle of the summer and our car's air-conditioning went out? Yeah, how could I forget?"

Rebecca touched his cheek. "Well, do you remember how mad your dad got? Because he wanted to fly, but I thought it was a good idea to drive? I did the math and estimated between mileage on the car, gas and expenses we'd save fifty dollars. Fifty dollars and an eighteen-hour drive, or a three-hour flight."

"What about it?"

Rebecca draped her hand over his arm and squeezed. "Well, it was the only time I can remember telling him he was right. I think that was where I messed up."

"What do you mean?" He asked, turning over to look up at her. She had never talked to him about what went wrong. She had instead expected to use the time during these few days to help him gain an understanding of what would happen next.

"I think he spent the last six months trying to find other moments where I was wrong. He's always supported me, no matter what, even when I messed up," she explained. "I was wrong to take this job and move us. I was wrong to make him quit his. I was wrong, and the only time I agreed was when the air-conditioning went out."

She didn't know why she was telling her son this. But it felt good and even helped her organize her own thoughts. She hadn't really gone into the deeper reason behind the divorce. She had instead pinpointed specific behaviors and blamed those, which never rang just right. The more she talked now, the more her feelings surfaced. She hoped it wasn't too much for Jr. to hear.

"I was wrong. I pushed him to make sure I always heard I was right, regardless of the truth, and I think it made him hate me. He couldn't tell me I was wrong. So he grew cold and distant," Rebecca trailed off. Tears broke her callous, calculated exterior and though she was with Jr., she felt alone.

"I'm sorry," she told him, but she felt so sad, she might as well have been telling James.

Jr. rolled over and stood up, then kneeled awkwardly in front of her, offering her his shoulder. Then, they hugged like they hadn't seen each other in months. It felt real, and she appreciated having her little boy in her arms again. He didn't seem like a teenager at that moment. He was her little boy.

Together they comforted each other for a while longer, then continued to share fun stories of the family together. And even though the day was still young, outside, the sky grew dark and foreboding.

Jr. noticed it first. He opened his mouth to mention the growing darkness, but there was a large thunderclap overhead that shook the cave and made Rebecca jump. Then, the clouds opened up, and the rain came down in a steady sheet.

Jr. stood at the mouth of the cave and stared as the forest was soaked in less than a minute, and water began to pool at his feet. Rebecca watched as well as the puddle grew larger. Then, a trickle escaped and ran into the cave, forcing her to lift up and out of the way.

Rebecca looked at her son.

The cave was going to flood.

22

JAMES

Joe's assault on James draped an awkward damper over the group. Edgar had remained silent throughout the entire ordeal. James now refused to speak to Joe, and instead focused intently on staying right on his heels. Joe's pace, despite his injury, was nearly breakneck. He felt simultaneously rushed and determined, pushing through the branches, quickening his footsteps in the clear zones and swinging around trees to propel himself forward. He was either in a hurry or he was afraid.

But James wasn't engrossed by the revelation that Joe was a secret piece-of-shit. There was curiosity. A curiosity that Edgar seemed sworn to hide. Whenever he looked back at Edgar, even just to gauge his reactions, he was already looking elsewhere. It was a painstakingly obvious game of cold-shoulder and James was right in the middle.

An hour's hike quickly became a climb as the landscape turned into a steep incline, and saplings were no longer springboards, but handholds, and they climbed at an angle, risking broken ankles to crest a mountain. Joe's prosthetic had begun to click with every step, but he didn't bother to check it.

Before long, the rock formation appeared in view and off to

the right, dug into the landscape. It was an outcrop, like a miniature Pride Rock. It was flat across the top and had a sort of cave near the back of it. He knew Pride Rock from passing the movie cover many times at work in the children's aisle of the store, almost committing it and every other movie in that section to memory — as they were always the first to go.

James had thought they were going to stop and rest at the formation, but Joe kept on. Not wanted to show any weakness, despite his obvious out-of-shape nature compared to Joe, he didn't gripe or mention their lack of rest. Edgar was either just as fit, which would be a feat considering his age, or he was silently protesting their near reckless pace. Whichever it was, neither he nor Joe said anything.

Two hours past Pride Rock and James was ready to beg for a break. His feet ached and there was an angry blister forming between his toes. By the time he remembered to change his socks, it was already too late. Joe didn't even wait up while he peeled the old ones off either — Edgar, however, did.

"Don't worry. I've got a copy of the map if he gets too far ahead," Edgar reassured him.

"What a tool," James replied. Edgar didn't disagree. What time it took to slip on clean socks was enough for his legs to catch up and remind him how out-of-shape he was. Now, as they pushed hour three, they screamed for a rest.

He put what he'd say together in his head, praying they were near a stopping point. Honestly, though Joe was a violent, scheming asshole, he felt safer when he was close by so he could keep an eye on him. His gut told him there was something off about the trip, and Joe knew all about it. Sentence at the ready, James reseated his pack as Joe ducked a branch and let it go, nearly smacking him in the face. He crouched in time and gathered the breath to speak, but before he could, the tree line broke unexpectedly into a clearing. He wouldn't need to beg for a break after all.

The clearing was a beautiful if not unexpected change from the packed forest. Flat in all directions, Mother Nature was trying to reclaim the forest she had lost to the ranger station. Waist high grass hid the ground leading up to the building, and more shrubs fought for sunlight. The building itself was on stilts, nearly fifty feet in the air. It was made of a single wooden structure, but there was a flood light mounted to the side, and a radio antenna. Near the bottom was a metal box. Joe was already heading towards it, but Edgar hadn't moved from where he entered the clearing. He was looking straight up towards the sky. James stopped and looked up.

The sky was a dreary overcast, with heavy clouds ready to drop their payload at any moment. The sun was hidden behind the thick wall gray and white thunderheads, and the temperature had dropped in the last few minutes. James could smell rain.

"Come on, let's get inside. I don't know about you, but I need to rest," James said.

Edgar nodded and took a step forward. Behind him, the trees rustled. There were heavy footsteps. A bear had emerged from the forest. It was a charging monstrosity of black and brown. The scene at the campsite replayed in his head. Everything moved in slow motion. James rolled, Edgar dove, and the beast snarled.

Lumbering towards them, its white dagger-like teeth in its mouth flashed. Its eyes were a soulless black. Edgar sidestepped, and when the bear changed course, James pounced. He drew his fixed-blade knife from his belt and swiped at it, aiming for its head and neck.

He felt the blade sink in, but it proved ineffective, only serving to distract the animal. James saw familiar cuts on its side as it changed course, realizing it was the same bear from before. Only this time, its wounds had scabbed over and it seemed more lively and less afraid. Now it looked like it was on the hunt. He didn't think bears normally wanted anything to do with people; it made sense then that there was something off about this one.

Edgar rolled over and struggled to one knee as the bear took a wide turn, then charged again. Edgar dodged its snapping, roaring jaws by jumping to the left, but as he did, it swiped at him, and the claws tore through his pants and into his calf.

He screamed. It was an agonizing, dreadful scream. The kind that cracked your ear drums and fried your throat. James felt his feet move automatically. Not towards the ranger station, but to help Edgar. He made it to him in seconds and hastily picked him up. He was clutching his bleeding leg while still attempting to hobble away. His pack laid open on the ground. James scooped him up and threw his arm over his shoulder before he could get to it. They labored towards the stairs and to safety, but Edgar tried to dislodge himself and retrieve his equipment.

"Leave it!" James cried, holding his arm firmly over his shoulder. He began to hobble along as the bear roared behind them, sending chills up his spine. He focused on getting to the station, but it looked so far away. Each step he took was intensely difficult, as Edgar had become dead weight in his arms. Then, as their mad dash was nearly over, James glanced back and immediately wished he hadn't. The bear was close enough he could count its whiskers.

He gave a burst of speed, nearly throwing Edgar. He waited for the beast to plow into them, its claws ripping them apart as it peeled the very flesh from their skulls. This is how it would end. With a damn bear.

Then there was a snap of gunfire above.

Shot after shot rang out, echoing through the clearing. James arrived at the steep wooden stairs and dropped Edgar in time to turn and see the bear retreating, bullets connecting with the ground at its feet. Then, with a final snort of disapproval, the beast trudged back into the woods, and James let out a triumphant battle cry.

Edgar screamed, holding his leg as Joe descended the stairs. Then together, without fuss or question, they draped Edgar's arms over their shoulders and hobbled him to the top, one step at a time.

Once they had safely climbed the three flights to the landing, they collapsed. James laid Edgar back while Joe dug in his pack for a first aid kit. It was a bloody mess under his pant leg. The bear's claws had flayed his skin in three perfect cuts right across the top of his calf.

"This will hurt, but you'll live," Joe said, ripping open a green packet with red lettering. "This will clot the blood. Then I'll have to stitch you up."

Before Edgar could protest, Joe emptied the bag into the wounds and they sizzled with white bubbles. Edgar screamed a way no man should ever scream. It was pathetic and heart-breaking. James could only stand idly by while Joe removed a hooked needle from his first aid kit and a piece of small, black, wire-like thread. He tied the end up, then sewed Edgar's skin back in place, one stitch at a time. Edgar moaned softly.

A few minutes later and Joe was covered in blood up to his wrists but appeared content with his field surgery. Edgar had gone quiet, sniffling to himself every so often. It was a terrible thing to watch an old man cry.

23

ARNIE

"Before I started, my brother ran this place. It hummed," Arnie bragged to an unimpressed new hire, a blonde with legs that went forever. She was in her third year of college, according to her resume, and needed a summer job. She was the obvious choice over a disabled veteran and firefighter. Arnie couldn't risk him stealing his thunder.

The girl, Melissa, whose name he had to refresh his memory of from the badge pinned to her very-real chest, sat prim and proper in one of the swivel chairs in the small back office where Arnie liked to nap during the day. He had his dirty boots kicked up on the desk while the girl waited patiently for him to finish reading her resume.

"Says here you enjoy gymnastics and cross-country running. How long have you been doing that?" Arnie asked, chewing on the eraser end of a pencil. He was nervous. She was hot.

"My boyfriend… and I met in high school. He's a gymnast too. I like to run on weekends," she said sweetly. *Fuck. A boyfriend.*

"That's great. Keeps you toned. Just so you know, you can't have any family up here. It's a safety concern. Is that okay?"

"Yes. Of course."

Arnie set his legs down and leaned back in his chair. His gut pushed his shirt out of his pants for a minute and he leaned forward, snatching a map to cover it up. He opened it on the desk and pointed at the various walking paths and campgrounds.

"We have our station here, and one main path into the park." He traced a line upward where a slit was cut through the dense forest.

"There are campgrounds lining either side all the way to the river. Some are pretty far back off the beaten trail, but there are wooden markers at their entrances. The campgrounds end at the river and beyond that is a fence. Do you have any problems following instructions? Like if I were to tell you to stay clear of that area?"

"What's the fence for?" She asked, her big blue eyes shimmering as she looked it over. Arnie could smell her sweet perfume wafting up from her shirt.

"It's the restricted zone, we just call it the zone. We've lost people up there — cliffs and such. We stick to the path, so do campers."

She leaned back and uncrossed her legs. Arnie's eyes drifted up her thighs, her form-fitted khakis leaving nothing to imagination. He licked his fat lips and slobbered a little out of the corner of his mouth.

Pretending to clear his throat, he wiped spittle away with his sleeve, then continued. "If someone doesn't report back at the end of their three-day pass, we do a standard sweep of everything south of the restricted zone. There are paths all through the grounds. Our radios work most of the time. A while ago we had a repeater on a tower deep in the zone. It helped us get service into the mountains. Now, you'll be lucky to get a signal in the parking lot."

He waited, using the natural lull in the conversation to steal a glance at her feet. *God, they're tiny. She's probably a size seven or less. I bet her toes are painted too.* Arnie felt pressure building between his legs and turned off to the side. *She probably wears high heels when she goes out. I wonder if she'll change in the locker room. He could give her locker 47. That one never shuts properly. She'll probably leave her socks...*

"So what happens if someone gets lost?" She asked, interrupting his fantasy. He had been staring out into the lobby.

He cleared his throat awkwardly again. "We patrol the campgrounds and walking paths regularly. It's almost impossible to get lost unless they go into the restricted zone."

"And what happens if they do go into the zone and we can't find them after their pass? Do we go in to find them?" *Never mind. She's too annoying to keep around. Why can't you just enjoy doing nothing like the rest of us? Where else can you make a living doing nothing?*

Arnie recited the policy in a monotone voice. He was the one who made it, after all. "When a camper's three-day pass is expired and they have not checked out, there is a three-day grace period in which we conduct thorough searches of all the campgrounds and everything on our side of the fence. If they are still not found, we call in a third-party search crew." *I bet she waxes...*

"Interesting."

"You think so? I wrote the policy. Well, rewrote it. After my brother died. I can go over a few more of them if you like. We have a really interesting one regarding the deer." He got excited. Did she really think the policy was interesting? Or maybe she thought he was interesting.

She dipped her head a little and looked away. "I'm sorry about your brother."

Stupid bitch. We aren't here to talk about him or your stupid boyfriend. I just need to know what color your underwear is.

"Yeah, it was a long time ago. I don't want to talk about him, ever, okay?"

She looked up, nodding apologetically. "I didn't mean to offend."

"It's fine," Arnie huffed, twisting around to look at a spreadsheet pinned to an overcrowded bulletin board. He wasn't really looking at it... all he could think about was her tiny little feet squeezing into some high-top boots...

"What's this thing?" She interrupted. Arnie rolled his eyes, swiveling around in his chair.

"The radio," he said, twisting a knob on the clunky metal box with several frequency dials, pre-programmed stations, and a speaker. It had a layer of dust across the top. He picked up the black goose-neck microphone and pulled it towards him.

"As you can see, it's been a while since we've had to use it. We hardly get any service anyway. Most of the time it stays off. Our rangers are good enough they don't need them," he bragged again. *Maybe that makes you hot. A man in uniform, not a fucking leotard.*

There was another awkward silence, then the radio squawked, causing them both to jump in their seats. A man's voice came through the speaker

"Hello? Hello? Can anyone hear me? Fuck! Are you sure this is even on? Hello?"

There was a rustling sound in the background. Arnie stared at it wide eyed. Melissa just looked confused. Timidly, Arnie leaned forward and pressed the *talk* button on the microphone.

"This is Arnie. Identify yourself."

"Arnie? Arnie, you fuck, it's Joe. Listen, you need to get to these coordinates. Edgar's hurt and you need to make pickup—." The speaker crackled, spewing feedback, and then cut off.

Arnie's hand was shaking. He could no longer keep up his routine with the girl. If Joe and Edgar had trouble, and were hurt that far into the restricted zone, that was exactly where

Arnie wanted them. He wanted them to suffer. He wanted them to hurt and feel pain and fear. He wanted payback for all those years ago. For days he sat in the parking lot of the forest, waiting for them to bring his brother out... only to see them emerge empty handed. Even when they went in a second time, they came back with nothing. Not even his body. It was their fault he was dead, and they should pay for it.

"Who was that?" Melissa asked. She had her back against the wall, staring down at the radio.

He wasn't about to tell her the truth. "Some of the guys playing a prank, is all. I'll ask around to find out who it was."

"I thought you said the ranger post was abandoned? It sounds like somebody needs help." She had genuine concern in her eyes.

"I just went over the policy. Look, here is their day pass." He fumbled on the desk and found their receipt. "They just went in two days ago. They still have another day before we go looking, then three days after that until we call in for a rescue. That's the policy. That's what it has always been." Arnie was nearly yelling at the poor girl. She had sat down and was looking away like a sad puppy. He immediately felt bad for yelling at her. Not because of how it made her feel, but because it increased the likelihood she'd quit before he had a chance to get into her locker.

"Look. Let me show you the four-wheeler, and we'll take it up to the river. If someone is hurt, we can bring them back with us. We have a wagon that can fit a person." He stood up and unlocked the door to the crowded office, and held it open for her. As she passed by him, her tight ass brushed up against his gut, and he engorged in his pants. Unable to concentrate, he instructed her to wait outside while he made a quick trip to the bathroom. And it was indeed quick.

24

ARNIE

AFTER PULLING up his zipper and tucking his shirt in, Arnie stepped outside. The air was cool and laden with humidity, ready for a summer rain. While generally okay with the stink near the forest, there was something about being engulfed by Melissa's perfume for nearly an hour, only to step outside into Satan's asshole, that made the air particularly disgusting. He hated the forest's stink, and the dampness in the air meant he might have to wash his shirt for the next day — he was wearing the only extra-large he owned.

Melissa didn't seem to mind. She was looking towards the wall of trees. He walked up from behind, his eyes locked on her just below the waist. She turned as he approached.

Though he had originally intended to take her into the grounds himself, his mind was clear now and the thought of being around her while she asked more questions wasn't worth a few more passing glances. Instead, while he was on his way from the bathroom to the shed behind the station, he remembered the radio call, and the fact that their vehicles were in the parking lot. He could hit them again by towing them. Normally, he'd be more direct about kicking someone while they were down, but this was different. It was personal. It was for what they did to his brother.

"Do you know how to drive a gator?" He asked Melissa.

She nodded. "I grew up on a farm. Four-wheeler or horse is fine by me."

"Good. I'm going to give you the keys. Here's a map." He handed her a sweat-laden park map from his back pocket.

"Head to the river and back. Get used to the path, the curves, and the different campgrounds. If it starts to rain, return immediately. The park floods at times and I don't need you ruining our ride on your first day." She nodded and beamed. She seemed excited to be given so much trust right out of the gate.

"Once you come back, it'll probably be the end of your shift anyway. There's a fuel pump next to the shed. Make sure you top it off." He handed her the keys and she scurried away. Arnie watched her hips dip as she walked, then returned to more important matters.

There were two vehicles in the parking lot. He assumed one was Edgar's and the other Joe's, or maybe one belonged to that guy James. He didn't know, he didn't care. They were together on this, and that meant they should all pay. He had already towed that car belonging to James's wife. *Asshole.*

Arnie returned to his desk inside and opened the top drawer. Inside was a black revolver, and under that was a cellphone. It was beat up, but always worked. He waited for it to power on, then found the contact he was looking for from the menu. A man answered with one word. "Yeah?"

"Sonny. This is Arnie over here at the park. I've got a couple of cars that have been abandoned here for a few days. Can you come grab them? Great." He ended the call and tossed it back into the drawer. Then, feet on the desk again, he relished the lightly scented, cool air blowing in from a wall unit. It hummed and rattled rhythmically, nearly causing him to drift off to sleep. Then, a thought forced him into immediate lucidity. He glared at the radio. *You left my brother up there.* He thought, as if the radio was personally responsible. But it wasn't the radio. It was Joe, and Edgar, and their friend Tim.

They left him up there to die. They came out without him, only to go right back in and leave him again. He felt his face grow hot, and beads of sweat formed in his armpits. *I'll get you. I'll get you.*

Outside, the four-wheeler roared to life then buzzed out of the parking lot, fading into the distance. Once he was sure Melissa was gone, he reached under the desk and found the feed wire for the radio. He unscrewed it and let it dangle. No-one came into his office, but he didn't need the girl getting any wild ideas. She seemed like the type to want to help everyone — to bend over backwards for charity and donate to the church every Sunday. And he hated her for it.

Those self-respecting types didn't make it very long under his management. He liked people who would sit down, shut up, and do nothing. It made for easy days in the air-conditioning, followed by easy nights alone at home in his favorite chair. For there was one thing for certain, he never took his work home with him. *Unless it was Melissa.*

With that pleasant thought, Arnie pushed himself up and headed for the locker room. There, he verified that locker 47 was the one that didn't close properly and returned to his desk. He set out the key for that particular locker on the desk and wrote the number down in Melissa's employee file. He smiled for the first time that day. All was well. All was good.

25

JAMES

JAMES RAMMED his shoulder against the stiff metal door once more before giving up, having only succeeded in bruising his shoulder. Joe groaned and pushed him out of the way, then reared back and kicked it with his good foot. The frame splintered and the door swung open, smacking against the wall. Together, they supported Edgar and dragged him into the musky cabin, having since ascended from the landing below.

As they went inside, James peered over the balcony, his eyes adjusting to the oncoming low-light. He was thankful for the early dusk — the view from three stories up would have made him queasy otherwise.

Below, he saw a dark shadow circling the tower. It didn't seem phased by the gunshots, as he was sure Joe hit it. It continued around once more before lumbering back into the woods. James pushed off from the railing and went inside.

It was a single room, frozen in time. It looked like it had been abandoned mid-shift. James first noticed papers laid out across a counter that was built to surround the entire interior of the tower. He noticed that the tower was a huge fishbowl, with ceiling high windows, all intact, giving an unobstructed view of the forest below. It was surprisingly well built, made from weatherproof wood, a tin roof and even a tiled floor. On the west side was an open-top cubby with a sink and a toilet.

James walked the circumference of the room, every so often peering over the edge of the counter and through the windows. A light breeze swayed the outpost and Edgar moaned pitifully on the floor. James turned to kneel by him while Joe scoured the cabinets.

"I think Joe is trying to find you some painkillers," James said. A cabinet slammed behind him and a bottle clinked.

"Aha!" Joe said. He held a dusty bottle with a brown liquid inside. The label had long since worn off. He popped the top off and smelled it, then pulled away, his nose scrunched up. "That's good. Better than painkillers," he said, taking a swig, then smacked his lips. He passed the bottle to Edgar.

"I'm fine. It's this damn tower swaying. My aching knee hurts more than this cut does, and that's only because it's going to rain." He sipped from the bottle.

"So what now?" James asked, reaching out and taking the bottle. He drank and was surprised by how the liquid was smooth yet it settled heavily in his stomach.

"Never mind that. What is this?" He asked, looking it over. He could see bits of something floating around in it as the moonlight passed through it.

"Honey wine. Mead," Joe said. "It was Tim's. He always had a stash up here. We used this station as a home base for our rescues. But as you can tell, it's been abandoned for some time. There's a radio, and it has its own generator, but the electronics are probably toast after all these years. I'll give it a go, and if we can get Arnie on the radio, he might meet us by the fence, and we can send Edgar out."

Edgar sat up on his elbows. "Fuck that, I'm good. Just give me another drink. We're too close for me to turn around."

Joe was already shaking his head. He stood up and his prosthetic clicked. Near what James would consider the front of the round room was a large hanging map made of stiff board. It was colored and showed the layout of the restricted zone. It wasn't complete, but it was more detailed than the map with the grayed-out section that James was used to seeing.

"If we hike from here then cut southeast, we can make it back to the fence. All Arnie would have to do is follow the river a half a mile, and he'd run right into you. Then, we can shoot up north to the coordinates," Joe said.

"This is bullshit, Joe. You've only got one leg and you aren't turning back. I can walk. You've got me all stitched up. I'll wrap up my leg and we can see this through, like we swore to. You know it takes three..." Edgar said, trailing off. Joe threw a disapproving look at him and Edgar pressed his lips together. He looked like he had said something he shouldn't have. James caught on.

"What takes three?"

"What?" Edgar asked stupidly. He had heard James. He was looking right at him.

"I said. What takes three?" James repeated, putting emphasis on each word.

"Uh. He meant it'll take us three hours to get us out, because of his leg." Joe said. He snatched the glass from James's hand and drank it while walking away. But James wasn't done with the conversation. He got to his feet, aimed to grab the drink back, but Joe held up a finger and opened his mouth. He began gulping the alcohol down by the mouth full. As he got near the last dregs, he tilted his head to finish it, and a small folded piece of paper fell out of his pocket. James snagged it and had it open by the time Joe noticed.

"Deadfall Trap. Spiked Log Trap. Feather Spear Trap. What the fuck is this, Joe? Are you going to try to kill me or something?"

For the first time in a while, Joe showed some emotion. It wasn't fear or anger, it was embarrassment, like he had been caught with his pants down.

He set the bottle down on the counter softly. "Give me that," he said calmly, his hand out.

James, realizing Joe needed what appeared to be a copy of the forbidden zone, stepped back. "Tell me what this is," he demanded.

"Give me. The map. Or I swear to God I'll break your fuckin' legs and throw you over the railing for our buddy down there," Joe snarled.

James froze. He was determined to hold his ground. To get to the bottom of it. Out of the corner of his eye, he saw Edgar roll over and crawl towards a chair near the counter. He tugged himself up, leaving his leg out at an odd angle, and fiddled with a metal box with a built-in speaker.

"You don't just want this, do you? You need this." James moved like he was about to tear the paper in half. Joe drew his weapon. James stared down the barrel.

Edgar cranked on a handle below the counter. It spun and made a whining noise.

"Tell me what this is, or I'll tear it up," James said.

Behind Joe, Edgar pressed a button, and the box squealed so loud, Joe covered his ears. James winced and took advantage of the distraction by drawing a lighter from his pocket. He flicked it and held it an inch from the flame. James's face was bathed in the lighter's glow. The whine of the gear on the radio faded into the background.

"I've got it closest to your notes. They'll burn first," he said. Was he really prepared to die for whatever this was? Joe had already shown he was cold and calculated. Would he shoot him over a piece of paper?

Joe clamped down on his teeth and looked like he was ready

to grind them down to nothing. His finger twitched on the trigger.

Then, in the midst of the standoff, James with his lighter, and Joe with the pistol, Edgar said. "I've got power. It's got some juice but only enough for a minute. Put your dicks away and get over here. It'll be Arnie answering, so be nice."

Joe lifted the pistol and showed his palms, then turned towards the counter. There, he grabbed the microphone and pressed on the *talk* key. There was a click, then nothing.

"What the hell, Edgar. I thought you said this thing was working? Normally there's a tone. Are you sure you know what you're doing with this?" Joe questioned.

"Yes, just talk, damn it! I have to keep cranking on this to hold what little power we have."

Joe groaned loudly, and he pressed the button. "Hello? Hello? Can anyone hear me? Fuck! Are you sure this is even on? Hello?" Edgar continued to crank on the motor. Joe smacked the top of it.

"This is Arnie. Identify yourself."

Joe leaned in. "Arnie? Arnie, you fuck-wad, it's Joe. Listen, you need to get to these coordinates. Edgar's hurt and you need to make pickup—."

The radio cut off, and there was a loud thump from somewhere below them. Joe mashed the *talk* key again.

"Hello? Hello? Arnie? Fuck!"

There was another loud thud, this time closer, and Joe looked at Edgar, then at James.

All was silent. All was still. James held his breath and the hairs on the back of his neck stood up.

Lightning flashed across the rolling clouds and the soft patter of rain grew to a raging torrent, drowning out all sound as water smacked hard against the tin roof. Then, above all other sounds, came a guttural, tortured wailing that made all three men turn to look at the door. The storm raged above, and over the clatter of heavy water droplets hitting the roof and rolling off the side in waves, came another thump, and another inhuman howl.

J R

Jr. CAUGHT his mom's eye, and together they shared a thought in the glow of Jr.'s little flashlight. *If the cave floods, they're subject to the elements, and there was no telling where it might flood in the forest.* The cave was their best bet. It was safe, a natural landmark, and not too far from where they were originally. It made sense to keep to it, but the question was how they could keep it from flooding.

He looked around anxiously. The cavern was empty, and they didn't have any supplies with which to scoop the water out if they wanted. Lightning snapped overhead and Jr. retreated to his spot next to his mother, sitting down, feeling defeated.

She didn't say anything. He wished she would. He needed her right now. He needed her to tell him it was going to be alright. He needed to know they'd both be alright. Instead, she leaned her head on his shoulder. If she was crying, he couldn't tell. The rain bounced off the cave walls and splashed their faces.

Jr. willed himself to remain strong. His mom was the one who was hurt, not him. He was nearing adulthood, which meant he would have to take care of himself in the very near future. He wrestled with the idea of going for help once more, but remembering he was pretty much lost quickly changed his mind. Instead, he tilted his head down and did something he hadn't ever done. He kissed her softly on the forehead.

He had hugged her, sure, but never once had he even allowed her to kiss him on the cheek. She had tried many times, of course, but he had always turned away. He didn't have a reason as to why he turned away, but she had accepted his decision anyway. She sniffed hard once and adjusted her leg. He peered over her head into the dark. Into the back of the cave where the water would start to pool...

He shined his light and stared at the other end. It looked odd, almost like another entrance, but up off the ground near the ceiling. He must have missed it before because of the way the cave sloped down.

"What's through there?" He asked.

She sniffled and looked at him first, then followed his eyes to the rear of the cave.

"What? Nothing. It's just a big crack."

Jr. crawled along his hands and knees, following the flow of water that had grown from a trickle to a few inches wide over the last hour and pooled near the back of the cave. Jr. had his eye on something else. He stood up and looked through the divide. It was flat except for a few smaller rocks, and it grew darker on the other end. He estimated it was six or seven feet across.

The ceiling was detached from the rear wall, and when he shined his flashlight in, he could see it was a passageway that appeared to open up on the other side. It looked just wide enough for them to squeeze through. It would be tight, but it would keep them safe from the water until it drained. Besides, who knew what might be seeking shelter from the rain.

No matter which way he looked at it, the water would be up over their heads before long, and with the onset of quick and powerful storms came mudslides, falling branches and flooding. He remembered reading something from the survival book about caves. *Caves were part of systems. Tunnels, caverns, running water, sometimes other entrances.*

He came up with an idea. He didn't have much time. He needed to know for sure if what he was thinking was possible. Immediately, he began ripping the laces out of his shoes and tied them together. Then, he rushed over to his mom and knelt by her feet. "I need your laces. There might be a cavern on the other end. I need to see if it will fit us both. If it does, we can crawl in and be safe from the storm and the water." He began pulling the laces from her shoes.

"What if the water doesn't drain once we get over there? What if there's no way out on the other side?"

Jr. looked around the cave.

"We just need to wait it out. Once the water lets up, we can come back through. There aren't any water marks on the walls, so I think the cave will drain once it stops raining as hard. With your leg as it is, we can't risk it getting wet or risk you getting too cold. This is our only choice."

She appeared to think it over and, to his surprise, didn't object. She worked to take her laces off but left her shoe on. "What are the laces for?"

He tied them together until it was one long piece, then secured his flashlight on one end. "Before I climb in there, I want to make sure we can get out. We'll use the light to see if there's a cavern." Lightning split the sky and more water poured from the clouds. This wasn't just a summer rain. It was a cataclysmic event.

Jr. waited for his mom to respond, but she only gave him a teary, firm nod before he pulled the flashlight away. He checked each link several times over before standing at the edge of the gap.

"Jr.?" She called to him from the dark.

"Yeah, mom?"

"I love you and I trust you."

Jr.'s heart thumped in response. "I love you too."

He held the flashlight in his right hand, and the end of the line in his left, then reared back and tossed the light gently into the passage. It clattered and spun on the hard rock, but the line held strong.

Unfortunately, it didn't quite reach the other side. Jr. pulled it out, then water seeped into his shoe. He was running out of time. Hastened, he added a little more strength to his throw and let out a sigh as the light landed on the edge, then tipped over and out of sight. It spun slowly, and he squinted into the dark. At first, he couldn't tell what he was looking at, but as the light rotated around again, he realized he was looking at a rocky outcrop — a stalagmite.

Jr. carefully yanked on the shoelace and the light twisted under the lip, then flipped up onto the edge. He quickly tugged on the line, dragging it back towards him and spooling the laces around his hand.

"We can get through! Let's go," he said, rushing to her side and scooping up her arm. She lifted her bad leg, and they splashed in the water as they hobbled to the wall.

"I'll help you up first," Jr. said.

He shined the light at the entrance and saw his mom shaking her head. "You first. I'll follow."

"Fine, but only because I need to help you down. It looks tight. If you start to feel stuck, don't worry, you're not. Just calm down, breathe, and push on through," he reassured her, half reassuring himself. Again, he was thankful for grabbing the book in the first place and sacrificing sleep to read through the night. It turned out to be well worth it.

Rebecca stepped forward and Jr. made a pocket with his hands. She used her good leg and an arm to brace herself, then lifted up on one leg. She had to practically dive into the mouth of the crawl space, but Jr. helped by pushing on her uninjured foot. She began to shimmy her way in, then moaned loudly as her swollen foot caught on the lip of the cave. Jr. helped turn it sideways, but it was awkward and swollen, and she screamed, causing Jr.'s ear to crackle as her shrill howls echoed off the tight cave walls.

"I'm sorry! I'm so sorry!" He called back to her.

"It's fine! Keep pushing! Just do it!"

Closing his eyes, Jr. pushed against both of her feet, igniting painful groans and a sickening crunch as bone ground against bone in her ankle. But, as she shimmied once more, lightning cracked above. She grunted loudly as she fell out onto the other side.

Water had nearly reached his knees by the time he managed to jump up and into the path. He smacked his head against the stone twice, sending stars shooting across his eyes. There was no point looking around; he couldn't turn his head. Instead, he took his own advice, shut his eyes, and focused on his breathing, inching his body forward, the rock pushing against his lower back.

It's just a low point. Keep going. You're fine.

"Almost there. Bring your hand around. There you go." A cool hand gripped his as he brought his arm up along his side, then reached out in front of him. Then, with a final twist and a heave, his upper half was free of the suffocating space, and his mom pulled him the rest of the way through. The path ended in smooth rock that allowed him to slip down easily, and he stood up, feeling accomplished and relieved to be out of such a tight fit.

Looking back through and out of the front of the cave once more, the lightning flashed, revealing a wall of rain. But as the remnants of the flash faded, there was another show of lightning. His heart nearly stopped as he saw something pale and skinny with antlers blocking the entrance.

REBECCA

DESPITE HAVING DRIED off since arriving in the deeper part of the cave, Rebecca shivered, and her hands were clammy. Just as she made it through the tight passageway, she collapsed and fainted. Jr. not only had to twist her broken ankle to the side, but he had to push on it to help get her through. Then, once she exited the passage, she hit it again before coming out. It was enough to make her vision swirl and her head heavy.

But before she passed out, she saw Jr. squeezing through and out the other side where she was waiting. Using what little strength she had left, she helped him to his feet and collapsed.

She awoke sometime later. The specifics were hazy. All she knew was the storm was over, and there was a steady drip somewhere nearby. She felt Jr. up against her and croaked. "Honey?"

"Yeah? Are you okay?" He asked, sounding strangely similar to James.

"I'm cold. I think there's something wrong with my leg. Will you turn the light on and look at it?" There was a rustling and a click, and Jr.'s face was illuminated.

Concern reflected in his eyes. He looked like he hadn't slept in weeks, not days.

"Sure, mom," he said robotically and still, he didn't blink. He stuck the flashlight into his mouth and knelt by her broken ankle, then carefully rolled the pant leg up. He shined the light down at it for half a second before looking directly at her. He took it from his mouth to speak.

"It's okay," he said, but his tone and the look on his face said more.

"Show me. It feels weird. It feels like I've got an itch."

She had been resting her hands in her lap and reached forward, only to have Jr. push them away. "What's wrong?" She asked.

"They're... they're cleaning it. Okay? This is bad, but they will help," he replied. Rebecca didn't have a clue about what he meant.

"Just show me," she said, waiting. Jr. slowly moved the light from her face down to her leg and she about passed out again.

Little white worms crawled all along the surface of her ankle. They covered her foot and were between her toes. Surprisingly, she couldn't feel them, but the sight of them all over made her want to hurl. She couldn't hold it back, and heaved, only to cramp painfully as her stomach was completely devoid of food.

Jr. was leaning over her leg. "You have a cut that must have gotten infected. That explains the swelling. Maggots are okay. They're cleaning it of dead flesh. Once it's gone, they'll drop off," He tried to comfort her.

She could hear him, but couldn't comprehend what he was saying. *Maggots. Under your skin.* The more she thought about it, the more she felt them, crawling between her muscle and the skin, eating. *Eating you. They're eating you.*

Her initial instinct was to panic and think insane thoughts like *cut it off* or *burn it until they're all dead,* but there was none of that. She had seen plenty of nature shows, and even heard of medicinal maggot use. This wasn't the same, but since she likely had an infection, it was probably best they were doing what they did. *Eating you.*

She swallowed the lump in her throat, whimpered, and felt Jr. lean over her. He clicked the light off and hugged her, and that was more than she had gotten from him in years. For once, she could feel him. She felt connected to her son again, and it gave her a renewed strength. A strength that filled her heart and dried her tears. It cut away at her hunger and her pain and pushed aside her negative thoughts. It was what they both needed.

"How long have I been out?" She whispered. Her every word bounced around the cavern.

"About two hours, I'd guess. I looked around. There's no way out, but the water is already draining back out the front. The storm is gone, but I saw..."

He paused mid-sentence and Rebecca raised an eyebrow. "Saw what?"

"N-nothing," he stammered. "I hate to tell you we have to go back through. We can't stay here, in case help arrives."

She nodded. She wanted nothing more than to sit in this cavern and wait for help, but it would be pointless if they had no idea she was there.

"This time, you go first, and you can pull me through instead of pushing on my leg."

He looked back down the path as if he saw something she couldn't. His eyes were locked in place. He only dislodged himself from whatever he was looking at after Rebecca rested her hand on his shoulder. He jumped when she did, but upon seeing her, relaxed, blinked, and smiled weakly.

Without another word, Jr. climbed into the mouth of the path, ducking his head to avoid the roof. He inched forward for the first few feet, then was forced to shimmy the rest of the way.

Upon reaching the other side, he spilled out and into a shallow pool. He shined the light away to avoid blinding her. There was enough light for her to see and grab any handholds available since her foot was out of commission. A brief wave of nausea hit her as she thought of the bugs squirming under her skin, but she shook it away. "Nope. Not here. You're not going to lose your shit here."

Finding comfort in the prospect of being outside again, she lifted herself into the hole using her good foot, and then pushing off with the knee of her injured leg. She nearly lost her balance and fell back onto the hard rock, but leaned forward and against the wall.

"Whoa, mom, are you okay?"

"I'm fine!" She called. Her head throbbed where she hit it, but at least she was in the narrow corridor now. Like it was made of glass, Rebecca lifted her injured leg further into the hole and kept her foot slightly raised. It was uncomfortable and awkward but it reduced the risk of slamming it into something. Then, she was able to pull herself along using the stone to her sides, and by pushing off with her good foot. In a few treacherous minutes, she made it within arm's reach of Jr., who locked onto her wrists and pulled. Then she was out of the cave and near the entrance, her leg suspended above the pool of water at their feet.

Jr. seemed pleased with his idea to escape the water and walked to the front of the cave. Though the flashlight gave them a meager amount of light, it was enough to see that the entire area was covered in puddles a few feet across, each one representing what could have been a wash-out or a hole to break another ankle in. To their right were downed trees, split from the wind, and to the left was a hill where shrubs, unsecured sticks and bramble were washed down in a mud slide. The whole area looked completely different from when they had arrived.

Rebecca was thankful they hadn't been caught in it, and she was thankful for Jr.'s quick thinking. She thought about what else she might say to him, because this would be the time, but nothing came to mind. She realized she didn't need to tell him anything. Together, through all this, she had shown she could still be tough, and that they needed to be strong as a family, because they were much better off that way.

Jr. pushed back into the cave and knelt in the puddle. He cupped his hands and drank from it. "It's probably the cleanest we'll get. Only drink a little. If we get sick, the more we have, the worse it'll be. We'll have some more in an hour or two."

Realizing the trouble she would have kneeling, Jr. helped her down to drink. Like a wild animal, she sipped from the puddle. It was cool and earthy and calmed her dry throat. She had to force herself to stop drinking. She hadn't realized how thirsty she really was.

But just before she pulled away, something under the surface caught her attention. She reached into the water and gripped the corner of a small package, soft and flat. She dragged it out of the pool and recognized it as a waterproof bag, similar to the one she had brought for the trip. It was a faded light green. She looked at Jr., then at the bag. There were initials sewn onto it. They read T.B.

JOE

YEARS OF MILITARY TRAINING, emotional hardening and callous withdrawal from the world couldn't prepare him for what he saw when he leaned over the edge of the lookout. He was first outside and had caught a glimpse of it at the last second. He was followed closely by James, who seemed oblivious. If he had seen it too, he would have said something.

The thing he had seen was beyond comprehension and shouldn't exist by any means. But that didn't mean it didn't. And just because Joe didn't want to believe in it didn't mean it couldn't still kill him. What he saw was his greatest regret, embodied and emboldened.

Antlers, fur, and bloody bones. It was a creature from the pits of hell and built from the devil's imagination. Joe considered James lucky. He hadn't seen it... yet.

But it had other ways of reminding you it was there.

Using a heavy-duty flashlight from inside, Joe saw the aftermath of the thumping sound. There were notches cut out from the support beams for the guard post. Three of them, all about seven or eight feet off the ground. From afar, they looked like deep gouges.

James broke the silence. "Here. Take this. I really don't care what happens to us at this point, just promise me you'll help me find my family?" He asked, holding out the map. "Take it and promise me you'll help. Promise me you aren't out here to kill me, because I'm not stupid. I may not know the specifics of the traps you mentioned, but I know you don't put three of them so close together. That means you're hunting something. What is it?"

Joe stared at him. How could he explain it? How could he give the man the information he desperately needed and wanted to know? How could he explain something that in and of itself was an enigma to him?

"I... I wish I had an answer. But I can promise you I will do whatever it takes to help you find your family. Our deal hasn't changed."

He had been angry for so long, at himself, and Edgar and others, for what had happened all those years ago. There was a sort of odd catharsis that happened when he saw it again. For a long time, it had been only a nightmare and a figment of his past. For many years, he thought it was just waiting to find him, lurking in the shadow of a doorway or around a blind corner. He spent most nights in a drunken stupor, imagining himself taking some leggy woman back to his hotel room. Only to have the thing burst through the door and skewer her with its giant...

"I appreciate that," James said. "I just miss my family. Between the storm and Edgar getting hurt, plus all that stuff you told me before we came out here. It just makes me worry about them is all." He spat over the edge of the railing and looked down at the three flights of stairs. Overhead, the storm had moved on to terrorize the nearby town, leaving the full moon to glow brightly in a clear sky. It cast shadows everywhere that twisted and danced, only fueling his already brewing imagination.

Joe nodded sharply. "Let's see what we've got for supplies, then we'll sleep in shifts."

James raised an eyebrow. "Shifts? Why?"

"The bear, of course? They can climb, you know," Joe lied. He didn't know if the bear could climb, and he didn't care. He knew why the bear didn't continue up the stairs and into the cabin. It hadn't walked off, it had run. It was afraid. They were just unlucky enough to get caught in its path.

Stepping through the door, Joe spotted Edgar snoring softly to himself. He had taken his jacket off and had it balled up under his head. His backpack was placed nearby and a large hunting knife, still in its sheath, was clipped onto the front. Joe quietly went to work searching the cabinets individually. Along the way, he found interesting relics but nothing of practical use.

In the last cabinet, he located a lockbox that, when rattled, sounded like it had something in it. He used a screwdriver to force the cheap lock to turn and found a handful of photographs. Most were old and in black and white, showing off some of the prettier parts of the forest. The first few were of the waterfall, a cave, the stone outcropping they had passed earlier, the newly built ranger station, and finally, a color photo of a group of men.

Joe set the box down and his heart pounded in his chest. He knew the picture. He was in it. Sliding his feet out from under him, Joe brought his knees up and looked the picture over, now having no choice but to live in the memories. In the photo was a much younger Edgar, Joe, Tim Breaker, and their friend and Arnie's brother, Roger House. Together, the five of them, all experienced foresters, stood in front of the newly created ranger station, placed deep in the modern-day forbidden zone. They all looked so happy, and Joe remembered the photo was taken just before it all started. Twenty days later, and Roger and Tim Breaker would never be seen again. They would be left atop a mountain with two bottles of water and a walking stick.

James walked around behind him to look at the photo over his shoulder. He stood nearby but didn't say anything.

Joe was lost in the memory.

It started with an injury. Then came the fighting, and the eventual splitting of the group. *Why didn't you just take them with you? You could have made it.*

Joe argued with his subconscious.

I could have. But I didn't want to. Roger pissed you off and betrayed you. Tim betrayed you. This was inevitable. The only difference was you got away with it.

James hadn't moved.

Joe lifted the photo up so he could see. "That's me, Edgar, Tim Breaker and Roger House, Arnie's brother."

James's eyebrows raised. "What happened to you guys?"

Joe sighed and laid his forehead on his knees. "Same thing as what's happening right now. Tim got hurt, nearly got his leg ripped off. We stopped the bleeding, but he couldn't walk. Roger chose to stay behind."

James sat down on the floor opposite of him but off to the side, so they both had a good view of the moon above.

"It's not your fault. I can see guilt on your face. They moved when you told them to stay put," James said. He was trying to help, but he was only making it worse. Mainly because he was completely wrong.

"I asked Roger to come with me. I asked him to leave Tim alone or with Edgar, and we'd go get help. Roger chose Tim over me."

"Were you two…"

"Together? Yes. For a few years." Joe confessed. He hadn't told anyone the specifics of his relationship with Roger. It was still new to him at the time. He hadn't even disclosed it to the police when they asked about Roger's disappearance. The only person that knew was Edgar, and he wasn't about to incriminate himself.

"I loved Roger. But Roger loved Tim. He had always loved Tim. He had loved Tim before he loved me. So I got angry and took everything while they were sleeping. I took the food, the water, the machete—everything that would have helped them survive. Then, I woke up Edgar, and we left them in the night."

James didn't say anything. He half-expected him to make a joke about his relationship with Roger, but he was silent and respectful. Joe appreciated him for that. James seemed to understand for as Joe talked, he was nodding. Joe took up the photo once again and put it back in the lockbox, then set it aside next to their bags. He'd bring it with him when they left.

"Get some sleep. I'll take first watch," he told James.

James nodded once, then set up his bedroll and laid his head on his pack. Joe sat and stared up at the moon for a few more minutes before spinning around to reach for a granola bar from his backpack, only to find Edgar sitting up on his elbows, a look of pure hatred on his face.

He looked devilish in the moonlight, the shadows enhancing the wrinkles around his eyes and neck, leaving a dark hole for a mouth.

Joe stared at him, slightly startled by his appearance.

"Liar," Edgar mouthed before lowering himself slowly back down.

29

JAMES

MOST OF JAMES'S SHIFT, the last one before sunrise, was spent either digging through relics in the old outpost or memorizing the trails on the large hanging map by flashlight. Joe had woken him up around 3:00 AM by kicking him in the boot then promptly passing out on his bedroll. It was a long day for them all, but with a few hours of rest under his belt, James felt better about what lay ahead.

From what he knew, Joe, Edgar, Tim and Roger were foresters together. Joe had a relationship with Roger, but when Tim got hurt, the truth came out. Roger chose Tim and stayed behind. Joe and Edgar escaped the woods alone to get help, only to return and find that neither Roger nor Tim were where they left them. *What a complicated mess.*

He wondered if Edgar harbored any hatred for Joe because presumably, if Edgar would have stayed behind, he'd be dead, and that seems to be exactly what Joe wanted...

He gave the map a rest and rubbed the sleep from his eyes. It was all starting to blur, and he was getting a headache. He had memorized most of the trails already, but there was nothing else to look at. Standing and looking at the old map was his strongest bet to avoid falling asleep.

He did his best to recall the trap locations on Joe's map how they worked. He decided to ask to see it later and perhaps capitalize on the newfound trust between them. Clicking off the light, he left the station and walked to the outer balcony. Not daring enough to look down, he instead looked out over the forest, the putrid, treacherous sea of trees with its foul stench and its rabid beasts.

He wanted to scream and call for his family. He wanted to tell them he was on his way and give them hope. Maybe Rebecca would see this as a change in him, to give him another chance to prove he could be who she needed. Maybe Jr. wouldn't resent him after this. Maybe they were already dead, and all of this was pointless...

James's conscious took a dark turn, and he had to shake his head to send them away. It was a long trip into the park, and they had been gone for a few days. That worried him. The location of the coordinates concerned him more so now that he knew a bit about why Joe and Edgar were interested in coming out here in the first place. Sure, a six-figure paycheck was nice, but why bring a gun? What is going on with the second map, and why is Joe so obsessive over it? What part of the history was he missing?

There was a lot to think over and just a few hours until daylight. Once it hit, the quiet peace of the night would be replaced with oppressive, humid air, the biting insects, and another day of blind hiking through the forest. He pushed off the railing and wiped the sweat from his neck, regardless of the cool, early morning air.

The moon, a waxing gibbous if he remembered correctly, gave plenty of light around the station, but it all seemed to stop at the forest's edge — like it refused to go in. James recognized this was silly, but he imagined the forest as some great entity. It knew they were there. It chose who to keep and who to let go, and right now, he and the group and even his family were on the edge of the entity's decision point.

He risked a queasy glance over the railing. Something told him to look. Call it instinct, or a sixth sense, or whatever. And he was right to listen to it.

Just on the forest's edge, something moved. Tall and pale, it passed behind the first layer of trees, so its vague outline was briefly illuminated by the moon. It skirted behind tree after tree, becoming hidden, then reappearing again. It moved like a person who's arms and legs were too long and foreign to it. James watched in awe of such an oddity and wondered what it could be.

No animal was that tall. Not even a bear on its hind legs, and even then, what bear was the color of pale skin?

It passed out of view once more, circling the vale and skirting the outpost. James scurried around to the railing to get a closer look. It was dark, and the night-bugs had stopped chittering. All was still.

A branch snapped. Leaves rustled. James caught movement out of the corner of his eye. Whatever it was, he could feel it watching him.

With bated breath, he waited, and tried to make the late-night visitor out, to try to understand what it was. But his mind was scrubbed of all ideas. He could only watch.

Suddenly there was a stillness that showered over the entire area—and then it howled.

Not like a beast or injured animal. But a very human, tortured howl that rattled him to his core and shook the outpost. It cried into the night, crescendoing to a painful wail. James clapped his hands over his ears as his eardrums crackled, forcing his eyes shut as they watered involuntarily. The very gates of hell were squealing open to take him.

He backed up, tripped and hit the wall of the building. He

tucked his head to his knees. He felt weak and begged for the thing to stop screaming.

Then it was gone, the echo fading away. He slowly opened his eyes.

Needing to see for himself, he got up as quickly as he could. His throbbing head felt ready to explode. Scanning left to right through the darkness, he checked the last spot where he thought the creature was. There were only trees, shrubs and leaves. His every bone shook to its core. His skin was covered in goose bumps.

A door slammed behind him and James spun about, wide eyed.

Edgar walked onto the balcony, closely follow by Joe. Both of them looked like they'd been awake for some time, and their faces said it all — they had heard it too.

He glanced at Joe's hands. They were shaking. His pistol rattled in one of them.

Joe seemed to be in a trance. Edgar, too, only he was sweating down his face and didn't seem to notice he was standing flat on his injured leg. Both had a glazed look in their eyes as they stared through James and beyond towards the woods. He waited to see if they'd snap out of it, but when they didn't, he reached out to touch their shoulders.

The instant his hand brushed their clothes, they both let out a great sigh and blinked, then glanced about confused. Joe glanced down at his own hand, not realizing he had been holding his pistol. He tucked it away, then looked sternly at James.

"Come inside. We have a lot to talk about," he said calmly. He eyed Edgar, who nodded. James hoped there was a rational way to explain what had just happened. He hoped Joe would be truthful and it would make sense. But at the same time, he didn't want to know. He just wanted to get as far away from the forest as possible.

Following them in, James entered the station and sat cross-legged on the floor. Edgar lit an old oil lamp, making him feel like they were out camping and one of them was about to start telling ghost stories.

To add to the effect, Joe stared into the flame, the light casting a warm yellow glow over his face. He sat like that for a long time. His thoughts were awash with a thousand burning questions, all of which came back to the same two. What was that thing? And what did they know about it?

Then he heard Joe speak in a way he had never done before. For once, he sounded unsure. He sounded like what he was saying was foreign and questionable. He sounded scared.

"We haven't been honest with you. But now that you've seen it, we will have to be, or you won't trust us," he started. James met his eye.

"It happened ten years ago, and it was all our fault." Joe readjusted the way he was sitting, then ran his hands down his face. "And we were so stupid to think we could kill it."

JAMES

It didn't take long for James to come to a few conclusions about Joe. The first of which was that he could not be trusted in any regard. His story, as he explained now, was almost identical to the tale about their friends Tim and Roger. Edgar sat close by as Joe talked about what happened. James could tell by the far-off look in Edgar's eyes that he wasn't just remembering, he was reliving it, too.

"Most of what I told you is true. Our friend, Tim Breaker, got hurt. But I lied about what we found. And Arnie is right to hate me, not for being with his brother, but for not bringing him out safely," Joe said, looking down and playing with a shoelace.

He took two deep breaths and continued.

"It was a simple rescue, but one of the first times we'd gone into the restricted zone. Tim and Roger were new foresters, but they had an interest in the park. Edgar and I were more seasoned and figured it'd be a good way to cut their teeth with the kind of stuff we did. Back then, the foresters went all over the park, not just the front section. Anyway, Tim got hurt, and we had to go get help. I asked Roger to come with me, but he chose to stay behind with Tim. It took us three days to get out and three days to get back again. By the time we got back up there, they were gone."

"Like dead?" James interrupted.

Joe shook his head. "Gone. Like they wandered off. We took the coordinates down perfectly, left them with enough water for a few days, maybe a day's worth of food. We weren't going to be long. Three days back, grab supplies and a litter, three more days to get to them. They were going to be fine if they stayed put."

James scooted so his back was against a cabinet and looked up at the wood slatted ceiling, trying to imagine being left behind for a week, alone in the woods. He immediately thought of Rebecca and Jr. He wasn't leaving this forest until he found them and brought them out.

He waited for Joe to continue, but he didn't seem to have much else to say. That wasn't going to fly with James. He had more questions. More questions that desperately needed answers. Questions that Joe would have to answer, one way or another.

"Tell me about the map. The traps."

Joe's eyes conveyed a look of utter sadness and regret. His face hung low, his once proud head drooped, and he picked at a scab on his finger. He looked like a child who had gotten caught with his hand in a bowl of candy.

"Do you know how long you can live without water?"

"Uh. A few days, right?"

"Yes. And food?"

"I have no idea." James said. He didn't know where this was going.

"Eight to twenty, depending on your body." Joe said grimly. "Tim was small. Really small. I know I'm jumping around, but it's for a good reason. Have you ever heard of the legend of the Wendigo?"

James raised an eyebrow.

Joe sighed deeply and ran a stubby finger across the floor in a circle. "Wendigo. Or The Spirit of Hunger. It's Ancient Native American lore. It's a spirit that comes for those who commit the most atrocious crime against the body— cannibalism."

James opened his mouth to object, not knowing where this was going, but Edgar put his hand up, silencing him. James sat back and Joe continued.

"Our friend Tim was gone. He had changed into something. Something inhuman. We can only guess what happened. Tim grew starved after so many days. Roger must have passed from dehydration or something else... so Tim did the only thing he could..."

"Wait, how do you know all this? Are you saying that Tim became this, Wendigo thing?"

"That thing isn't Tim!" Joe bellowed. His eyes were wild, white stuff forming in the corner of his mouth.

"Tim became that thing because of what we did. We left them out there alone and the Spirit came to him. It marked him, and became him," he screamed, his chest heaving up and down. "Edgar and I barely escaped the first time, because it's stupid fast and, as you can tell, scares the living piss out of us. We barely got out alive. A few years later, we came back and set up the traps you saw on my map. They're made of steel and high tensile cable, so I know they're still there. When we came up the last time... we vowed to put Tim down... but it was going to take three of us to run the traps... we almost paid for that bit of knowledge with our lives that time." Joe lifted his prosthetic leg, revealing more of his life to be yet another lie. "I'd been deployed and blown up. But I was in a truck. This was from that monster."

James was on edge. If any shred of what Joe was saying was true, it meant his family was in more danger than he realized. Or, if Joe was absolutely bat-shit crazy, then it meant he was sitting around waiting for a psychopath to guide him safely through the woods. Either way, the danger he and his family were in hadn't changed, it just became clearer. He'd search the location of the coordinates, find them, bring them to the tower, and back out the way they came in.

Quietly, on his own, he stood up and prepared to leave. He couldn't sit around anymore. He wasn't one to believe in the supernatural. Joe was probably just traumatized from losing his friend and making up some shit about a flesh-eating monster as a reason to go back and search for his dead-friend's remains. After all these years, would there even be anything left?

"Where are you going?" Joe asked.

"To find my wife and kid. It's either that, or sit here around your shitty campfire while you tell ghost stories. I don't know what that thing in the woods was, but it was probably some rabid bear, or maybe I'm just high as a fuckin' kite. Maybe I'm just as crazy as you are. Either way, I'm not sitting here any longer."

James reached for his bedroll and Edgar's strong, calloused hand shot out and seized him around the wrist.

"Let go, Edgar," he commanded, towering over the old man, whose skin was lackluster, and his eyes shimmered with tears.

"It's true, James," he said. "It's all true. We came back later, and it was too late. Then, we returned to finish it once and for all, to put our friend down because we couldn't stand to leave him like that. But it's not him anymore, James. This thing, it's the most terrifying thing I've ever seen. I don't want to be here. I want to go home. Hell, part of me wished I had died on this mountain instead of Tim. Because every night for years, I've had to relive the memory of the choice we made that day. The choice that made our friend what he is."

Tears dripped from his face. James didn't try to pull away. He felt terrible watching a man as old as Edgar cry.

"I didn't think twice about leaving Tim behind. I didn't want to risk not getting out myself. Now, that thing obscures my memories of Tim. We have nothing left but this. So please, stay. We'll help you find your family, but we have to end this. If we don't end this... I don't want to think about what it will do to your son if it finds..."

James reared back to hit him. "Don't you dare talk about my son like that's even a possibility! I will find him. And we will get out of here. And I don't give a shit about your ghost story anymore!" He screamed until his throat hurt. Joe had his head up against his knees, and James plucked the map with the traps on it from his breast pocket and looked it over. The traps were northwest of their location, and the cavern was north of that. Joe had circled an area around the traps and the cave, indicating the general area where the coordinates pointed to. Good. If he went north then east, he could check the cave, then circle out from there. That would only leave the entire area leading east to the fence line.

He tossed the map on the floor at Joe's feet and once he had his bag packed, opened the door to leave, but stopped in the doorway. It was still pitch-black outside, yet his watch said it was nearly 7:00 AM. He tapped it twice, as it couldn't possibly be right. The sun should be fully in effect by now. James turned back to Joe.

His face must have said enough. "What's wrong?" Joe asked.

"It's still dark but my watch shows 7:00 AM."

"It knows we're here. It hunts at night. From here on out, nobody sleeps until it's done," Joe said, standing up and dusting off. "Your family won't make it the next few hours if we don't kill it. It will mark them, hunt them, make them turn on each other... and then it will eat them."

31

J R

Jr. LOOKED at the package his mom was holding. It wasn't there earlier. He remembered the thing in the cave... the thing with the antlers appearing in the entrance. Could it have left the bag?

He took it from her tenderly and saw the end was folded over in a tight knot and tied off with wire. He handed her the flashlight. Whoever T. B. was, they took a great effort into making sure the bag was sealed.

The material itself was of the same waterproof fabric that his mom had brought to store their electronics and clothing. This bag looked worse for wear, however, as originally it was probably a deep shade of green. Now it appeared faded and sad, leaning more towards a gray, like it had been cooked in the sun. Rebecca leaned in as he turned it over. There was nothing else distinguishable about it. He decided to open it.

The wire wrapped around the top was easy enough to unwind. Jr. opened it and removed a black notebook and a slightly rusted space-pen—the kind that could write no matter the weather. He examined the notebook.

It too was faded, and many of the pages were stuck together, but otherwise it was intact. The writing inside were scratchy flourishes at odd angles, sometimes running over each other, as if the person who wrote it was doing so in the dark and lost track.

June 4th 1989

We've been up here for 8 days now, but it feels like more. Tim's leg has gotten worse, and he feels clammy, like a fever is coming on. He keeps looking at me in the most peculiar way. He seems strange. Like he's not himself.

I've tried to talk to him about what he's feeling and about our plans for the future, just to keep our mind off of things. Now, with our relationship exposed to Joe, I think we can finally move on with our lives. He should leave him now. He doesn't need him anymore. He has me.

But Tim won't talk to me. The only time he does is to ask for food when he knows we don't have any. I've emptied my pockets for him to see. He accused me of hiding it. I think the woods are getting to him. I'm going to try to find clean water. I was trying to keep fluids in him but when I searched my bag for my bottles, they were gone. I found him dumping them out. I don't know what to do. I don't feel safe with him, and I don't know if Joe and Edgar are coming back.

ROGER HOUSE.

JR. FLIPPED THE PAGE. There was another entry in the same jumbled writing. He had trouble reading it and fumbled a few times as he recited it to his mom.

JUNE 5TH 1989

I had to leave him. I had to leave Tim. There's something wrong.

Something I can't explain. He's gone insane. I woke up to him chewing on my leg, like it was a fucking drumstick. So I ran and now I'm lost. But if you find this letter, just know that I haven't given up hope. I'm still me, but I don't think Tim is himself anymore. We tried to sleep, but the night never seems to end around here. I don't have a watch. If you find it, it has a green band with an electronic face. Time feels like its standing still. I'd sleep for hours, and wake up still in complete darkness to find Tim standing over me. One time, he threw back his head and howled like a monster. And this last time, he ripped off a piece of my skin with his teeth. So I ran. I ran, and I left him. I ran until the battery in my light died. I'd write this by moonlight if I could. But even that is covered by a layer of clouds.

Just know I'm going to keep heading east until I find something, a landmark or shelter, or someone comes to find me. I'm going to leave this at our last known location. I don't think Tim will see me, and if he did, I don't think he'd care. Please be good to him. Please don't hurt him. I still love him.

Roger House.

JR. turned the page but there was nothing there but the remains of a few dark red fingerprints, like the book had been ripped from the writer's bloody hands.

He flipped through the pages one more time to make sure he didn't miss anything, then clicked the pen open. He put it to an empty page and started scribbling. At first he was worried it wouldn't write, but gradually, the pen marked the page. He read aloud as he wrote.

Sometime in May 2009

My name is Jr. Pope. Though there are no walls, I am trapped in this forest with my mother, Rebecca Pope. She's hurt, and we don't have any supplies. We're lost up here, and tired, and hungry. We never knew you, Roger House, and we never will, but we feel you here with us. I pray you and Mr. Tim made it out alright, and that we might meet sometime. Until then, we will do all we can to survive. We have each other.

HE STOPPED READING out loud but hurried out one last sentence. He was careful not to let his mom see what he was writing.

WE AREN'T ALONE.

J.R. Pope.

JR. TURNED the remaining pages over and felt a lump. He found a bracelet made of dog-tags and a simple chain taped to the inside back cover. The smooth metal was a dull but comforting weight. Etched below it were the initials T. B.

Jr. quickly slid the bracelet over his wrist, closed the book, and tucked it in his pocket. His concentration was interrupted by his roaring stomach. His mom hadn't said much, and he wondered if she was as hungry as he was. His biological clock told him the sun should have been up by now and in full force. It was dark and late when they fell asleep, but now, when it should have been morning, there was no sign of the sun. It was pitch-black outside, even darker than the inside of the cave, it seemed. Now Jr. was getting worried. *This is just like what happened to Roger.*

Then his stomach began to cramp. He hadn't noticed it

before, or hadn't wanted to notice it, but three days without eating was starting to wear on him. His mother tried to comfort him by reaching out, as she had trouble standing at all now due to her swollen and discolored ankle. He pushed her hands away and waited for the stabbing pains to subside. He knew they would eventually, it was his body reminding him to eat. But he knew from the survival textbook he had at least a week before he'd really start to hurt from not eating.

He was lanky, just like his dad, and Rebecca, a thick but well-built woman, would probably last longer due to her size. Jr. tried to keep his mind off the hunger pangs, but they dug into his side. Hoping more water would help, he knelt by the pool again, sipping loudly off the top. He felt like an animal at a watering hole, bowing its head to some beast watching from the back of the cave.

The water did little to help his stomach. Jr. looked up at his mother, who had her eyes closed and was leaning against the cave wall.

Jr. crawled over to join her, then stopped. A branch snapped outside somewhere. He looked outward. Rebecca clicked the light, and it sputtered on, then went out again.

"Come on, come on!" She said, shaking it. It faltered again, then went out for good. Frustrated, she threw the light over Jr.'s head. But instead of the flashlight clattering to the ground, it collided with something standing in the mouth of the cave and he suddenly saw something he wasn't prepared for.

It stood taller than the cave. It had a humanoid body, and it was the color of maggots, fleshy and gray, almost white. Jr. caught a glimpse of multi-pointed antlers atop its head, shiny sharp claws attached to long, spidery arms. Its every tendon rippled beneath paper thin skin. Jr. caught sight of a single eye, beady and lifeless. It had a glassy surface and was embedded within the white skull of some poor animal, maybe a deer or a horse.

Then, when the light fell to the floor, it clicked on.

Jr. gasped. His mom whimpered. But there was nothing. All was still. The cave was empty. And they were alone again.

He let out a sigh of relief. His heart threatened to burst from his chest… then… the creature howled.

32

JAMES

JOE'S WARNING RANG OUT, dire and without a filter. But James had made up his mind. He needed to get to his family first. Once he had them, he could deal with Joe and Edgar's paranoid delusion. There was no way he was going to believe that a flesh-eating monster had it out for them, let alone that this horror was what remained of their friend after they left them on the mountain to die. *Guilt. That's what this is. Paranoia and guilt.*

James shouldered his pack again, but Joe stepped in front of the door. It was dark, and he was conserving his light, but he stared at Joe's shadow, hoping his message was clear. *I'm leaving,* he said with his presence, *you can't stop me.*

Truthfully, he didn't think Joe would have a problem stopping him if he wanted. It wouldn't get him anywhere. He was needed according to their plans.

James huffed and tried to step around him, but Joe matched his movement.

"What are we, twelve?" James said.

"Didn't you just hear what I said? Your family won't make the next few hours if we don't kill it. We have to kill it. Don't you understand? If not, it will come for them, and it will come for us, and we will have saved nobody."

"It's your friend. If this thing is real, then it wants you, not me. Now get out of my way." James made a move and felt a hand on his chest.

"This thing preys on the weak first. And if you're not weak, it will drive you mad until you are. We know more about it than you realize."

He forced a laugh. "You honestly believe some big gray Native American monster is going to rip me apart? It doesn't exist. I honestly would have seen it by now."

"How did you know it was gray?" Edgar asked from the floor in the dark.

"What?" James said, looking over his shoulder.

"Gray. You said it was big and gray. You described it perfectly. So you've seen it and you've heard it too. If you've seen it, how can you deny it?"

He didn't know what he saw. Something in the woods. Something that was tall and howled in a monstrous way. He had seen and heard something... that he could agree to.

"I don't know what I saw. But if you'll get out of my way, I'd like to find my family. Then you can deal with it."

He stepped forward and Joe actually moved out of the way. Just as James reached the door and had his hand on the knob, Joe said quietly, "It's a curse. I hope they don't get it."

James paused. "What? What are you going on about?"

"It's not just one. There could be many. But we know of at least one. It marks you, that we know is true. It drives you to the brink of madness — I think it feeds on your fear first, you know, before it eats you. And once it does sink its teeth into you... it becomes you."

"What're you saying, Joe?" James was already confused. He had never heard of a Wendigo, but these two obviously believed in it. Felton forest was so vastly unexplored, it was possible some unknown animal could have been up here all along, undiscovered.

If he thought about it that way — made it real in his head instead of some ghost story — then he could justify following Edgar's and Joe's instructions. If he went with them, killed this animal, then he and his family would be safe to leave the forest without worry. *What about bears?*

A fluke. We must be in its territory. It didn't bother chasing you up the tower, so it's probably gone.

"I'm saying if you even believe for a second that something dangerous is in these woods, call it a Wendigo, call it a monster, call it whatever — the truth remains. Your family is at risk if the thing is still alive. They held their own before against a large animal on the other side of the fence, and I don't doubt they could do it again if they were still in the park. But we aren't on the other side of the fence. We're in its territory, the place you hired us to take you through."

For once, Joe sounded both sincere and apologetic. He seemed to take note of the entire situation and put it in terms James could understand. Putting it all together, it made sense. Sure, he had memorized the routes, but he was a blind man searching for a needle in a haystack out here. Joe and Edgar at least knew how to handle their own, even if they couldn't perfectly navigate this part of the forest.

He made up his mind then that, instead of rushing to a judgement and running aimlessly through the woods hoping Rebecca and Jr. would just be hanging about, he would stop arguing and follow them, but he had one thing he needed to clear up. "I'll go. But we change the order of things. My family first, then we kill this thing."

They were silent for a moment, then Joe broke the standoff and said, "Deal. We need you, James. This will take three of us."

Nothing more was said as the trio packed up their things, took what they needed from the guard tower, and headed down the stairs. Once they were on solid ground, their heads were on swivels. Guided only by an intense glow from the moon, they crossed the valley of tall grass, lightly swaying in a breeze. Everything about the atmosphere, from the temperature to the way the bugs called out to the feelings in their gut told them it should be daytime. But the moon was at full strength and showed no signs of surrendering to the sun. James watched it pass by as he navigated through the wall of trees and into utter darkness. Below their feet, the leaves crumbled, but all else was quiet.

A few feet ahead, Joe's headlamp blazed to glory, and he consulted his personal map from his pocket. James stole a glance over his shoulder and, to his surprise, Joe let him look. On it was a clear depiction of three separate traps arranged in a triangle formation.

"We should be less than an hour from the cave. The traps are near there. We can check the cave first for your family, then move east towards the coordinates you gave me," Joe whispered. James nodded, then Edgar's flashlight clicked on.

It was an eerie place. It should be teeming with life. From little critters to birds circling overhead — everything was either asleep, dead, or too fearful to announce their presence. They were alone in the woods, and yet James felt as if there were eyes everywhere.

Joe moved on, pointing at a gnarly vine in their way and scanning the ground more than looking up. If James listened carefully, he could hear Joe counting the steps to himself. He was pacing himself to better get a handle on how far they had come. James tried to remember how many steps made a mile, but found it pointless. Being able to walk and calculate a mile was pointless if you didn't know what direction you were supposed to be walking in.

A few hundred paces later, and James noticed a temperature drop of a few degrees, which was odd, considering it got warmer first thing in the morning, then drifted into the mid-seventies at night. Now, it felt more like the latter.

Alone with his thoughts, James tried to image Rebecca's face when he showed up with two experienced woodsmen instead of two strangers with a message *from* him. She would never expect him to come out to get her. She probably thought he wasn't capable. Maybe this would restore some of what she was missing.

A branch snapped in the dark and Joe froze. Edgar did as well. Regardless of the seriousness of his injury, the old man either didn't notice it, or didn't show he noticed it. They were moving at a pace a few notches below a jog, but Edgar kept up just the same.

But he had stopped, and was now sitting on the ground, breathing heavily and looking about the immediate area with his flashlight. Nothing moved in the endless dark, but Edgar was able to take a rest. Upon closer inspection, James could actually see him now. His lips were chapped, and he was pouring sweat.

"I'm fine," he said. "Just gotta catch my breath." He heaved, clutching himself above his heart. He reached into his bag and, with shaky hands, pulled out a medicine bottle and popped the cap. He upended a bottle of pills in his mouth and crunched on them.

James gave him a concerned look. Edgar continued to chew like a cow.

"Sugar. My blood sugar is low." Edgar said once he saw James looking at him cross.

"I promise you, I ain't about to die of some dumb shit after I climbed this God forsaken mountain and slept on the floor of some dusty ol' station." Edgar pushed himself up and leaned, stretching his back. "I'd rather be fed feet first to the Wendigo."

33

JAMES

"How much longer do you think you'll need, Edgar?" Joe asked him.

"Not long. Twenty minutes, tops. I just need to catch my breath." Edgar sipped on a water bottle. "How's your leg?"

"Fucked. Alright, I'll be first watch. We should be less than an hour from the first trap." James opened his mouth to protest.

"We have to pass by it to get to the cave anyway, relax. Take twenty, back-to-back on the ground. I've got watch."

Edgar settled in next to a tree and James sat down, then turned and leaned against him. His back was bony, but once they got the hang of it, they could rest that way. James needed the time off his feet. He just wasn't about to show any signs of slowing to the other two. He didn't need a reason for them to leave him behind. Plus, he wanted to show he was serious about his plan to get to Rebecca and Jr. first.

Trusting in Joe, James closed his eyes and near instantly fell into a daze where. he wasn't quite asleep, but he definitely wasn't coherent. He listened to whatever sounds the forest had to offer before his eyes felt heavy and he shut them.

JAMES AWOKE to a sharp pain in his leg. Thinking first he had been bitten by a bug or even a rodent, he was surprised to feel something didn't just bite his leg, it was still biting him. He yelled and shook it off. Warm blood oozed into his boot and it stung. Fumbling with his flashlight, he jumped up and shined it down where he was sitting.

He couldn't believe what he saw. It was Joe. He was down on all fours like a dog, his mouth ringed with bright red blood, and his eyes were solid white. He had a piece of flesh dangling from his teeth. James was horrified.

"What the fuck, Joe? What is wrong with you?" James screamed at him. Joe didn't seem to notice. He was shirtless, and there were three jagged cuts across his back. The one in the middle was largest, and the skin around the injury crawled and rolled like it was alive. Still, Joe was frozen.

By this time, Edgar had come to and was pushing himself to his feet. "What's the commo—Jesus!" he stumbled back and James caught him. Together, they both looked at Joe. He looked like a great beetle caught out from under a damp rock.

"What the fuck is wrong with his eyes?" Edgar leaned in and reached out, aiming for his back. "Wait... I've seen these before..."

He touched Joe's shoulder and, in that moment, Joe screamed in his face, his eyes white and wild. Like a spider, he crawled on his hands and feet at an impossible pace, his head-lamp on, sending sickening shadows dancing about.

"Jesus, the fuckin' thing got to him!" Edgar yelled, throwing his pack on and digging through Joe's bag. "You see the scratches and his eyes? It got to him. Now there's only two of us. We have to hurry!"

James followed in shock, still shaken and confused at what just happened. With each footfall, the bite on his leg sent him a very real, very painful reminder. *Joe lost it. He lost it and started eating you. His own ghost story got to him.*

He didn't have time to think anymore. He didn't have time to consider what this meant for the traps. All bets were off. He was going for the cave, and Edgar would have to deal with it. Because now, Joe was out there in the dark, crawling around like a lunatic, and who knew how dangerous he could be to his family.

Edgar kept a decent pace despite his age and his leg. Spurred on by adrenaline, he would eventually slow, but for now, he looked to be comfortable as the two of them ducked, dodged, and weaved through the brush.

Edgar held up a fist and James nearly ran into him. Then, he looked around, pausing at each tree before settling on one to the east. At first it didn't look any different from the others, but up close, James saw it was marked. Three claw marks, just like Joe's back, had torn through the bark and left permanent scars. But just below the marks was the letter W. It was carved.

"This way." Edgar said, coming around the tree to the left until he reached a miniature clearing. There, he stopped and dropped his pack, then rummaged about sliding dirt sticks and leaves aside. A few moments later he popped up, holding a tiny metal cable in his palm. It stretched along to two trees on the opposite ends of the clearing. Edgar traced one to the right, then followed it to the back side of the tree.

"Aha!" He said. Then, a mechanical clicking started, and the wire was slowly lifted up. It vibrated on its own a few inches above the ground. Edgar skirted the tree, looking pleased.

"What's that do?" James asked.

"Look up."

He did so and was surprised to see a metal frame with a handful of tubes aimed towards the ground. Individual slits had been cut out of the tubes and there was a wire attached to a taunt recurve bow on each of them. James caught a glimpse of a razor-sharp point glinting within the tube.

"Spear trap."

James backed out from under the square housing. "Jesus, you guys weren't kidding."

Edgar shook his head. "I'm telling you. This thing is crazy fast. Let's go. We're close to the cave."

Despite James not being sure what to believe at this point, it still meant something to Edgar and Joe. They believed their ghost story of some creature haunting the woods. And that meant they'd be willing to do whatever they perceived as necessary to kill it. He didn't even want to consider what these traps would do to a person.

Edgar carefully stepped over the wire, then turned to illuminate it so James could do the same. They went around the tree where the mechanical gear was mounted to the backside. He saw it had a large lever and a gearbox with the heavy-duty cable running upward until there was another bracket to change its direction. It was an ingenious contraption, and he understood why Joe thought it'd be here even after all these years. The damn thing was industrial.

A few minutes beyond the spear trap and James was no longer walking behind Edgar, but next to him. "So what happens now? Are you going to leave Joe out here?"

Edgar was quiet. James, thinking he was being ignored, was about to repeat the question, but Edgar said, "I won't leave him, no. And I will help you get your family out of here. Once all three traps are set, I have one shot to do this. If it fails, I'll do Joe, then myself."

James was utterly confused. *Why would he kill himself?*

"Suicide? Why? Some sort of punishment?"

"It's simpler than that. We told you it's like a curse, right? It can spread like an infection. Once you get it, you're on the list. Joe was marked, and eventually it will come for him, but there is someone weaker than him that has its attention. It's probably going for your family. But now or later, it will come for me, because I am weak and only getting weaker. If Joe or I are marked and we leave this place, we can spread it. You got lucky." He nodded at James's bleeding leg.

"It didn't have Joe fully, yet. And if it had when he bit you, I would have put you down like a dog."

They continued in silence. It was hard to believe such an elaborate story, but at the same time, it was impossible to ignore some of the facts about it all. He *had* seen something in the woods. Heard it too. And Joe had just been caught, eating the flesh off his leg. And then there were the marks across Joe's back. He hadn't done that to himself. Regardless, if James didn't believe in all of this, they certainly did, and that made Edgar and Joe dangerous.

It was all so possible and impossible at the same time, and Joe and Edgar had lied to him more than once.

James wasn't ready to accept that this really was a plague brought on by a creature that fed on your fear, the *Spirit of Hunger*, he called it. The facts, however, didn't point out any reasonable explanation to what was going on.

He just needed to stay focused.

34

JAMES

It was definitely taking longer than he expected to get to the cave, and James was growing suspicious. Edgar was quiet, no longer freely sharing his thoughts. James, on the other hand, was rattled and on the edge of a total breakdown. He was abandoning what little courage he had left. At any moment, he was ready to hand over determination in exchange for utter cowardice.

Since Edgar had stopped talking, it let James' mind switch from secure, analytical thoughts about his plan to rescue his family from the dreaded forest, and over to paranoid delusions about things that go bump in the night. Then there was the irrational fear of Joe crawling out of the dark to sink his teeth into his leg again. Then there were the terrible what-if scenarios that played over and over in his head. Scenarios that lead to his wife alone in the cave, her body flayed, her corpse bloated and her son knelt over it like a cur, ripping off strips of flesh...

He tried to shake the thoughts but found it even harder the longer they hiked in silence. Ready to scream just to hear something other than his own footsteps, James decided to approach Edgar, but he suddenly dropped to his knees and started digging again. James wondered if he was about to bite his leg just like Joe, but he only kept scooping out fist-fulls of dark, damp earth.

A few moments of furious thrashing in the tick infested leaves, and he lifted a cable for James to see. Instinctively, he hopped back, expecting another contraption over his head, but there was only the thick canopy. This time, James followed Edgar around the largest of the trees near him. On its backside was yet another handle attached to a gearbox. This one was slightly rusted, but with a grunt and a pull, it moved freely with a few grinding cranks on the mechanism. James looked around, using his flashlight for signs of the trap. He spotted something odd, high up in the canopy. It looked like a log. *A log suspended in the trees?*

Spear trap, swinging log, deadfall. That must be the swinging log. James could see how it was held in place but didn't ask about it further. Using the flashlight, he traced the cable from the gearbox to a pulley high above his head. It continued across to the log where he assumed another pulley was waiting. Once released, the log would swing down with immense force and pulverize anything in its path.

He was growing impatient, and Edgar was holding something back.

"Where's the cave?" James whispered, unsure of why he was doing so in the first place, but given the situation, where sound echoed off every tree, it felt right to keep his voice low.

"Shut up." He turned and met his gaze, but lowered his headlamp so it was pointed directly into his eyes. It gave his mouth a hollow, shadowy look and made his crooked teeth appear like the jaws of a monster.

"I need you to understand something, James. This thing, the Wendigo. It wants me, and it wants Joe, but it will take whatever it can get. And that means your family too. Want to prevent that possibility from ever happening? Help me kill it. We got two traps set. With any luck, we can prepare the third and lead it down the path. Then I can die in peace knowing its gone. But I can't do any of these things without your trust. This takes three people, and now with only two," he poked James hard in the chest, "I have to be the bait. It's a miracle we've made it this far. I didn't want to die tonight, but if it means making things right and killing this thing for good, so be it."

James was left awestruck. *He was going to be the bait.* He wasn't an idiot. That at least made sense. Edgar had easily set up the first and second trap. It meant the third was to be manned by him, the weakest. He would lure the monster in. But that had all gone to shit when it chose Joe. Joe, with his prosthetic limb and broken character, had been chosen.

He stepped away, symbolically ending the confrontation. *Chosen... now you sound like you actually believe in this thing.*

Edgar readjusted his headlamp. He nodded toward a set of trees, four of them sharing a space. They were set up like pillars to a blasphemous temple. Wide at their base, growing thinner near the top, then leaned in as one and created a make-shift tunnel. James could see the path narrowed so much they'd have to walk in a single file. It looked like it wanted to swallow him.

Edgar started walking towards it and stopped abruptly, his ear tilted off into the darkest part of the forest. James heard rustling, growing louder each second. It sounded like it was heading in their direction.

"It doesn't matter if that's Joe. He's not himself anymore. Quickly, and quietly, stay on my heels. The last trap is through that path," he whispered, his culminating anxieties manifesting as a fresh coat of sweat on his brow. He wiped it up and over his head, then massaged the back of his neck nervously.

Just let it come through here. Let the traps work. Let this be over. Edgar turned, cinched down his belt and adjusted the height of his headlamp. James held up his flashlight down the path and stayed as close as he could to Edgar, matching his steps. They crossed the invisible threshold, marked only by a sudden drop in temperature. Now, he felt like the branches that created a dense thicket around them were closing in, rubbing against his shoulders. He had to focus on his breathing to avoid a bout of claustrophobia.

The rustling grew louder.

James's heart was pounding in his ears.

"Almost there. Be ready to move. It's coming," Edgar said, pushing a thorny branch away from his face. He stepped over a dark brown root and nearly lost his balance, but James squeezed in next to him and caught him before he fell. Edgar kept going.

Now, there were branches cracking behind them, the footfalls like heavy stones dropping in the sand.

If there was an end to the tunnel of tree limbs in sight, James couldn't see it. Edgar kept on at the same pace. Neither of them dared to look back.

As the cracking branches came to a terrible crescendo, the path opened up and spat them into an area significantly less populated with trees. Edgar ducked right, James left, and together they skirted a large square patch of dirt. It was out of place, and easy enough to spot.

Where there should have been grass and sticks and brush, was just a dead zone in a symmetrical square approximately five feet wide. Once the dirt patch was between them James finally dared to look. He shined his meager light into the path, but the entrance swallowed it all. Edgar seemed to be torn between digging at his feet and seeing what was coming their way. James, unwilling to sit and do nothing, dug too.

Hands scooping up dirt, lodging it under his fingernails, he dug, flinging it everywhere until at once, both he and Edgar felt the corner of a tarp. They seized it upward and pulled, dragging it back and revealing a gaping hole in the clearing.

Chunks of dirt and debris fell into it and Edgar tilted his head inside briefly.

It was a massive pit. At least eight feet deep and just as wide, it had a series of sharpened branches sticking up from the bottom like an ancient spike pit. *Punji sticks. Deadfall.*

Then, the stampede through the forest came to a halt. It was deathly quiet. James and Edgar waited. James prayed the thing would come through, fall in, and die. He prayed they wouldn't need the other traps and that this would be the end of it.

What thing? You don't believe in it, remember? It's just Joe. Crazy Joe. Joe who lost his mind.

All was still.

Then something screamed from the dark path with a voice cracking from unbridled, animal rage.

Joe came barreling out of the path. His body was devoid of all clothing. His pale skin nearly reflecting off their flashlight beams. He sprinted at an insane speed despite his prosthetic limb, which looked out of place on his naked body. His eyes were wider than any man's should be, black as the forest itself, his mouth, bloody and tongue chewed off at the base. He appeared to be crazed, more animal than man.

He howled, leaping across the pit and landing on Edgar, who crumpled.

James recovered, jumped up and planted a kick square in Joe's ribs. They cracked under his boot, and he rolled off and over the edge into the pit. There was a dull thud and then silence. After catching his breath and checking on Edgar, James peeked into the hole, his hands shaking and lungs on fire, struggling to keep up.

35

EDGAR

"THAT'S NOT IT. That's not it," Edgar panted, clutching his heart and leaning up against a tree. Everything hurt. He had deep gashes across his face, but even those were minimal compared to the rest of his body. He had shooting pains up his legs, his feet felt heavy, like his shoes were made of bricks, and there was a fresh bruise flowering out from his elbow.

He struggled for air. *Damn it, Joe.*

James was looking over the edge of the pit.

"Help me up," Edgar grumbled.

"He's dead. God damn it I killed him," James declared, his face long. He was clearly shaken up by what had happened. His skin was pale, and his lips quivered.

With clammy hands, he pulled Edgar to his feet.

"You didn't kill him. It did," Edgar replied. "This is what it does. It whittles you down, one by one." He looked into the hole at Joe's corpse.

He was, as he thought, impaled on the spears built into the bottom of the trap. He was left dangling, blood running from wounds in his arm, leg and chest. His mouth opened and closed like a fish. His eyes were bloodshot. Edgar gave him one last look. *Goodbye my friend. May our souls rest forever.* It was a sweet, short goodbye. There was no time to mourn.

Mourning was for those with the rest of their life to live. If this plan unfurls properly, you won't leave this forest, but at least the curse would be over. It was the price to pay for what you did, or at least failed to do. Maybe God will take pity on us and see our ultimate acts on the earth and grant us grace. Goodbye Joe Corrinth.

"Did you hear it? It was right behind him. It knows something is going on," Edgar said to James, pulling away from Joe's final resting place and mapping out the area according to his memory. He walked along the edge of the perceived clearing, though it was not nearly as definitive as the other trap areas. They hadn't had a lot of time to prepare this one, compared to the others.

He pushed the tall shrubs aside, scanning the bottom of the trees until he found his mark. Another W, carved into the base of a massive oak.

"I heard it. Does that mean the traps didn't work?" James asked.

Edgar shook his head, then motioned for James to follow.

"It must have come through the woods. It isn't like us. It moves differently. It's strong and thin and powerful. Now that things are set, we will have to guide it back onto the path." Edgar passed beyond the tree without waiting for James. He didn't need him now. The pieces were in place. All he needed to do was get to the first marker, and then he could lead it right through the gauntlet.

He heard James swear as a leafy branch scraped across his face. Edgar moved more slowly than ever. He couldn't seem to draw enough air into his lungs. Each breath sent a stabbing pain into his chest from the backside. But he couldn't stop. Not when they were so close.

"We get it on the path. The spear trap will slow it down. The log trap will weaken it, and then the deadfall will finish it off,"

Edgar said. It sounded great in theory. The reality of it was much more flimsy. He'd have to push past the pain and his aging, aching body, and lead the foul creature to its death. Alone.

"I'm taking you to the cave." His statement came weakly as his voice was hoarse from a lack of water. They couldn't go on like this. It'd been at least a day or more without anything to drink, and about the same for food.

"What was that?" James asked, lending an ear.

"I said I'm taking you to the cave. We're as well off as we can be. Now it's a matter of fulfilling my end of the bargain. You have a family to protect, which is admirable. Me, I only have mistakes that need corrected."

He swung a leg over a fallen log and kept on.

"I had a daughter. Miscarriage. Since then, my wife and I never tried again. She's all I have. Will you tell her goodbye for me? Tell her I made things right? Or at least tried? I don't want her to think I'd come back up here for nothing." Edgar stopped and appeared to contemplate something, staring down at his feet, then kept going.

"There's no money." James blurted out.

Edgar didn't miss a step. *Of course, there's no fuckin' money. Even I knew that. I could tell just by looking at you that if anyone had money, it would be your wife. I could tell by your damn car that you had no money.*

"Figures. Fool's gold, though, right? It all seems to work out that way. He stopped by a long sturdy branch and picked it up, then used it as a walking stick.

"I can help you get off this mountain, though. There has to be another way," James said, louder than he would have liked, as his hopefulness even in the bleakest of moments shined through.

Edgar gave a forced, wheezing laugh. "Son, I doubt either of us are getting down from this mountain. And if we do, we never met. This secret dies up here. No one has disturbed the Wendigo in many years. Not since we tried to kill it. No one came looking. Everyone stuck to the trails. Everyone was happy."

"I don't understand. Why wouldn't you tell anyone? Send the military? Soldiers?"

This time, Edgar laughed, hearty and full. It hurt, but he let it happen. He hadn't laughed in a long time.

"Military? For what? A seven-foot-tall flesh-eating God of Hunger that possessed my friend? They'd send a white van. Not the damn military. If we don't kill this thing...and the curse is passed on where there are more people...it could be the end of everything," Edgar trailed off. Ahead, the trees were thinning, and there was a rise in nocturnal sounds. The forest was beginning to sound more normal.

Edgar picked up the pace, his every step jarring his skeleton all the way up to his back. He had forgotten the angry cuts across his face and the budding bruises on his legs and elbow. Anything was better than the thicket. Anything was better than the path. But as the path sprung outward like the mouth of a river, Edgar stopped, turned and grabbed James by the shoulders.

"Listen. Around the bend on the hill is the cave. You'll see the shadow. Get your family and go. Even if they aren't there. Don't go searching for them. If I were them, that's where I'd be. There is a path, just north of the cave. It will take you to a rock formation, then to a deer-blind in the trees. After that, you only need to head south until you hit the fence. Do you understand? Do not come back here." Edgar gave him the most stern, serious tone he could. He looked at James as he would a son. He portrayed all he could through his eyes, without saying anything more. He begged that James would listen, and he prayed he'd find his family. But most of all, he begged he never told a soul about this place.

James sighed and placed a hand on Edgar's bony shoulder. "I can't promise—" he started, but it was cut short. From deep within the shadow of the trees came a blood curling scream. Inhuman, much higher than any person could produce, it ended in an animalistic howl.

"It's coming. Remember the directions. Go!" Edgar shoved him off. "Go now!" He yelled, then turned back to the trees. It was like an impassible wall that he didn't want to go through. Like he knew he was walking toward his demise. He lifted his foot and paused. *C'mon. Don't be a pussy. Man up. Kill this thing. James has a kid. Do it for his kid. You'd have done it for yours.*

It was enough. Edgar stepped forward, and the other followed. Soon, he was marching deeper in the woods, James at his back, disappearing up a hill and into the night. A few minutes in and the screech sounded again. The Wendigo was calling to him. Challenging him. And he answered it. "Tim! Breaker! I hear you Tim Breaker! And I'm coming to fucking kill you!"

Then the forest grew entirely still. His eyes refused to focus on the trees ahead. The scratchy bark surfaces absorbed all light and didn't reflect any back. Then came the mountain-shaking footfalls, the cracking of branches, and a rancid smell so fierce it watered his eyes.

"Tim Breaker!"

REBECCA

"LET'S GO!" Rebecca screamed after stumbling to her feet and throwing her arm over Jr's shoulder. Pushing herself beyond her body's limits was not something she had planned to do, but fueled by sheer terror at what she had seen, it was enough to flood her body with life-saving adrenaline. For a moment, she was able to forget the maggots crawling through her skin. Jr. looked petrified, but his face quickly became hardened and determined.

Together, they prepared to hobble out. Whatever the thing was that screeched at them, it was gone, and both of them refused to be stuck in this cave with it. And in order for them to escape it, they would have to run past it. Rebecca had made the decision on her own that she was not going to be confined any longer. She had hoped Jr. wouldn't even suggest crawling into the back cavern between the walls again.

Luckily, he didn't. Instead, he took up her arm, picking up his half of her weight, and lining up with the cave entrance. She did her part by holding the flashlight. With that, she hoped he could focus on getting them out.

She looked at him and saw the faint outline of his face with his angular jaw and sharp nose. He looked like James, and, in that moment, she missed him dearly. All of her grievances seemed so trivial now. Her career, pointless. Money, forgettable. Her own bloated ego and sense of self-worth, at this point, an afterthought. She looked at Jr. and saw the only thing that mattered — family.

"Ready, Mom?" He asked without looking at her. She nodded. He must have felt it because he began walking out of the cave, each step followed by the swing of her bad leg and a wince when she misjudged the ground, bumping it. A few steps to go, and the thing in the dark didn't reappear. Then they were outside, and once again under the forest's oppressive ceiling. Jr. looked around and Rebecca did her best to follow his vision with the light.

"Now where?" He asked.

She didn't have an answer. *Anywhere but in the damn cave* wasn't good enough. "Let's go over by those trees. We'll follow it until it breaks or we find water. I think we're close to the river," she lied through her teeth. They were impossibly lost.

Jr. steered them up near where she was pointing and cut left, every so often dodging a branch or a large stone. Soon, they were forced to slow as the forest grew thicker and they spent more time turning than walking straight. Rebecca, sure they were getting further lost, tried to fill the silence.

"You know, before, it was your dad that worked a lot."

Jr. didn't answer. He stopped at a branch devoid of leaves and pushed it up and behind them.

"He was a workaholic before he started. You know. Drinking."

"Dad has never been a workaholic," he argued. "He's been like this since I can remember."

"Sure, but I remember before. When we were first married, he worked two jobs to keep the lights on while I finished my degree. It paid off, as you can see, but I think it did something to him when we moved."

"What do you mean?" Jr. asked softly. He didn't seem to be scathingly mad by talking about his dad in this light. Rebecca appreciated that she could talk to him, even when they were in dire straits. It helped the time go by and lessened the pain in her foot. It would be easy for her to sit down and give up, but that wasn't who she was.

"He was happy. I forced him to quit his job, the one he had worked at for years, so I could take the one I have now. He pushed hard, got promoted, and fed the family. Then, when I was ready to move on, he didn't get to reap the benefits of his hard work. I think he hated me for that."

"For what, exactly?"

Rebecca sighed and her heart skipped a beat, brought on by the thought of what she was about to say. "Because I minimized what he accomplished. He worked for us. I wanted more, so I took it, and he suffered. I can only blame myself so much, but I can think back on it now and say I would have done it differently."

Jr. walked around a large hole in the dirt that she hadn't seen, her vision refusing to focus. She squeezed his hand, signaling for him to stop so she could adjust. He slid to her other side, and she transferred the flashlight to her opposite hand. Then they continued walking.

"So what happens now?" He asked, his tone changing from troubled to hopeful.

"Well, as soon as we get back, I know I'm going to take a bath longer than any human should. Then I'm going to take out a second mortgage to fund the meal I'm going to eat." She tried to make light of the situation, but it fell flat. He wasn't buying it.

"No. I mean with dad. With us? We're a family."

She had to think long and hard about her response. She didn't know what this all meant. She didn't know how she felt about James. She loved him. She'd always loved him. And she recognized the mistakes she had made. At this point, if they survived, it would be a matter of explaining what she had learned and finding out if he felt anything similar.

"I don't know, honey. I think we should focus on getting out of here. Once we get to the river, we can follow it back to the break, then cross over. By then, someone should be there to meet us at the campground."

"I don't think anyone is coming, mom."

Rebecca's stomach turned over. There was so much sadness in his voice, it was almost unbearable to hear. *And probably true. He sent that message days ago. If someone was coming, they would have found them by now.*

"Someone will come. They have to. We've been out here for days. The forest rangers will have seen our tents and—,"

"It's not the forest rangers who got my message. It was dad. And even now with him being our only hope, you're trying to take that from him." Jr.'s voice rose quickly and unexpectedly. He didn't stop walking, however, but she could feel his shoulders tense up under her arm. *What the hell was that about? Why the sudden anger?*

"What's gotten into you? You were so hopeful when you sent the message. I do believe he'd come. Or at least get the help here that we need. And I know you did everything that you could, so I in no way blame you for the situation."

"How could you blame me, mom? You're the one who fucking brought us out here," he snarled.

He's right. Try to change focus, and the facts still remain. This wasn't on James. This was on you. You better fix this, or Jr. will hate you forever, and James will never forgive you.

Rebecca paused, "You're right. I did. But my intentions were pure. I wanted to be with you…"

Jr. stopped. She felt him looking down at something. She lifted her arm up and over his neck, then found what he was studying. At first, she thought it was nothing, a stick or bug or maybe just a gnarled tree stump. But upon closer inspection, she could make out the letter W, clear as day, carved into the bottom half of a tree.

"What does it mean?" She asked, her mouth running before she could think.

"Mother Nature doesn't grow in straight lines," he said, pressing his fingers into the letter. "There are knife marks."

Knife marks. That meant someone had been here recently! Her heart beat faster and she clasped her hands to her mouth. It was something — better yet, it was a sign of rescue.

"Can you tell how long ago it was made?" She asked, hoping he had gleaned a magical fact from the survival book.

He ran his fingers over it again, then nodded slowly. "Actually, yeah. The bark is damp, meaning the liquid held in the fibers hasn't evaporated yet. This was probably done within the last day or two," he said, standing up. He took the flashlight from her hand and leaned against the tree, poking his head between it and into the denser part of the forest.

He popped his head back out, a huge smile across his face, "There's a path."

JAMES

JAMES STRUGGLED UP THE HILL, his feet moving faster than his mind could keep up with, causing him to slip repeatedly. Eventually, he was forced to slow down or risk breaking an ankle. It was an arduous climb to the top. He thought of his wife and son, and the look they'd have when he came crawling out of the dark. He wondered what they'd say, or if they'd say anything at all.

A few more steps and he would be there. His flashlight bobbed into the mouth of the cave. Soon, Jr. would come running out to greet him. Something shiny reflected from a branch hanging just outside the entrance. It was a CD, tied through the middle with a headphone wire.

"Jr.! Rebecca!" He called. "It's James!" He piled into the cave.

"Rebecca?" He was greeted with his own echo, and a feeling of a complete loss of hope. The cave was empty. Gray with smooth walls, his footsteps echoed as he walked its length and he began inspecting every inch of it. It was bone dry, and there were no signs of footprints. But the CD was a telltale giveaway that Jr. had in fact been there. He inched toward the back, taking in every speck of dust or loose rock, until his eyes met a lip near the rear-most wall. Lifting his hand up, he could feel a narrow gap where someone could slip through. He reached and felt a smooth piece of cloth. Latching onto the corner, he pulled it down and looked it over.

It was a faded green bag with a wire wrapped around the top. Waterproof by the looks of it. James transferred the flashlight to his mouth and unwrapped the opening with trembling fingers. He noticed the initials T.B. were written on the side. *Tim Breaker. No way.*

James got the bag open and dumped a notebook into his hand. It was dry, and the writing was legible, despite some fading of the ink and a stiffness to the paper. He read through the first few entries, signed by Roger House, and noticed some similarities in how things took place. First the injury, then the fighting, then nothing. He gave a silent prayer for Tim and for Arnie's brother.

Then he flipped to the last page and nearly dropped the book. There was a note from Jr. and from what it said, he knew Rebecca was hurt. He could hear his son's voice in his head as he finished the line. *We're not alone.*

Nothing followed after that, and James made sure to check the book twice. What did Jr. mean by, *we're not alone? Could someone have found them?*

You already know the answer, don't you? It found them. The Wendigo.

"No. They're out here. Waiting for you. Go find them," James coached himself. He shoved the book into his back pocket and left the bag behind. Why, he didn't know, only that it felt right. Maybe he could share the notes from Roger with Arnie. Maybe he could have some closure from it.

Or he could learn from the relationship with Tim, and how they were all friends, and how Edgar and Joe really did leave them up there to die.

He decided it was best to figure out the details of that

conversation later. Rebecca and Jr. were close. He could feel it. With a final glance into the crevice above, his better judgment told him they wouldn't dare to go in there. That was beyond Rebecca's comfort zone. With even less hope than he had when he went in, James exited the cave and headed to the left, against Edgar's instructions. Edgar's directions would take him out of the park. But James didn't need to get out, not yet. Not without his family.

JR

THE PATH LOOKED like it had been gutted from the top down. Jr. and Rebecca walked in a single file, and she used the trees for support. It was too tight to walk abreast, but above their heads there were broken branches, missing leaves and signs that something big had just come through there. *Not big. Tall. And thin by the looks of it.* Jr. stopped to wait for his mom to catch up. The deeper they went into the woods, the more Jr. felt like they were entering hell itself.

He imagined a massive archway made of bones, with *Abandon All Hope Ye Who Enter Here* written in blood. He looked back at his mother, who was clearly struggling, and he felt sad. If they were truly passing through the gates of hell, it meant she was going too. He thought about his dad. While his wife and son were walking through hell, where were you? *The bar.*

The last thought didn't even make the most remote bit of sense, and he shook it from his head. *His wife and son were missing. He got the text. He'll be here. Somewhere, sometime, he'll be here.*

But how long is some time? Your book says you can go three weeks without food and three days without water. How long do you think your mom can keep up before the infection from her leg poisons her?

Negative thoughts clouded his mind as Rebecca caught up. She was sweaty but appeared hopeful. She forced a weak smile, and he returned it with a blank stare. "Tell me we're going to be okay," he said, the words coming out in a child-like fashion. He wanted to start over. To leave this all behind as some sort of terrible nightmare.

"We'll be fine, as long as we stick together," she replied. There was some comfort in that for him. They had each other.

Ready to move on, Jr. spotted a stick laying in their path that would have been devastating to Rebecca if she would have tripped on it. He stooped, grabbed it up, and noticed the tip had been sharpened to a needle point. He held it up for his mom to see. She glanced at it, then at him.

"Mother Nature also doesn't do that," he said. Though it was morbid to think about who might have needed such a thing, the stick, which was just taller than him and a comfortable inch around, gave him some sense of security. If he needed it, he had something.

But would it be any good against that thing with the antlers? The thing that watched you in the cave, would it work against that?

More negative thoughts clouded his mind to the point he hadn't even realized the path became a clearing. A clearing that also looked man-made, for there were rough saplings hacked apart at the middle, various bits of tall grass stomped down, and a spot in the damp mud where it looked like someone had been digging with their hands. Jr. stopped a few feet from it and upon closer inspection, saw a razor thin wire humming and vibrating softly, six inches off the ground. Then he held out a hand to prevent his mother from coming too close. She carried her leg up like an injured dog and placed a hand on his shoulder to balance.

"What is it?" She asked, looking around. Jr. looked up.

"Tripwire," he said. "Look at that."

Rebecca looked up as well as her mouth fell open. It was a

spear trap, but expertly made with welded metal, high tensile wire, and multiple chambers. He traced the wire with his light off to the right and followed it around a tree. He reached out and guided his mom through each step, then helped her pass over the wire. Together, they checked out the tree and confirmed his suspicions as he found an industrial gear box with a crank shaft mounted to the trunk.

When activated, it would skewer the victim instantly with over five half-inch needle-point shanks. Jr. admired the craftsmanship of the mechanical components.

"What is this thing doing here?" Rebecca asked, looking around for any more traps or out-of-place parts, her eyes eventually settling on a small digital watch with a green and black band lying face up at the base of the tree.

"It's a spear trap. The rule with any trap is you want to use enough pressure or force equal to the thing you're trying to kill. It's why you won't use a brick to kill a rhinoceros," Jr. explained.

Rebecca wiped the face of the watch off on her pant leg. He looked at her and she frowned, but he continued. "Whatever this is meant to kill, it's over seven feet tall. See the frame? It's probably about eight or nine feet up. And there are five spears, not one or two, which means it's wide."

Rebecca didn't answer. She had the watch up near her face and was staring at it. Without asking, he took his watch from her to see what had her so captivated. On the face was a simple number readout, showing the time to be near 1:00 AM. What didn't make sense was the date. The date showed it was Tuesday. Which was impossible because they had arrived at the park on a Tuesday.

"It's broken. Don't worry about it, mom," he reassured her.

She shook her head. "Those things run on satellite. They're new. Expensive. That's the same one I bought for your father last year that he never wore. It looks like someone had been using that one. There's blood on the band."

Jr. turned it over and, sure enough, there was a maroon stain on one side near the clasp.

"So what? Someone lost it. The same someone who left the stick for us. Do you really think we've only been up here for a day? It takes at least a day to hike up to the camping spot and we've slept a few times."

Rebecca didn't answer. She looked absorbed in thought, her eyes darting side to side. She glanced from the watch to Jr. and back to the watch again before settling on the path ahead.

"I suppose you're right," she said, "But it's odd, don't you think? If the watch was correct, it means we have two days left on our pass, and the foresters wouldn't come looking."

Jr. grumbled. "Or it's just broken, like I said. Come with me, you look exhausted. Do you want to rest for a bit?"

She nodded, looking pitiful. Jr. was tired too. His body relying on his last glimmers of hope to make each step just a little above unbearable. Every moment felt like it was lingering twice as long, and the fact that his mom didn't sound like she had any hope in their rescue didn't help either. Jr. thought about what he should say. What else could he lean on to help her? But as he tried to come up with the words, his flashlight flickered, there was a thud, and something touched his ankle.

Jr. spun around.

His mom was sprawled out, face down, on the ground. Jr. dropped to his knees.

"No! Mom? Mom!" He rolled her over. Her eyes were closed, and there was dirt plastered on her face. She looked pale, and when he touched her skin, it was burning up. Her fever had risen.

"Oh my God, no. Mom, wake up!" He cried. Hysterically, he ran through what the book had said to do, but nothing stood out as pertaining to the situation. Tears began to flow freely as he knelt by her side. He didn't even notice the heavy footsteps and the creaking of the trees as he tried to figure out what was happening to her. He pressed his fingers to her neck and was thankful to find a faint but present pulse. Then he checked her breathing by listening in over her mouth. It was raspy but consistent.

Without any other ideas on what to do, and pure panic setting in, Jr. cried. He cried like a baby. He cried for his mom and his dad. He cried for himself. Between his shimmering tears, he spotted another W carved into another tree nearby, and he sniffed heavily.

But then the approaching pounding of feet on dirt became impossible to ignore, and Jr. did the only thing he could think of. He dragged his mom between a set of trees with leafy branches growing low on the trunk and covered her up as best as he could. Then he placed her flashlight in her hand. Taking up the spear, he left whatever was coming up the path behind him and ran, following the markers into the next clearing. He had to find help. Someone had to be nearby.

39

REBECCA

WHATEVER JR. WAS SAYING CAME across garbled and had an unnatural echo behind it. She was drowsy, her eyelids drooped, and her vision was a kaleidoscope of colors. Before she could stop herself from falling, there was a weakness in her knees, and she lost all strength in her legs. She tried to shield herself from the fall, but the message never reached her arms. Her face met cold earth and at the same time, her brain shut itself off. It was dark. Not the kind of dark you experience when you wake up from a dream in the middle of the night. This dark was perpetual.

Her eyes couldn't, or wouldn't adjust, and for a brief moment, she thought she went blind. But then it all started coming back, and when it did, her head pounded with fervor. She became aware of how she laid first, realizing she was on her back. The world spun and here was an odd taste in her mouth. Not blood. But maybe just dirt and grime.

Then she became cognizant of a distinct heaviness in her arms and legs. She tried to call for Jr., but her tongue was so dry it ached in her mouth. A leaf danced on her face. Then another on her neck, her shoulder and her arm. In fact, there were leaves covering her all over. Sliding her hands slowly over the ground, she felt for her flashlight. She felt a cool metal cylinder and found the small rubber button with her forefinger. It took all that she had to press it. When it did, it shined on her feet. There was only more forest, more trees, and more endless dark.

She wasn't just hurt. She was sick, and it was sapping her energy. Jr. had clearly moved on, leaving her behind. He couldn't carry all of her weight forever. It was already difficult enough with her bad leg. With the light off, she cried softly to herself. *Good. He has a better chance of survival without you. You'll only hold him back.*

She tried to fight through the negativity, but it was impossible. She was tired, in mind and body, and fighting imminent negativity by exacerbating what shreds of hope she had left wasn't going to cut it. There was complete despair on the table and she was eating it, alone, until the fever took her for good. For some time, she laid there, a mad mix of tears and sorrow and frustration not only for her negativity, but for not forgiving herself.

She didn't want her last moments filled with regret. Instead, she focused on a goal, even a small one, like sitting up, so she could die comfortably. Right now, a jagged rock dug into her face, and she was sure her hair was crawling with ants. It took a while, but after what she figured was about ten minutes of belittling herself for being weak and desperate pleas to God for strength, she was able to drag herself to a nearby tree and sit up against it. From her position, she could at least see if Jr. was coming back through the entry into the clearing.

Crying seemed easier while sitting, and after a while, her well of sorrow dried up. Tilting her head back, she closed her eyes, but kept herself awake by reliving her best memories with Jr. and James. From their wedding venue in a quaint Catholic Church in the heart of Tennessee to their honeymoon in Kauai, where they spent many days and quite a few nights wrapped up together. She thought of when Jr. was first born; he looked like her clone, but quickly grew into his father's looks.

She thought of their beautiful two-story home in Barhill, and the sound their feet made as she and James ascended the stairs, giggling like idiots, their hands interlaced, already half naked. But as the memory faded away, the footsteps didn't, she peered into the distance. There, in the dark, someone was heading her way. Their light bobbed, and she shut her eyes again. It was all just a dream.

"REBECCA! REBECCA WAKE UP!"

She opened her eyes a hair, though it was laborious.

"I'm okay." She whispered. "I'm okay, Jr. Go on. Get out of here. Mother Nature doesn't build in straight lines." She forced a dull smile with the corner of her lips, which probably came off as a grimace.

Jr. didn't reply, but she felt her hand lifted up, and fingers interlace with hers. It was rough, and there was a ring at the base of one of the fingers. Her eyes flew open. She must be hallucinating. But something bumped her leg. There was a bolt of pain, and she had clarity. It wasn't a hallucination. It was James.

He looked terrible. Deathly thin, the skin on his face had pulled tight, and his clothes hung loosely on his body. He looked like he had aged ten years. He had his flashlight on between his legs, one hand on her forehead, and the other gripping hers. She cried, but no tears came. The same couldn't be said for him. His tears left clear streaks on his grimy face.

Together, they shared a moment they hadn't had in a long time. She felt connected to her husband, felt the love that she had for him when they were first married. She found that spark that kept them in sync, and she mumbled, "I love you."

She waited for him to say it back. To hear his deep, rich voice tell her the words she knew were true. But they never came. She willed her eyes to open and lost all hope. She was alone. James wasn't with her. There was only a rock in her hand that she was squeezing painfully. She felt a profound misery in her heart that traveled to her throat and sat there. It choked her, and she wished it would just end her life then and there. She was tired and broken.

"I'm not ready," she whispered, "I'm not ready."

She didn't want to die alone in the dark. Reaching down again, she found the flashlight and shined it down the path where she and Jr. had come. *Where you came to die. This was your death march. Now, you can close your eyes and drift off alone. Forever alone.*

More footsteps.

Her head wavered, her neck unable to keep it straight. It lolled onto her shoulder and, with her last bit of energy, she kept her eye open, staring down the path until a light bobbed into view again. *That's fine. I liked that dream. I could die living that over and over again.* But the longer she waited, the faster the light came in her direction. She became aware that there was something that hadn't been there before. Something she recognized.

James's voice, clear and free of distortion from her memories.

"Rebecca!" He cried.

"I'm… here," she croaked. It came out raspy and broken.

Rebecca opened her eyes fully in time to see James running towards her, a flashlight illuminating his quick feet. She watched him barrel down the path. Her gaze drifted upwards. *The trap.*

James burst into the clearing, his foot slipping through the trip-wire. There was the clank of metal on metal, the twang of a wire snapping, and light rumbles as something hit the ground. She didn't want to look. She couldn't bear it. She was too late.

She tilted her head up, begging the Lord to strike her down now, so she didn't have to witness what was in front of her. But it didn't happen. There was a scuffling sound, and she felt rough fingers on her face. She opened her eyes to see James kneeling at her feet, just as she imagined him. Over his shoulder, she caught the outline of the polish steel bolts, lodged into the ground in the middle of the clearing. James had made it. He had made it back to her.

"Hi honey," she whispered. The corner of her mouth crept up with her words.

"Hello, my love."

Then his rough, blistered lips met hers and they kissed gently. She closed her eyes and relished in the moment. She felt him sit down next to her, and she leaned off to the side, so her body rested up against his. She allowed her head to fall onto his shoulder, eternally thankful that God had answered her prayers. Then the ground began to shake.

40

J R

Jᴿ. ᴏᴘᴇɴᴇᴅ ʜɪꜱ ᴍᴏᴜᴛʜ ᴡɪᴅᴇ, sucking in as much air as he could. It was no use — a tightness gripped his lungs unlike anything he had ever experienced. Wheezing, he dropped to one knee and hoped to keep himself from passing out. He couldn't understand where it was coming from; what had his chest so tight? But the answer was clear and present. He was terrified, to the point his fear wanted to snuff him out. Then, in a tag-team ensemble, guilt and shame were waiting for him when he was finally getting a grip on his nerves. Guilt for leaving his mom behind, and shame for being a coward when she needed him.

But that thing in the dark... it was coming, and his mom was growing weaker. He couldn't carry her onward through the dense path. If he had even tried, it would have been on him in seconds. At least with his mom tucked away, they both had a chance. A far away branch snapped and Jr. almost pissed himself, choosing to dive into the nearest bush and hide his face behind a plush of leaves. He clicked the light off and listened, his eyes adjusting to impenetrable darkness.

No branches snapped, no critters scuttled. It was a new world, devoid of life, yet teeming with it if you knew where to look. Just when he was about to click his flashlight back on, he heard something no child should ever suffer through. He heard the painful, agonizing wail of his mom, then a gargling, choking sound that made him wish he were dead. When the echoes of her scream faded, Jr. caved and planted his face in his hands, curling up like a toddler. He cried painful tears, stifling whimpers and growing the knot in his throat.

"Get up," he told himself. "Get up and live, you pussy."

No. I'm going to wait for it. It's coming, and I want to go. I hate it here. I hate all of this.

He banged his fist in the dirt.

Cowards are forgotten. Do you want to be forgotten? Would you want your mom, or your dad, to forget you? No? Then get up. Grab your spear and move on. You're not done.

It was enough to stop the flow from his eyes and the welling of snot in his nose. Blinking in the dark, he felt around until he found his staff and stood up slowly. All was quiet again, and there wasn't another sound from his mother. *I won't forget you.*

If he was going to survive, he needed a plan to kill this thing.

Whoever had set these traps had intended to do the same. Tim or Roger or whoever knew what it was capable of and had planned the traps accordingly. The spears could have killed it, but that was way behind him. Risking the flashlight, Jr. clicked it on in his hand, unfolding it for brief glimpses at his surroundings. He was near another clearing. Odd, as it was in line with the path and the spear trap. He prayed whoever had set the first trap had done something similar for a second.

Remembering the lessons on primitive survival from the book, there were only a handful of signs to look for if you wanted to spot a simple trap, and if you knew what you were looking for, you could spot them easily. Laying down flat on his stomach, he shined the flashlight so it skirted the ground floor, and he was elated to find another ultra-lite wire strung across the vale. He followed it up into the trees and saw it was connected to a pulley system. Though he couldn't spot the wire anymore, there was a clean-cut log suspended just below the canopy. It lined up with his position. *Mother Nature doesn't use chainsaws. That's a clean cut on the face of that log.*

He checked the positioning of the line and saw it ran directly in front of the path he had come through. He realized how lucky he was at that moment. He must have barely stepped over it.

Still using quick darts of the light, he found another tree that looked out of place. There was a pile of branches laid at its base. *Mother Nature doesn't stack things like that.* He followed the edge of the clearing, checking for more wires. It was slow going, but he eventually made it behind his target tree. Relief came on so hard it touched his very soul when he found another carved W into the bark, and a path leading deeper into the woods. It followed a route naturally easier to navigate than the rest of the surrounding forest. *Smart. You were luring it.*

He didn't know who he was complimenting. Maybe Tim, maybe Roger, but it felt right to give the masterminds behind this some credit. Without further constraints, he rounded the tree and continued on. With each step, the sticks and branches seemed to reach out and try to touch him. He had to crumple his shoulders in just to avoid the glancing scrape or tickle of a leaf. If he had, he was sure he'd scream. And that would bring the thing to him before he was ready.

Further on ahead, the path ended abruptly, and he froze. His toes curled over and pointed downward. He swung his arms, spinning them wildly, the feeling of falling taking over. He willed himself to lean, throwing his head back and attempting to fall away from the pit at his feet.

Jr. tilted and he lifted up his toes, anything to avoid falling. His weight shifted, and he fell painfully on his elbows, jarring them and biting down on his teeth so hard he felt they might crack. Using the light, he could see there was a massive deadfall before him. It was several feet wide and took up almost the entire area. He glanced over the rim to see how tall it was and pulled away. There was a body at the bottom of the pit, a man impaled through the chest on the punji sticks below. He wasn't prepared for that, and a whimper escaped. Fearing he had been heard, Jr. shut off his light and huddled near a tree, the man's twisted, frozen face imprinted on the back of his eyelids. He couldn't unsee him. But there was one thing that stood out about him. One thing he did notice in the brief moment he was looking at him.

He held a piece of paper in his hand.

What would be so important that he would be holding it in death?

Jr. contemplated what the paper could be, and liked to imagine it was a note to a lost love, or a picture of his kids, or maybe a final confession before he died.

There were sharp sticks at the bottom of the pit. They weren't particularly thick, but the hole was deep, meaning his fall had been long, and his death gruesome and painful.

Maybe he had a map.

The thought was alluring. He withheld his immediate desire to fish the paper out just to fuel his burning curiosity and told himself to stick to the plan. Indecisiveness leads to poor knee-jerk decisions. It could serve to be analytical now. He had little choice, and the options were trash. Run to nowhere, because he was lost, or hide and wait for a someone that was never coming.

Or fight. If Jr. could throttle his inner thoughts, he would. *Fight? Fight it how? You've got a stick.*

It's all right here in front of you, dummy. The traps. The path. The stick. You have everything you need. You could end this right now, then go back for your mom.

"Or I could sit right here, and it could leave," he said, quieter than a mouse.

Hide all you want. It's hunting you, and it knows you're afraid. It showed itself in the cave. It let you hear its cries. It wants you to be scared.

"It's feeding on my fear," he mumbled. To his displeasure, what should have been a question came out as more of a diagnosis. "And if it's feeding on my fear, then I need to starve it to death."

Cowards run. Cowards are afraid. Are you a coward?

"No. But I know I'm probably not making it out of here alive. So fuck it. I'm done being afraid. I'm done running. I'll control the stage. I set the rules. I'll bring it here. I choose how I die," he mouthed the words, daring not to speak again until it was time. Even if he lost a limb, he was determined not to let another sound escape his mouth.

"I choose how I die," he uttered.

Or how you live.

JAMES

WHAT SHOULD HAVE BEEN a passionate reunification with Rebecca was a heartbreaking, morbid descent into fear and panic. The ground shook at his feet. His first thoughts that it was an earthquake, but those were nearly unheard of in this region of the states. His head jerked around without any real direction or pattern, checking for the source of the quake. *A large panther. Or maybe a landslide. There were boulders on the ridge, and it had been raining that day.*

Whatever the cause, he didn't have time to waste and relish the moment with his wife. He needed to at least get her out of the path, for *it* was surely nearby, and their best bet to survive was not constricted to the narrow forest trails. Bending over, invigorated, he seized Rebecca up by her arm and threw it over his shoulder, then heaved her into a fireman's carry. She groaned in pain.

"Hold on baby, I've got you," he said, then shoved his flashlight between his teeth and clamped down hard. He needed his hands to juggle rebalancing Rebecca's body and navigating the tunnel of branches up ahead. It was slow going, but the further he got from the clearing, the more he realized there was a rhythm to the earthquake. There were moments between the beats, and he soon found himself walking in line with it.

There was an odd familiarity about the beat. And then he connected something he had remembered from many years ago and now. When he was a boy, no more than seven, there was a local family who were Indians. They lived on a reserve and, every so often, music carried on the wind along with the scent of burning herbs and mesquite wood. That's what he was hearing; drums, and the further they got away from the epicenter, the clearer they became.

Rebecca's head flopped and jarred the side of his cheek, but it didn't faze him. He had Rebecca. He had found her. Against all odds, he had found her, and she was still alive. But where was Jr.?

He couldn't ask Rebecca, she wasn't conscious. Hell, his own body was barely functioning. Only the deepest stores of energy fueled him on. Otherwise, he'd be weak, clammy, and ready to sleep for days. The sound of the drums seemed to envelope his every fiber. He felt them in his chest and in his achy feet. The deep, resonating tones rattled his eyes, and his teeth chattered on the aluminum light.

As he drooled uncontrollably, the beat ended when he and Rebecca cleared the tunnel and arrived at the second clearing. The one he knew to be loaded with the log trap. The nearly invisible wire hummed softly above the ground. Waddling to the left and overtop the wire, James set Rebecca down in the brush and peered down the pathway, preparing himself not to jump in case the drums started again. But it was still until the crunching of footsteps down the path drew his focus. They were quick and soft, unlike the others he had heard before.

James held his fists up, the aluminum flashlight clicking between his teeth as he used his tongue to rearrange it. Then there was a flash of pale flesh, and a naked, bloody man sprinted through the dark. It was Edgar, and a great shadow followed him, matching his step.

He was bone-thin, and his skin was devoid of all color. His stringy hair flowed behind him as he ran faster than any person his age should. But it was disjointed and obtuse, like he wasn't used to running and struggled to develop a rhythm. James flashed the light into his eyes. They were like white marbles, and his eyelids had been peeled off. His teeth were jagged, there was only a stump where his tongue should have been, and his chin was covered in blood. James yanked the flashlight from his mouth as soon as his initial surprise had subsided. "Edgar, stop! Stop! Stop!" James screamed.

But it was no use. Edgar was gone. What was left was just his animated body. There was no life behind his eyes. He snarled like a beast as he ran down the path. James prepared himself to fight. His eyes caught something in the outer rim of his flashlight. The tripwire vibrated.

Then, realization. His vision shifted to slow motion. Now, he could make out every gray and white hair on Edgar's naked body. He could count every rib and measure every bruise. He entered the clearing, and he caught his ankle on the trip-wire. There was a pop, a whirring of gears, and the soft whistle of the log releasing from its housing and soaring through the air like a pendulum.

James tried to look away but not before catching Edgar's eyes shift back to normal, and then there was a brief moment of confusion as the five-hundred-pound log sung through the clearing, sending the old man flying up against a wide tree. It crushed him with a sloppy pop and the thud of wood on wood. There was a gentle creak of the cable as the log bounced off, swung and tilted off its axis, dripping bits of Edgar's body into the tall grass.

James kept his eyes averted, instead focusing on Rebecca, who remained unconscious, her head lolling off to the side. He almost puked when he saw the spatter of blood on her face and chunks of skin in her hair. Then he lost what composure he had.

In the process of turning to Rebecca, he had to dodge the spinning log, and caught a glimpse of what was left of Edgar. He was a stain of bloody pulp on the face of the tree. Some of him stuck to the log, while other parts of him were scattered around, but almost every tree within arm's reach had chunks of flesh, muscle, and blood stains on them.

James's legs felt weak, and he broke into deep upheavals from his diaphragm, which only cramped around his empty stomach. He was about to pass out, but there was a rumble from beneath the earth again and the drums resumed.

Remembering what he saw the last time, he couldn't bear the thought of what would be upon them next, and with the log trap gone, he was out of options. He and Rebecca couldn't stay there. Not with what had just happened.

Mustering courage and nursing a cramping stomach, James prepared to carry her again. When he tried to pick her up this time, she was even heavier than before. He realized she must have been semi-conscious the last time he carried her, and she was trying to help. But now, with her completely out, she was dead weight.

In any other scenario, he could have carried her without a problem. But out here, after a few days without food or water, and with the mental toll the entire journey had on him, Rebecca was almost too heavy for him to bear. But he had her, and that's what mattered and now. There was only one thing left to do — he had to find Jr.

With Rebecca's weight spread as evenly as he could across his back, James turned around the bend and walked the narrow path sideways to make it through. He tried to keep his eye on the way in front of him, but whenever he did, he felt eyes on him. He was tired of things coming out of the dark. He was tired of always being afraid. He was tired of those damn drums.

A few hasty steps later, the path broke into the final clearing, and remembering the closeness of the deadfall trap, he hurried against another wall of trees where he had more room to move. But just as he was about to set his Rebecca down, something shuffled in the dark. Someone screamed, and then there was a searing pain in his upper arm. He dropped her at his feet without meaning to. He had lost all feeling in his arm only to have it return as a white-hot burning sensation.

He muffled a scream, so it came out as a growl and grabbed at where something had jabbed him and was currently sticking out of his bicep. He felt thick blood near the base of a sharpened wooden stick. He pulled it out then tossed it aside. Applying pressure, he ducked and shielded Rebecca's body in the dark.

His light was too far for him to reach without risking falling into the pit that loomed just off to his right, the smell of damp earth wafting upward.

Then, a hand gripped his flashlight and lifted it up, shining it in his eyes. James turned away.

"Dad?" A familiar voice called.

"Jr.?" James replied.

"It's me."

James pulled his palm away from his bleeding muscle. "I think you stabbed me, son."

JAMES

JAMES HAD time to hug Jr. briefly, but it was done out of habit. His arm was bleeding, Rebecca was on the ground unconscious and the drum beat still pumped in the background. He did, however, take the time to look his son over. He looked just as haggard, if not more so than he himself did. His face was gaunt, his hair hung about, matted with dirt and oil, and puffy bags had formed under his eyes. He bore a look of a boy who had aged into a man overnight.

James gave a superficial arm-wrap over his shoulder then pulled away.

"I got your message. I brought help, but they didn't make it." He looked his bicep over. It wasn't deep, but there'd be a scar. He applied pressure.

Jr. shook his head. "Jesus, dad. I'm sorry. I thought it was that thing. I wasn't even expecting you. I wasn't sure, but I shouldn't have doubted you." Tears formed in his eyes.

"No no, it's okay. I'm here. We can get out of this now, together. But I need to ask you something."

Jr. sniffled.

"Do you hear the drums?"

Jr. stopped, tilting his head to the side. "No dad, I don't hear anything. In fact, I haven't heard anything from this forest since I got here. It's like this place eats light and sound."

James shook his head. Jr. couldn't hear the drums. *How couldn't he? The fucking earth was shaking.*

"Never mind. Where's the creature? Tell me you've seen a creature and I'm not losing my mind?"

Jr. froze and for a moment, James thought he was about to say no, but his head tilted forward and back again. They met each other's eyes.

"It's tall, and fast," Jr. said. "I think these traps were meant for it. It's horrible dad. The sounds... God... and the antlers..."

James nodded. "I know, Jr. I know for a fact they were. The people I came with, they tried to kill it before."

"What is it?" Jr. asked.

"I didn't believe it at first. But after what I've seen over the past few days, it'd be impossible for me to deny it. It will kill us all the same." James stopped and breathed deep once. "It's called a Wendigo. It's an ancient creature, a spirit of the forest or something. Something terrible, and the consequence of the ultimate sin against the body." As he talked about it, he felt right to do so, like he was telling a story around a campfire.

"It was created. Not on purpose, but as a punishment. The people I came with, Edgar and Joe were their names... they left their friends on this mountain a long time ago. Their names were Roger and..." He trailed off, remembering Edgar marching into the dark, taunting the creature, calling it by its name. He dared not repeat it now.

"Something happened, someone got hurt, and they were forced to leave their friends behind. When they returned, they only found a monster."

Jr. didn't answer, but his face was still, and his attention focused.

"They tried to kill it and failed. They left and came back,

then set up these traps, and again, they failed. Now, when you went missing and I came to find you, they used me as bait so they could finish what they started."

"Did they kill it this time? Did it work?"

James shook his head. "No, son. It's still here. It'll feed on our very souls before it feeds on our bodies. It feeds on our fear. We mustn't be afraid of it. We must fight it. Do you understand?"

James became aware he had seized Jr. painfully by the shoulders, then his arm throbbed, and he hissed at it. "Damn it," he said, covering it with his palm. Jr. found a weak spot on his shirt and pulled. It ripped easily, and he tied the bit of scrap around James's arm.

"We can't run. We have the pit. I think I know what we have to do," James said, looking at Rebecca, who was resting on her side.

"I can be the bait. You have to get mom out," Jr. interjected.

James shook his head. Jr. had become a man overnight.

"None of us are going to be bait. We face it. Lure it into the pit, then we put it down. We just have to figure out how to get it here. How to get it so riled up, it can't help but fall right into this hole. The other traps are a bust, so it's on us to finish it off," James said confidently. He felt like he was planning a great battle, and that was fun to envision until he realized what was at stake — his family. Their lives. It all came down to whatever decisions he made. Even if Rebecca could see him now, he was sure she'd lean on him, see him for the husband he could be, and the father he needed to be. She'd see he was strong, and she'd trust him.

"So tell me, what do we need to do?" Jr. said. He kept glancing over James's shoulder.

"Help me get your mom behind the trees right here. Then you're going to lower me into the pit. I'll take this," he held up the spear. "And put it down once it falls in."

"Then what do I do?"

James stepped in and seized Jr. in a one-armed hug. "Protect your mom and promise me if that thing crawls out of the hole, you'll leave me and get her out of here. Promise me."

Jr. nodded. James pulled him in close then planted his chin onto the top of his head. He had his boy and his wife, and yet he felt like he was about to leave them again.

"I'm sorry. I'm sorry about everything."

"It's okay, dad," he mumbled.

James pulled away as the drums grew so loud, his teeth vibrated. He saw Jr.'s expression hadn't changed.

Without anything left to do, James and Jr. walked over to Rebecca and together, carried her around the pit and set her down gently just off the trail, leading out and back towards the cave. There, she was nearby but almost invisible in the dark.

Then James shuffled up next to the pit, his toes draped over the edge, and sat, allowing his feet to dangle. Jr. shined the flashlight into the hole. It was a long way down. Joe's lifeless corpse stared at him from the corner.

James gulped and turned around, stabilizing himself with his arm, then slowly lowered himself down. There was a moment in which he was afraid he'd be impaled if he let go, as his feet didn't touch the ground, but Jr. rushed forward and clamped onto his wrist and helped lower him. Once on solid ground, Jr. dug into his pocket and removed a small silver bracelet attached to a set of worn dog-tags. He held it out for him to grab.

"For luck," Jr. said. James slipped it over his wrist. The metal was warm. James played with the tags with his fingers. He didn't know how they were lucky. He just assumed it was something Jr. liked to wear. He accepted them graciously. Then Jr. tilted the spear in. James grabbed it, shook it in his good hand, and checked the point.

"I'm ready," James said.

Jr. backed away from the hole, out of sight.

Together, they waited. The drums pounded and James had a

splitting headache. They waited for what felt like hours, and still, nothing came.

Jr. scuffled over the edge, causing him to jump.

"Sorry. What do we do?"

He thought back on what all had been said about the creature, then, remembering Edgar marching into the forest, he got an idea. An idea that went against everything common sense told him. An idea that was contradictory to his unbridled desire to flee.

"We need to taunt it. To call it. To bring it here. It's what it wants," James responded.

"What do we say?"

"We call it by its name," James said solemnly. "Its name is Tim Breaker."

43

JR

Jr. PULLED BACK from the hole and tucked into his spot behind a shrub. Just a few feet away, his mom's labored breathing broke through the dark. He hoped she'd wake up to see his dad, to know he had done something heroic for them both. But at the same time, he hoped she slept through this nightmare, because nothing in her dreams could be as bad as what they were about to do.

"On the count of three," James said. "One."

Jr. settled in.

"Two."

A branch snapped in the dark.

"Three!"

Jr. took a deep breath. So deep, it was painful as his tired lungs expanded against his rib cage, then with his mouth open wide, he screamed. "Tim! Breaker!"

James yelled at the same time, his voice thunderous, despite the deep hole. Their voices echoed off the trees, then died down. They waited, counting the seconds, not daring to look beyond the narrow path in front of them. Jr. held the flashlight aloft, his hands quivering, his teeth chattering, and an unexpected chill laid across his back. He felt cold, and there was an itch building in his nostrils.

He couldn't help but stare and wonder if his dad's plan had failed. He wondered if the creature would come when called, or if it was slowly tracking through the woods, looking to ambush them from the darkness. He tried to push the negative thoughts away, but he was growing colder by the minute. A dull, achy throb built under his kneecaps.

Then his flashlight began to dim. Ripe, child-like panic filled his soul as he smacked at the light, willing it to stay on.

There was what sounded like something falling in the dirt up ahead. Jr. was torn between keeping the dying flashlight pointed where they needed it and smacking it against his palm. "Not now, Jesus, not now," he said, shaking it at its base so it rattled.

He caught movement out of the corner of his eye and looked up in time to see five shiny black claws attached to long, tendril-like fingers wrap around a tree at the end of the path. Then the light died, and they were plunged into darkness.

Jr., remembering his mother's light, felt around in the dark for her feet and traced them up to her pocket. He fished the flashlight out and flipped around in a flourish, then clicked it on.

The creature emerged from between a pair of trees. It was there, in all of its terrible glory, it was there. It barreled down the path, clawing and pulling itself with the trees to either side of it.

It stood well above the lower branches and its skin was life-less, like it had never left the dark. It used massive, shiny black claws attached to bone-thin arms to propel itself forward. With bipedal legs, skeletal and bird-like, it kicked off the ground, running down the path.

But Jr. fixated on its head. It wore the face of an animal, a deer or a goat or a horse, but with enormous, sprawling antlers.

It roared, powering through the brush, barreling straight towards them. Its bottom jaw opened from under the skull, revealing a black, snake-like tongue and a thousand pointed teeth. It howled in a way that no human ear should comprehend. It was like a symphony of voices cried out for help at once, but no-one answered.

Jr. did his part, his frozen petrified body holding him in place. He heard his father yell out again in response to the commotion ahead.

"Tim! Breaker!" He yelled.

The creature stopped, then continued on slower, hunting for the source of the sound, sweeping its great head side to side in a wide arc.

"One more time, dad," he whispered.

"Tim! Breaker!"

Then the creature broke into a mad dash straight through the middle of the clearing. Jr.'s bones locked up and he was forced to watch as this beast of lore, this monster in the dark, this inhuman creation of terrible evil, tumbled into the deadfall trap. There were a series of grunts and another chorus of wailing. Jr. didn't dare to look into the hole. But still, the grunting continued. After a while, there was only a soft squish, a dull thud, and more grunting. Then it was quiet.

Desperately wishing his father could just crawl out of the hole, it took every ounce of courage for Jr. to lower himself to his chest and point his light inside.

It was a hellish scene from a horror movie. The creature was impaled on its side. James was stabbing it blindly with the spear, all the while reaching between the punji sticks towards the corpse's hand in the corner. The creature snapped at him or swiped with its claws. James dodged, then struck again. A squelch followed every blow. Jr. watched hopelessly from above as his dad, cold and calculated, speared a monster that shouldn't exist. And then it hit him. The stench. A smell so wicked, he nearly had to turn away. It was emanating from the monster. He knew that now, as wave after wave escaped its mouth with every tortured cry, that the smell from the creature was that of the forest. James seemed unaffected, his eyes cold. He jabbed, spewing blood over his face.

Jr. watched as a pattern of short, quick thrusts released a mind-bending howl, followed by a stressful grunt as his dad tried to reach the corpse. The sticks were in his way, and he stretched his arm between them, forcing his shoulder between the crack. Jr. didn't know what James needed, but it must have been important to risk getting that close to the monster. He was far better off continuing to jab at it out of reach of the shiny black claws.

A final shove forward let James snag a piece of paper from the man's hand. He dove to his hands and knees, and crawled under the monster, between the sticks that impaled it, and over to where Jr. was waiting. He looked at his dad, who stopped without reaching up to take his outstretched hand.

"What're you doing? Come on!" Jr. pleaded with him, but James was lost to all words. His face was locked onto the monster, its bone-covered face opened up wide to reveal rows of long, spine-like teeth. Its eyes were shallow pits of dark nothingness. It swiped a claw at him, then writhed in pain.

Jr. saw his dad slip the bracelet off his hands, rubbing his fingers over the top of it. He held it in front of him like a talisman. The creature became still.

James tossed it at the creature's boney head. It hooked around an antler, then locked eyes with him.

He reared back, blood-soaked spear up high, and plowed it through the monster's mouth. It burst from the backside of its skull.

"Die!" James screamed in agony, twisting and bending the stick so it distorted the creature's skin, spewing forth more blood. Then, with a massive sigh, the creature was still. Its arms went limp, and its head lolled to the side.

A few minutes later, James pulled himself away, turned his back to the monster, and took a few labored steps to the edge of the hole where Jr. was still waiting. Jr. pleaded with his eyes for his father to join him, and James lifted a hand to accept his son's aid climbing out of the pit. Once he was on solid ground, James rolled over and collapsed next to his son, and together they stayed like that for a long time.

At some point, Jr. clicked the light off, only to click it on again. James touched his hand. He felt like that was his father saying it was okay to turn it off. When he did this time, he thought he was closing the chapter on a story and starting a new one. It was an awesome feeling, different than when he saw his dad in the woods. He was getting to know his dad all over again.

After resting for a bit Jr. asked, "What did you have to get?"

James unfolded the piece of paper he had risked his life to get.

Jr. clicked on the light. James explained, "I remembered Joe had this" as Jr. tried to make out the details on the little piece of paper.

Jr. couldn't tell what it was at first, then he realized it was a map of the grounds. It showed some distances, elevations, directions and even a few landmarks. On it was also the name of the three traps, the cave, a set of rock outcroppings, a ranger station, a deer-blind, and finally, the break in the river where they could cross.

"He had this on him. Kept me out of the loop. But I have it now. I think it's time we leave this place for good. Do you agree?" James asked.

Jr. didn't have to answer.

Soon, with Rebecca's arms spread over their shoulders, the map in hand, and two flashlights to guide them, they were on their way out of the path, beyond the cave, past the rock outcropping and to the deer-blind.

"How did you know what it wanted? How did you know to give it the bracelet?" Jr. asked.

James bowed his head. "I didn't know. I just wanted to believe there was a bit of Tim still in there."

Jr. shrugged as his mom was starting to stir.

Then, up ahead, the most pleasant sound came over the hill, and a most welcome sight. A small gas-powered cart arrived at the water's edge. Driving it was a pretty blonde girl in a forester's uniform. She dismounted the vehicle and waded confidently across the river, took one look at the family, and helped lift Rebecca's feet so they stayed dry.

With Jr. in the front next to the young woman and James and Rebecca riding in the bed, they drove back through the forest on the main road, bypassing the campgrounds and bursting into the afternoon sun. Jr. traveled in a surreal haze, wondering if his parents felt the same.

They covered their eyes as they burst into the daylight, the warmth of the sun an oddity compared to the sticky heat of the park. The cart rolled on, the blonde girl silent. The next few minutes passed in a blur and soon they were inside in the cool air, resting in the wicker chairs in the lobby. Somebody said the police and an ambulance were on the way.

Jr. and James stared at a blank wall while the young woman administered an IV to Rebecca, every so often looking her over and checking her pulse.

Meanwhile, Arnie seethed in the corner, biting his nails.

44

ARNIE

ONCE HE HEARD the four-wheeler returning sooner than he had expected, he peaked out the window to see what was going on. The blonde was already returning on the gator. She was driving way too fast, and there were two people in the back seat and a young kid in the front. Arnie was ready to chew her out when she came around the blind side of the building but was instantly lost for words when he saw who it was.

He recognized the guy on the back first. It was James, the asshole who pissed in his bucket, and he looked terrible. He had blood all over his face and down his arm. In fact, all three of them looked horrible. They stunk. They were covered in grime and bruises, and the lady's leg was wrapped up in a rank cloth. Melissa started helping them into the building without his direction. He couldn't object, not with how worse for wear they looked. He saw a handful of maggots creeping off the bed of the vehicle.

He gagged once before returning inside to see Melissa with an IV bag in hand, working on the lady who was moaning softly to herself. She was lying on the floor with her leg propped up on a little black book.

James didn't say anything. Instead, he chose to stare at a bare space on the wall in front of him. The teenager with him, his son, he assumed, based on his looks, also had a blank look on his face. The three of them didn't say a word, and neither did Melissa.

About twenty minutes later, there was the sound of tires on gravel and Arnie looked out the window to see the ambulance arrive alongside a Sheriff's Office squad car. From then on out it was a flurry of uniforms until finally the family was being escorted out the door, with the woman on a gurney and her husband and son right behind her. Before the son left, he turned around and ran back to the coffee table. He walked over to Arnie and held out a worn black book. Arnie took it, and as he did so, confused, his mouth worked on a toothpick.

The kid didn't say a word as he hurried off to his family. But as he did, Arnie saw him scratch at his back where there were five long, angry gashes left unbandaged. Thinking nothing of it and unsure of what kind of backlash he would soon be facing, he returned to his spot behind his desk in the corner of the lobby. He laid the book on the table and flipped it open, gasping as he read the handful of entries. Most of them, to his utter amazement and later, crippling grief, were from his brother. He read through them several times before moving on to the final message.

It was written by the kid, Jr. A few of the pieces fell in place. Coupling what he knew about what happened the day his brother went missing, with the rumors about the park, he began to plan his exit strategy. His dirty truths were soon going to come out.

Melissa, the new hire and bleeding heart, would surely tell the police about the radio transmission he had ignored. They'd check the logs and see that rescue attempts were never made. They'd see a lot of things wrong with the park, and all fingers pointed at Arnie.

They'd see the theft and the fraud and all the buried sexual harassment complaints. They'd see the history of hikers gone missing and discover his policy, which prevented any kind of potential rescue from the restricted zone. They'd see the company credit card was used for thousands in unapproved purchases. They'd discover the pornography on the desktop, some legal, most of it not. They'd test him for drugs. And after all that, he'd be ruined and left to rot in prison. But with the black book in his possession, he had the answers he needed and had sought for so many years. His brother had been left to die. He had started to change too… and with the marks on the kid's back…

They were answers he wasn't prepared to deal with from a jail cell for the rest of his life. He had been safe for so long, and up until now could bury secrets as he needed out here. This was his kingdom. He had never needed to defend it. He had never been investigated, but he knew one would be coming soon.

Carefully, he locked the door to his office and reached to shut the aluminum pull-down barrier, but someone was standing at the counter. He was a head shorter than Arnie, and fatter. His face was round, and he bore an eccentric smile. He held out his hand to shake. Arnie, skeptical at best, took up the offer briefly, but it was floppy handed and weak.

"My name's Dwain Cooper from Caprock Haunts Investigative Firm. I was wondering if you had a few minutes to talk." His pudgy face, bulbous eyes and ridiculous smile made him look like a circus clown without makeup, and Arnie already hated him.

"I don't have time for your shit," Arnie spat, pulling up his shirt from where it was loosely tucked into the front of his pants.

"Oh, but I think you will soon."

Arnie ignored him and dug into his pocket for the socks he had stolen from Melissa's locker. Then he opened the desk drawer and removed the black revolver. Under the desk he checked that there was a round in the cylinder.

"I think we have a lot to talk about," the pudgy man said again.

Arnie stared him down with a wicked grin, brought the used socks to his nose and took a deep whiff and exhaled loudly.

"Talk about this," Arnie replied, and in a fluid motion, he brought the pistol up from under the desk, stuck the barrel in his mouth, and pulled the trigger.

BELFORD MANOR

THE OTHERWORLD ARCHIVES

ONE MANSION's foundation creaks with the weight of its secrets.

Marcus, a convicted felon, serves out his sentence, dreaming of his life before his days were spent eating slop and narrowly avoiding being shanked in the shower.

Release day comes, and it's not as sweet as he thought it would be.

Abandoned. Broke. Entirely alone. Maybe he was better off in prison...But opportunities for felons are few and far between and the famous Belford Manor needs a caretaker. Where others may see a spooky, crumbling estate, Marcus envisions a future for himself, where he can heal and move on. But everything isn't what it seems, and questions about the house quickly become impossible to ignore.

Now, Marcus is entangled in a mystery older than the dirt the house is built on. Its walls pulse with a fetid horror that makes the lonely felon wish for his cell. The manor wants more than Marcus's attention. It may very well want his soul too.

Looking for more terrifying tales? Start reading The Haunting of Belford Manor. Available from Amazon and on Kindle Unlimited.

Building a relationship with my readers is the very best thing about writing. I send newsletters with details on new releases, writer-life, deals and other bits of news related to my books. And if you sign up to my mailing list I'll send you something I think you'll like, my terrifying novella, *Peel*.

Tell me where to send the book by clicking here: Send my Book!

Or visit www.davidviergutz.com/freebooks

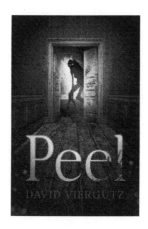

HOW YOU CAN HELP

Did you enjoy this book? You can make a big difference.

Reviews are the most powerful tools I utilize for gathering attention for my books. As much as I wish I could, I can't load the newspaper with massive ads, or slam the subway with posters.

At least not yet.

But I do have something more effective than that and it's something major NYC publishers wished they could get their hands on.

My committed and loyal cohort of readers.

Honest reviews of my books help other readers know what to expect.

If you enjoyed this book, I would be eternally grateful if you could take a few minutes of your time leaving a review. (It can be as long or as short as you'd like)

Thank you!

DAVID'S CATALOGUE

To see an entire list of David's titles, simply tap the link below.

David writes a lot of books and his library has grown too large to list them all here. Tap the link to see the covers, read the blurbs, and find your next read. David writes in many shades of horror from dark fantasy to pure terror. Tap the link to check them all out.

David's up-to-date catalogue

ABOUT DAVID VIERGUTZ

Disabled Army Veteran, Law Enforcement Veteran, husband and proud father. David Viergutz is the author of stories from every flavor of horror and speculative fiction.

Take the plunge into David's imagination as he delivers chill-bringing adventures where the good guy doesn't always win. David remembers dragging a backpack full of books to class beginning in middle school and leaving his textbooks behind.

David takes his inspiration from the greats and fell in love with complex universes from the desks of Nix, Tolkien, King, Stroud and Lovecraft to name a few. David's imagination, combined with his experience in uniform give his books an edge when it comes to the spooky and unnerving.

One day, David's wife sat him down and gave him the confidence to start putting his imagination on paper. From then on out David's creativity has no longer been stifled by self-doubt and he continues to write with a smile on his face in a dark, candle-lit room.

"It can always get worse." - David Viergutz

DEDICATION

I write what scares me. If I can put it on the page. It no longer lives in my head rent free.